S0-BDP-847

Praise for

The Talk Show Murders

The Midnight Show Murders

and

The Morning Show Murders

by

Al Roker and Dick Lochte

"As well-paced and thoughtfully prepared as an Alice Waters tasting menu."
—*Kirkus Reviews*

"Great fun, full of nifty twists and turns."
—CARL HIAASEN

"The laughs are frequent and belly-deep, and the personable tone is akin to a television mystery/comedy like *The Rockford Files* or *Columbo*."
—*BookPage*

"Fast-paced, exciting . . . Wry humor lifts this above most celebrity-written fiction."
—*Publishers Weekly*

"The authors succeed in entertaining readers with a crime drama flavored with some of Roker's familiar charm and humor. . . . for a murder mystery, it's great fun."
—Fredericksburg *Free Lance-Star*

"Al Roker's first mystery thriller is a winner. Terrific plot, fast, funny, and full of action and adventure with even a touch of steamy romance. And I love his leading man, TV personality, restaurateur and amateur sleuth Billy Blessing. Billy's not only heroic, witty and self-effacing, he can whip up little snacks in his kitchen that taste better than Butterscotch Krimpets. I think Stephanie Plum would love him, too, even with some of the misguided things he has to say about New Jersey."

—JANET EVANOVICH

"Roker brings his A-game to the table when it comes to giving reader's a bird's-eye view into the behind-the-scenes action on a television show."

—*Chicago Sun-Times*

"This is a funny, funny, very funny mystery that really gallops along and has several cool twists. Maybe Al Roker should quit his day job."

—JAMES PATTERSON

"Great fun! Al pulls back the curtain to reveal what really goes on when the cameras go off."

—HARLAN COBEN

BY AL ROKER AND DICK LOCHTE

The Morning Show Murders
The Midnight Show Murders
The Talk Show Murders

The

TALK
SHOW

Murders

A BILLY BLESSING NOVEL

AL ROKER
and DICK LOCHTE

DELL | NEW YORK

2012 Dell Mass Market Edition

Copyright © 2011 by Al Roker Entertainment

Published in the United States by Dell, an imprint of The Random House Publishing Group, a division of Random House, Inc., New York.

DELL is a registered trademark of Random House, Inc., and the colophon is a trademark of Random House, Inc.

Originally published in hardcover in the United States by Delacorte Press, an imprint of The Random House Publishing Group, a division of Random House, Inc., in 2011.

ISBN 978-0-440-24582-7
eBook ISBN 978-0-345-52930-5

Cover design: Carlos Beltrán
Cover illustration: Ben Perini

Printed in the United States of America

www.bantamdell.com

9 8 7 6 5 4 3 2 1

Dell mass market edition: December 2012

The
TALK
SHOW
Murders

Chapter
ONE

At roughly six-thirty on a Thursday morning that dawned bright and clear, members of the Chicago Police Department's Homicide Division and Forensic Services were lured to the city's Oak Street Beach by a body that had been deposited on the sand by Lake Michigan's ebbing tide. A drowning in the lake, accidental or otherwise, was not exactly remarkable. But this one was clearly unique, though that fact was not presented immediately to the public.

The CPD had dropped a cone of silence over the discovery. Even the hapless early-morning jogger who'd nearly stumbled over the corpse was being forced to pursue his cardio perfection in seclusion somewhere off the grid.

Surprisingly, in this era of instant information, where members of the media are as persistent as they are plentiful, the news blackout lasted for nearly thirty hours. It was broken by a gray-haired, ill-tempered former cop named Edward "Pat" Patton. Since his retirement, Patton had begun a second career with a blog, *Windy City Blowdown,* devoted primarily to outspoken and often outrageous political critiques, right-wing rants and, adding a much-needed patina of credibility to his efforts, an ex-lawman's insider take on the city's criminal activity.

Blowdown's popularity had led to Patton's frequent appearances on local talk shows and on a few network offerings, such as *Midday with Gemma,* where the eponymous hostess Gemma Bright had just welcomed him to share a periwinkle-blue couch with her previous guest, Carrie Sands, a young vibrantly blond actress who was starring in a new motion picture filming in the city.

When the applause of the primarily female audience began to subside, Patton plopped down on the couch. He leaned in close to the actress and whispered something in her ear that caused her smile to lose its perk. Then he turned his attention toward the show's hostess, adjusting his face in what he probably believed resembled a Gene Hackman–Popeye Doyle half-grin. "Okay, Gemma, I'm here," he said in his familiar, gruff voice. "So what d'ya wanna talk about today?"

"Oh, I think you *know,* Pat." Gemma Bright's Australian accent was elaborate, slightly nasal, and made more distinctive by her odd habit of emphasizing words and syllables in a seemingly random fashion. This, combined with her fortysomething zaftig but stylish good looks, an extroverted personality, and an ability to convey what seemed like genuine interest, had positioned her as the second-most-popular television personality in the Second City. "We want some *dish* on that mys*ter*ious body that washed ashore yesterd*ye.*"

"Dish, huh? Well, lemme tell ya, babe, it ain't all that appetizing."

"Death rarely is," Gemma said.

"That's probably why all those health-conscious wimps kept jogging past the body without stopping," Patton said. "Or could it be that they were just too caught up in their own petty little lives to wanna get involved?"

"That's not fair," Carrie Sands chirped, evidently feeling he was talking about her people. "When you jog you get in the zone and you block out a lot of what's happening around you."

"That explains why most of you bubbleheads voted for our illustrious illegal-alien president. You were in the zone." Patton winked at the audience, which, surprisingly, rewarded him with scattered applause and laughter.

"Holy shit, Billy," my assistant, Kiki Owens, said. "Who is this trog?"

"You know as much about him as I do," I said, which was the truth at the time.

"After the president's release of his full, authenticated birth certificate, this guy must be the last idiot spewing the birther crap. On our network!"

"Oh that pesky First Amendment," I told her.

We were in the studio-six greenroom of Worldwide Broadcasting's Chicago affiliate, WWBC, watching the midday show unfold while I awaited my turn on camera. We were sharing the space with a pale, undernourished-looking guy in his twenties. His black hair was bowl-cut in what may have been an homage to the late Moe Howard, may he rest in Three Stooges Heaven. His concave chest was wrapped in a black

T-shirt emblazoned with the statement "Down is the New Up" in yellow letters. His faded black jeans had slipped low enough on his hips to show an inch or two of candy-striped boxers, which in its way complimented his oversized pink high-top canvas shoes.

"Patton's a local celebrity," he said. "A real asshole who treats his employees like dirt."

"You work for him?" I asked.

He frowned. "Me? I'm Larry Kelsto. Why would I work . . . ? I'm a comic," he stated, adding defensively, "I've been on a bunch of network shows. *Last Comic Standing, Comedy Brew, Last Call with Carson Daly.* Anyway, if you want to know about Pat Patton . . ."

He then went on to provide a Wikipedia-lite explanation of Pat Patton's semi-fame, concluding with, "The guy never met anybody he didn't hate. He's the opposite of Roy Rogers."

"I think you mean Will Rogers," I said.

"Who the hell is Will Rogers?"

"Roy's father," I told him, dismayed that a comedian, even a young one, would have to ask that question.

Larry Kelsto was not really interested in any of the Rogerses, including, I assumed, Kenny or the late Mister. Lowering his voice, he said to Kiki, "You're an actress or a model, right?"

Kiki stared at him. She's an attractive, diminutive black woman who seems as fragile as an orchid, but, as I once witnessed, she can make a six-foot-four, 290-pound Russian Mafia enforcer break down and cry like a baby. Her best weapon is a British accent with which she can draw blood faster than a buck knife. Judging by the look she was giving Larry, she didn't seem to be into younger guys. Or maybe it was the candy-striped boxers. Or the shoes. Probably just Larry.

"Stick to comedy," she said, and focused her attention on the monitor.

That didn't seem to improve her disposition. "I'm picking up a really toxic vibe from Mr. Patton. We should leave now, Billy."

"Are you kidding? What business are we in, again? *Show* business. And what's the cardinal rule? The show must go on."

"I can fill for you," the comedian said.

"Thanks, Larry, but I think I can handle it."

Kiki shook her head. "Big mistake, Billy."

"Relax," I said. "It's just a talk show. After sharing a couch with Carrot Top, listening to him expound on the joy of weightlifting, and Sean Hannity just being Sean Hannity, this will be a breeze."

"Really? Listen to the guy. He's rancid, Billy. He makes Hannity sound like Walter Cronkite."

"Bite your tongue," I said.

On the monitor, Patton's face had turned a sanguine shade as he replied to something the young blond actress had said. "Okay, I give you that, missy. Out of a couple hundred self-absorbed, gotta-stay-in-shape me-firsters, one little wimp shows some sense of civic responsibility by pressing a button on his cute little iPhone to call the CPD. Give 'im the friggin' key to the city, why not?"

"We *tried* to get him for the show," Gemma said, diluting the man's vitriol by choosing to ignore it. "But the police are treating this as if Homeland

Se*cur*ity were being threatened. We couldn't even find out his name."

"All you had to do was ask me, Gemma," Patton said. "It's Shineman. Carl Shineman. They got him locked up tight in his million-dollar high-rise apartment on Elm."

"Why all the *see*crecy?"

"Ah. If I told you that, Gemma, you'd know as much as me."

"How is it, Pat, that you *all*ways seem to be in the *know* on every *crime* story?"

"Honey, as I've told you before, I put in a lotta long, hard years with the CPD, and I was payin' attention every minute. I understand how things work and where to go to get the info that citizens have a right to know."

"Then maybe you should *tell* us why the police are being so *see*cretive."

Patton hesitated, then said, "It's . . . all about the corpse, Gemma."

"The *corpse*?" It was our hostess's turn to address the camera. "This *bad* boy will never even give me a *clue* about what he's going to say once he's out here."

"Where would the fun be in that?" Patton asked with a guffaw. "I get a kick out of seeing your reactions." He faced the audience. "You like to be surprised, too, am I right?"

Applause and giggles.

"Point made, Pat. So what's the big *see*cret about the *corpse*?"

"The police don't want to look like clowns, but the fact is, even with all their state-of-the-art computer toys, they're having the devil's own time making an ID."

"Had the body been in the lake that long?" Gemma inquired.

"The water and the fishies did some damage, to be sure," Patton said. "But that's not the real problem."

I noticed a tiny crease appear above Gemma's right eyebrow. Love that high-def quality. She seemed to be getting a little peeved at the way Patton was drawing it out. "And the *real* problem *is* . . . ?" she demanded.

Grinning, the ex-cop ran a thick finger across his neck. "The corpse's head had been chopped off clean. And they can't find it anywhere."

Enjoy your lunch, kids.

Chapter
TWO

Gemma blinked.

I'd written off as nonsense her comment about not knowing what Patton was going to say. Even if Standards and Practices didn't have their own often too-rigid rules of dos and don'ts, talk show hosts are usually control freaks, at least professionally. But from where I was sitting, it looked like genuine surprise on her elaborately pancaked face.

She waited for the gasps from the audience to

subside and asked, "You're *say*ing someone de*capi*-tated the victim?"

"He sure as heck didn't do it himself," Patton said. "His hands and feet were chopped off, too."

"OhmyGod!" Carrie Sands exclaimed. "Then it had to be murder."

The view switched from a two-shot of Patton and Gemma to an angle that included the actress.

"The missing hands do kinda rule out suicide, babe," Patton said. "But like the old joke says, they could always use what was left for third base."

"That's disgusting," Carrie said.

Patton shrugged. "All in the eye of the beholder. I know people who say pole dancing is disgusting. Personally, I'm a fan."

Carrie glared at the grinning man.

"If you can get your *mind* off of *pole* dancing for a few more minutes, Pat," Gemma said, "is there anything else you can tell us about the mys*ter*ious body?"

The camera moved in on Patton.

"Sure," he said. "The vic was Caucasian. Male. That much is still in evidence. Wherever the head is, it's got brown hair. In his forties, they think. No DNA match so far. The feeling at Homicide is that he's somebody whose identity would point the way to the killer or killers."

The camera closed in on Patton and Gemma, catching a glint in her green eyes. "And they have no i*dea* who the poor soul might be?"

Patton lowered his head and tried another Gene Hackman grin. "They don't."

"But you do?"

He shrugged. "Let's just say I've got a hunch. If it

pans out, you and your audience will be the first to hear, Gemma."

"Does your *hunch* have anything to do with the work you were doing before your retirement? Back when you were on the Organized Crime Task Force?"

He smiled. "Good try, Gemma. But no. Those Outfit guys usually didn't bother cuttin' off parts of the body if they were using the vic for fish food. When they put somebody in the drink, they stayed in the drink."

"W-whoever did this didn't try to keep the . . . d-dead man submerged?" Carrie Sands asked, catching the camera operator off guard. By the time he found her, Patton was answering the question.

"They tried. The theory is the body had been anchored by a heavy weight but broke loose when the fish came to dinner. Judging by the teeth marks, they say it mighta been a bull shark did most of the dining. I been living in Chi my whole life and I never knew there were bull shark in Lake Michigan."

Gemma Bright must have realized the idea of a shark nibbling on the corpse was one nightmare image too many for her lunchtime audience. "Yes. Well. *Nas*ty business, in*deed*."

She turned to the camera and said, "A real-life murder *mys*tery, and we'll be bringing you the events as they un*fold*. Now, coming up is a *charm*ing man— you all know him from *Wake Up, America!*, seen every *week*day morning from seven to nine right here on WWBC Chicago, and on his own cooking show on the Wine and Dine cable network, Chef *Billy Blessing*.

"But first . . ."

As the show cut to a commercial, I stood, fully aware of Kiki's gimlet eye. She was on the verge of saying something, but Larry Kelsto interrupted her.

"Only fourteen minutes left," he whined. "I'm getting that bumped feeling. I knew it as soon as Patton showed up, the asshole."

I took a few deep breaths and tried to relax. A young woman appeared at the door, wearing denims, a white WBC T-shirt, a barbed-wire tattoo on her left wrist, and a headset. Whispering into the headset, she approached and quickly and efficiently checked a tiny wireless microphone before hiding it behind my tie.

"This way, Chef Blessing," she said.

"Lose the goofy grin, Billy," Kiki advised. "It's inappropriate with all the talk about a headless dead body."

As I followed my guide along the darkened backstage area, I heard Gemma announcing, "Here he is, one of your *fav*orites and my *very* good friend, super-chef *Billy Blessing*."

A stagehand pulled back a flap in the dark curtain, and I stepped into bright lights and a response that sounded, to my ears, at least, a little more enthusiastic than the blinking APPLAUSE signs usually produced.

The other two guests shifted on the couch as I took our hostess's hand and kissed it. I can be debonair when I want to. I gave the still-applauding audience a friendly wave and took my place on the end of the couch.

Gemma smelled of magnolias. Patton smelled of a spicy aftershave and, unless I missed my guess, a mid-morning gin.

"Billy, it's *won*derful to have you here again," our hostess said. "It's been *much* too long since your last visit."

"About three years," I said. "Definitely too long. This is a great city."

Gemma faced the camera. "This is the busiest man I know. In addition to his so *very* entertaining television work, he has a *mar*velous restaurant in Manhattan. He writes cookbooks and—"

"He was mixed up in some murders on the West Coast," Patton said.

A shadow of annoyance flitted over Gemma's face. She wasn't used to being upstaged, especially by a guest who'd already moved to the less-active middle of the couch. "How right you are, Pat," she said.

She leaned closer to me and, using a softer, more intimate voice, said, "You went through *quite* an ordeal in Southern Cali*for*nia last year, Billy. And before that, you helped the police with a series of murders in New York *City*, as we know from the fascinatingly suspenseful *book* you wrote. What was it called?"

"*Wake Up to Murder*," I said. "It's available in trade paperback."

"You're becoming a regular *super*sleuth, like . . . Monk."

I myself would have opted for Alex Cross or Easy Rawlins. Or even Guy Hanks.

"The police did most of the work," I said.

"Well, I'm *sure* you contri—"

"You were right in the middle of the West Coast murders." This time, it was Carrie Sands, speaking up from the never-to-be-heard-from far end of the couch. "I just read poor Stew Gentry's book and he says you did all the detective work."

"Ah, yes," Gemma said coolly. "*That* book. We had the young man on the show who helped poor, *sad* Stew write the book. Harry something . . ."

"Harry Paynter," I said. There'd been a time when Harry was supposed to have helped me with my book, but he'd declined, in favor of *Fade-out: The Stew Gentry Story*. Just as well. Harry was a little too much of a hack for my taste.

"His and Stew's book garnished un*ani*mous critical raves," Gemma said. "And it's at the *top* of the bestseller lists."

"In second place, actually," Carrie said. "Gerard's latest, *The Thief Who Stole Big Ben,* is number one."

The French novelist Gerard Parnelle had begun a series of thrillers about a scruffy Marseilles orphan who, through several improbable encounters, had been transformed into a beautiful, remarkably resourceful master thief. Book one, *The Thief Who Stole the Eiffel Tower,* had been the basis for a motion picture so successful in Europe and Asia it had heralded a Newer Wave for the French film industry. The movie Carrie was making in Chicago was an American version, *The Thief Who Stole Trump Tower.* If they wanted to steal something really big, they could've ripped off Trump's ego.

The recently published sequel, *Big Ben,* had arrived at the tipping point of the series's international popularity.

"Gerard's book is *numero uno,* of course," Gemma said. "And, Carrie, I want you to remind that *bad* boy that he owes me a visit."

"He's in Paris, Gemma," the actress said. "He flew there weeks ago."

"Well, he'll just *have* to fly back," Gemma said before turning to me and, without batting an eye, asking, "Do you ag*ree* with what Stew had to say about you in *his* book, Billy?"

"I . . . I haven't read it."

That was a lie, but from what I've observed, lies don't count on TV talk shows any more than they do in politics.

"Sandy Selman's making a movie based on Stew's story," Carrie announced. She was apparently the source of all that was literary in Hollywood.

"Really? Will you be *in* it, Billy?"

"Doubtful," I told her. Hoping to close down the topic and move on to the reason the network's public relations team had arranged for me to be on the show, I added, "That whole thing is pretty much old news."

"Still, it's ex*cit*ing to hear about it first*hand*. As I recall, it was only by the *merest* stroke of good fortune you weren't killed. I'm sure our audience would love to hear what that was *like*."

Sighing, I dutifully obliged with a brief wrap-up of my brushes with death, being careful not to say anything that was not part of the public record. Having returned to Los Angeles for the trial, I'd had my fill of courtroom command performances.

"Do you think the punishment *fit* the crime?" Gemma asked.

"Happily, that was not my call," I said.

"What the hell does it take for those touchy-feely idiots in La-La land to put killers away?" Pat Patton exploded.

"They didn't go free," I said.

"No. But they could be out in eight. And then they might come looking for the guy who helped put 'em away. Something to think about, huh, Billy boy?"

He was actually grinning. "Anything to make you happy, Pat," I replied.

Then, assuming that even a lame segue is better than none at all, I said, "Speaking of 'looking' for something, Gemma, I hope your audience will be looking in on Monday when *Wake Up, America!* begins the first of two weeks' telecasting right here from Chicago. We'll be reminding the rest of the country about what a great city this is."

Thankfully, Gemma hopped right on board and we went back and forth on the glories of the Second City for a while.

I'm usually relaxed even in this kind of environment, but I was thrown off a little by the sight of Patton in my peripheral vision. He kept staring at me—not in fascination or awe or even professional courtesy but with narrowed eyes, as if I were an irritant that was causing him some internal distress.

I tried shifting on the couch until he was out of my line of sight, but that left me at an awkward angle. Which was making Gemma nervous.

During the commercial break, I turned to Patton and said, "So how do you like me so far?"

He continued to glare, ignoring my question. Then, lowering his voice, he said, "We've met before, right?"

"Not that I recall. But I'm on TV every morning. Sometimes people—"

"I've seen you on TV. Not so much on your show.

I listen to the radio in the morning. It was on the news coverage of those murders. But I've got a crappy little screen. Eyeballin' you up close and personal, I'm pretty sure we met way back, Billy, when you had a lot more hair and less pounds. Yeah. Only the name wasn't Blessing. Billy . . . something else."

"We've never met," I said, wondering if that was true. Hoping that it was.

"We're chatting with one of our *fav*orites, Chef Billy Blessing," Gemma said, signaling to us that we were back on camera. "He and the rest of the *Wake Up, America!* team will be greeting you *live* from Chicago for the next two weeks over WWBC."

She turned toward me. "Will all the cohosts be here, Billy?"

I'm sure I answered the question and that I continued to keep up my end of the conversation, but my thoughts were definitely elsewhere.

I heard Gemma announce tomorrow's guests and apologize to Larry Kelsto for bumping him once again. She then informed the studio audience that each and every one of them was getting a complete makeover, courtesy of several local entrepreneurs. With the squeals of their delight almost drowning out her goodbyes, *Midday with Gemma* drew to a close.

As was the custom, while the credits rolled, Gemma, Carrie Sands, Patton, and I all stood and pretended to be chatting among ourselves as if we were old pals. Actually, Carrie was saying she'd be seeing me on Tuesday's *Wake Up*. We were giving her movie a big push because we'd made a first-look deal with its writer, Gerard Parnelle, for a TV series idea he was putting together.

Patton was not playing our game exactly. He remained silent, staring at me, sly smile in place.

Given the all clear, I headed for the greenroom and Kiki, but Patton blocked my way. "Billy Blanchard. That's your real name, right?"

The sight of his smile had taken the surprise out of it. I stared at him, unblinking and unemotional. "My real name is Billy Blessing," I said, walking around him.

"Now, maybe," he said, keeping pace. "But back at the tail end of the eighties, pal, you and I both know it was Blanchard. And you claimed a body that turned up in Cicero. I'll have the stiff's name in a second."

"I don't know what you're talking about, Patton," I lied.

Kiki appeared at the far side of the set. Frowning, she marched toward us. "I'm sorry, Billy, but we have to go now."

I nodded to Patton and allowed my very efficient assistant to pull me away.

"Judging by the hooked-fish expression on your face," she said, "I assumed you didn't want to continue your conversation with that creep."

"Absolutely not."

"What was he saying to you, anyway?"

"Nothing very pleasant."

"I told you," she said. "He's a monster."

I turned.

Patton had been joined by a very tall, very muscular, very black man, neatly dressed in tan slacks and a tight white T-shirt. He was in his twenties, but the slicked-down hair and thin mustache belonged to another generation. He shifted from one foot to the next, somewhat impatiently, while Patton continued to stare at me.

The ex-cop raised one hand and gave me a jolly finger wiggle, as if seeing me off on a pleasant journey.

"A monster," I agreed.

Chapter
THREE

The monster rested uncomfortably at the back of my mind until that night, when I met for dinner with a few newly arrived members of team *Wake Up*. Namely, coanchors Lance Tuttle and Gin McCauley; ex-starlet Karma Singleton, our latest entertainment reporter; producer Arnie Epps; and executive producer Trina Lomax, who'd opened up the purse strings for a lavish feed at a pricey but genuinely unique restaurant in the city's Old Town section that owes as much to scientific innovation as it does to Cordon Bleu.

Our culinary adventure began with little round, crisp morsels that tasted like the best peanut-butter-and-jelly sandwich I'd ever devoured. This was followed by eleven equally playful and unusual mini-courses, ranging from the essence of shrimp cocktail to lobster with vapor of rosemary (boiling water poured over rosemary leaves at the table), all proffered on delightfully odd dinnerware. The pb&j, for example, arrived nestled in something that resembled the legs of a steel spider resting on its back. The shrimp cocktail essence was sprayed into the mouth via an atomizer.

To bottom-line it, our senses (including sense of humor) were happily occupied for nearly three hours.

We'd just polished off an extraordinary dessert (flash-frozen chocolate mousse, complete with spray dried coconut milk, cocoa crumbs, anise, and a few other ingredients) prepared directly on our dining table by the restaurant's owner, when Gin McCauley asked me a question that turned my heart chillier than the mousse.

"Say again?"

"Ah was wonderin' what you can tell me about this Pat Patton charactah? He said you and he wah ol' friends." Gin's Southern accent had been intensified that night by several strawberry margaritas. Usually I found it sweetly charming.

"When were you talking with Patton?"

"This evenin'. Soon's ah got unpacked."

"And why were you talking with him?"

"'Cause ah'm interviewin' him on Monday's show. Ah'm guessin' he was exaggeratin' your friendship?"

"A little," I said. "Why interview *him*?"

"Because Trina tole me to."

"He claims he has inside information on the headless corpse that all Chicago is talking about," Trina Lomax answered. "And Gemma tells me he's something of a local institution."

"He belongs in an institution," I said. "He's a right-wing nutjob."

Trina waved the comment away. "Who isn't these days?" she said.

"Ah'd like to think ah'm not," Gin said.

"Nor I," Lance added. "How bad is this guy, Billy?"

"On Gemma's show he was still calling the president an illegal alien," I said.

"Well, for Christ's sake," Lance said. "After the final certificate disclosure?"

"Le's dump this turkey," Gin said to Trina.

Our executive producer opened her mouth, then paused, as if censoring herself. She frowned and spent about a thirty-count watching the staff clean the dregs of our dessert from the tabletop. Finally, she took a deep breath and said, "I was waiting for a slightly less public moment to have this conversation, but . . . I'm sure all of you must be aware of the criticism Worldwide has been receiving lately from . . . some quarters. That we're White House lackeys. That we're biased, anticonservative members of the liberal elite."

"Bullshit," Lance said. "We have Republicans on the show all the time." He glared at Karma Singleton. "We even have 'em on staff."

"That may be," Trina said. "But ratings are down and according to Fields and Fields's most recent survey, a lot of our viewers think our programming is ignoring the neoconservative trend in America. Gretchen is . . . concerned."

That would be Gretchen Di Voss, the current head of Worldwide Broadcasting, whose family has been in charge of the network since her grandfather, Harold Di Voss, created it in 1931.

"How concerned?" I asked.

"She has requested we consider making a few changes," Trina said. "Nothing more drastic than adding an occasional voice from the right. Like Mr. Patton."

"If he's a right-wingah, maybe Karma oughta do the interview," Gin said.

"That's a brilliant idea . . . ," our entertainment reporter said.

She was a tall, willowy redhead who had appeared as a tall, willowy redhead in a couple of movies that no one but late-night cable watchers have ever seen. She had recently played a tall, willowy redhead weathergirl in a short-lived Worldwide sitcom, *Fair and Warmer*, set in a small-town television station. And now she was our tall, willowy redhead. The difference being that, suddenly freed from the confines of a prepared script, she was able to speak her mind—which belonged to someone a little to the right of Genghis Khan, as played by John Wayne.

" . . . and this is brilliant news, Trina," she continued. "Finally, we'll have a politically balanced show."

"Fair and balanced," I said.

"An' brilliant," Gin said.

"Exactly," Karma said, a little too pleased by the news and herself to realize she was being ribbed.

"Well, that may be," Trina said, "but Gin will be interviewing Mr. Patton. Now, who's up for a nightcap at the hotel bar?"

* * *

On the cab ride to the nightcap, I played back a message left by Cassandra Shaw, the remarkably efficient hostess-manager of my restaurant in Manhattan. The tone was typically acerbic. "Too busy out on the town to answer your phone, Billy? Well, no matter. We had another power outage in the main dining room just after seven. I reset the breakers, but needless to say, the early diners did not take it well. Complimentary desserts for all.

"At nine-thirty, the place was packed and that asshole city councilman Baragray dropped by with some of his friends, sans reservation, causing quite a ruckus and demanding a table. I suggested they join the mayor and his friends in the LaGuardia Room. Upon hearing that His Honor was on the premises, they scooted away as quiet as church mice. Other than that, all was well on this very busy Friday night. Over and out."

"Ever'thing okay?" Gin asked. "You got that worry crease in your forehead." She was sitting beside me on the rear seat. Arnie Epps was up front with the cabbie. We were trailing a cab transporting the others.

"We had a power outage at the Bistro earlier this week," I said. "Our electrician didn't find anything obvious. His solution, naturally enough, was to rewire the whole building. Mine was to wait and see. But there was another outage tonight. It looks as if I'll probably be paying for his kid's college education."

"Bummer," she said. "Uh, Billy, why do you think Trina's so insistent on me interviewin' this Patton charactah?"

I shrugged.

"Arnie?" she asked.

Arnie Epps continued to stare out the window, pretending not to hear. Which wasn't a good sign, since it indicated he possessed info we wouldn't like. He's an odd dude, our producer: a tall, ungainly man with a penchant for Hawaiian shirts loud enough to make your eyes bleed and an often-unnerving passivity. But he wasn't a bad guy and was actually a fair conversationalist if the subject was television history, the works of Charles Dickens, early jazz recordings, or East Coast flora and fauna, heavy on the flora.

"Hey, Arnie," Gin said louder. "What's the deal on Patton?"

He hesitated briefly, then replied, "Trina wants to see the guy in action."

"She should check today's *Midday with Gemma*," I said. "That'll tell her all she needs to know."

"Trina's not exactly a fan of Gemma's," Arnie said. "She wants to see the compatibility between Patton and Gin."

"Why?" I asked, though I thought I knew.

"The guy's an eyeball magnet. He's on Gretchen's short list for new regulars."

My fears confirmed, I slumped against the car seat. Then I brightened. "He struck me as a die-hard Chicagoan," I said. "I can't see him moving to New York."

"Actually, the plan would be for him to come in only once a month or so," Arnie said. "The rest of the time, he'd be reporting from here."

"Plan? There's a plan already in place?"

"Predicated on how well it goes on Monday," Arnie said.

I turned to Gin. She winked. Then she gave me a sweet smile and drew her index finger across her neck.

Chapter FOUR

In the suite of rooms above my restaurant that I call home I'm usually up at five on weekdays, getting ready for the morning show. Weekends find me sleeping in a little longer, till nine or even ten on Saturdays. Because there'd been more than one nightcap in the hotel bar (which we'd closed at three, by the way), I could have used a little extra bedtime that Saturday. But I didn't get it.

Something—exactly what I wasn't sure, only that I was dreaming of birds chirping—woke me at a little after eight. I opened my eyes, blinked a few times, and wondered where I was and why I could see sky outside my bedroom window. Sky but no birds.

My head felt as if it was filled with Kleenex. Used Kleenex. In an effort to inject a small element of kindness in an unkind world, I will not even begin to describe what the inside of my mouth resembled.

I staggered to the bathroom and did everything that had to be done. Revived by a hot and then cold shower and the taste of strenuously applied toothpaste and wrapped in a plush terry bathrobe provided by the hotel, I plopped down on the sofa in the suite's sitting room and dialed room service.

I put in a request for the biggest omelet on the menu, two servings of crispy bacon, toast, and hot coffee, and plenty of it. Then, confident that the ball was rolling, I leaned back against the sofa cushion and began working the TV's remote control. I flipped through a morass of brightly colored kids' cartoons; of live, recent, and classic sporting events; movies that I hadn't liked the first time I saw them; sincere-looking hucksters peddling cosmetics and cures; and screaming-head news channels. Finally, I arrived at a relatively calm oasis, the repeat of last night's Charlie Rose interview.

Charlie was talking to a Democratic congressman whom, I'm sorry to say, I did not recognize. Charlie asked him if he thought the Dems would reclaim the House in 2012. And—surprise, surprise—the congressman's response to that lobbed puffball was: "Heck, yes." From that point, he and Charlie engaged in a somewhat laid-back battle for control of talking points. I'm not sure who won, because a gong announced what I assumed was my breakfast waiting at the door to the suite.

I could almost taste the omelet as I danced across the carpet. Reaching for the doorknob, I exhaled, intending to breathe deeply of the comforting aroma of coffee and eggs mixed with melted cheese, peppers, and onions.

Instead, my nostrils were filled with the overpowering scents of Old Spice mixed with morning cigarette breath.

Eddie "Pat" Patton was at my door, wearing dark

gray slacks, a matching gray jacket, a gray Kangol cap, and a nasty grin. He reminded me of an evil Disney rat, specifically, the one threatening the baby in *Lady and the Tramp*. (If you'll pardon the digression, it's always struck me as odd that a company built on the popularity of a mouse would be so quick to demonize rats.)

"Morning, Billy," he said, taking a step forward, so that his right shoe blocked me from slamming the door in his face. A move perfected by door-to-door salesmen. And cops. "I hope you don't mind my dropping by. I phoned, but you didn't pick up."

"You phoned?"

"About a half-hour ago," he said. "Right, Nat?"

"About then." Nat had been standing to Patton's left, out of my line of sight. The young muscle with the slicked-down hair who'd been with him after the midday show telecast. Today, he was wearing tan poplin slacks and a cocoa-brown T-shirt that fit him like a second skin. He was clutching a bright red folder in his huge right hand.

"Guess you mighta been on the throne," Patton said.

"I was asleep," I said, realizing now that the bird chirp had been coming from the hotel phone.

"Well, I'm glad I took a chance you might be here," Patton said. He turned to Nat. "Gimme the file, boy. And go wait for me in the car."

The big man's mouth tensed. He handed his employer the folder. Then, with some reluctance, he drifted away, presumably to do as he was told.

"This won't take long, Billy," Patton said, walking past me into the suite. "Not that you seem to be in any hurry to greet the day."

"What can I do for you?" I asked, closing the door and following him into the sitting room.

He did a 360 of the room, took in the floor-to-ceiling windows, the French provincial furniture, the Degas prints on the pale blue walls, and the average-size TV monitor. "Looks like an expensive French whore's boo-dwarr," he said.

"I'll take your word for it," I said. "What do you want?"

He lowered himself onto the sofa with a combination grunt and sigh, emitting a softer grunt when he leaned forward to place the folder on the coffee table. "You wanna go put on knickers, be my guest," he said. "I'm in no hurry."

"I repeat: What do you want?"

"You gonna stay in your robe, Billy, close it up and park."

He took out a pack of cigarettes and looked around for an ashtray.

"Nonsmoking room," I said, tightening the robe's belt and taking the chair near him.

"You fucking with me? You payin'—what?—four or five hundred bucks a night to stay in this antique showroom and they don't let your guests light up?"

"You're not exactly my guest, and even if you were, I wouldn't want you lighting up here. Kill yourself if you want. But don't take me with you."

"I'm surprised you're so gullible, Billy," he said, slipping the cigarettes back into his jacket pocket. "It's all bullshit scare tactics, you know. Second-hand smoke. Global warming. Cholesterol. From the white-coat whackjobs who brought us the bird flu pandemic."

Oh, yeah, he'd be a cherished font of information for our morning show. I indicated the red folder. "That for me?"

He nodded, edging it toward me with one finger. "It took me a while to dig the original out of the boxes of case files I got stacked away. Then getting it all copied."

He checked his watch. "Aw, hell. I don't think I got time for you to order up some coffee for me."

"That is too bad," I said.

"Price of being a busy man. Just look that over," he said. "Nothing you don't know, of course. Just a kinda show-and-tell that I know, too."

Chapter FIVE

He was right: There was nothing in the red file's newspaper clips that I didn't know.

On April 19, 1986, one William "Billy" Blanchard had been arrested in Detroit, Michigan, for "obtaining money by fraudulent means." As the printout in Patton's folder detailed, the specific crime was an attempt to sell a controlling interest in what was then known as Motown Records, a company with which Blanchard had no legitimate association.

By then the owner of record, Berry Gordy, had moved from Motown to Showtown, Hollywood and its environs, and it had been well reported by the media that he was thinking of divesting himself of his holdings in the music company. According to the printout, Blanchard and an unknown associate, posing as representatives of Gordy's organization, had convinced a local African American businessman, Marcus Aurelius "M. A." Kibbler, to "acquire for a specific purchase price" a majority interest in the corporation and "bring Motown back to the real Motown."

Until then, I'd been assisting my foster father, Paul Lamont, in his cons. But I had researched Kibbler, discovered his unwavering pride in the city of his birth, and created what Paul called the playbook for the job. As a sort of rite of passage, he had suggested I take the lead position in the scam.

High on adrenaline and the self-confidence of youth, I'd closed the deal by providing the mark with a reason even more potent than Detroit pride. "Though Mr. Gordy would want his money in cash as clean as your baby sister's soul," I'd told the mark, "a successful record company would provide an ideal legitimate enterprise through which one might freshen funds, should one happen to have any such funds in need of freshening."

Kibbler, owner and operator of the largest illegal drug dealership in the Michigan-Ohio-Indiana tristate area, took less than a minute to make up his mind. "I'll have the money for you in two days," he said, shaking my hand.

The upside of taking a mark like Kibbler, I remembered thinking at the time, was that he could not go running to the law. The obvious downside was that my life wouldn't be worth a scratched Motown CD if we ever met again. Which was why Paul and I planned to depart the USA for a long while, as soon as we got our hands on Kibbler's cash. Europe, we were thinking. Paul had always wanted to spend time on the Spanish island of Ibiza, telling me he would be "in his element" at a place that had been home to the infamous art forger Elmyr de Hory and the even more infamous author of the fake Howard Hughes autobiography, Clifford Irving.

I often wondered what my life would have been like if we'd taken that trip. But it was not to be. Hours before the loot was to be exchanged for totally bogus shares of stock, Kibbler was arrested by an undercover DEA agent. Even more unfortunate for me, the agent had not only been present for my pitch, he'd been wearing a wire.

Kibbler was sentenced to a couple of decades at Milan Federal Correctional. Because no money had changed hands and especially because I'd lucked out appearing before a judge with a sense of humor, I went away for only a year and a day to Marquette Prison on Lake Superior. And Berry Gordy, never knowing the part he'd unwittingly played in the whole affair, sold Motown to Universal MCI for considerably more money than I'd dare try to con out of even an easy mark like Marcus Kibbler.

"I'll need that back," Patton said, holding out his hand for the folder. "It's just copies. I've got the original newspaper clips in a safe place."

I presented him with the folder.

"I don't know when you turned yourself into Billy Blessing," he said. "I know you were still Blanchard in April of '87, when you came out to Cicero to claim the body of your con-man buddy Lamont."

I stared at him and remained silent.

"You're right about us not meeting. But I was there at the mortuary. Know why?"

I didn't know. I didn't care. But that didn't matter to Patton.

"I'd heard Lamont had been trying to game some dangerous locals, and it looked like Louis Venici, one of my favorite goombahs, had done the job on him. Probably with his cousin, one Sal Bassillio. But I had no proof. Then this ex-con kid shows up out of nowhere to roll Lamont's bones home to the Big Apple. I was hoping Louie and Sal might try to take you out, too. But unlike Lamont, you did not dawdle getting out of town."

"If you'd told me your plan, I might have stayed longer," I said. "Worn a target on my back."

"*Mox nix,*" he said. "Not long after you went on your way, the two punks wound up out at O'Hare, stuffed in the trunk of Sal's famous yellow Caddy. You wouldn't know anything about that?"

I was never aware of the specifics, only that Paul's boyhood friend, New York City original gangsta Henry Julian, had told me he'd "taken care of the situation."

"Enough of the history lesson," I said. "What's your point?"

"Just a friendly drop-by." He used the sofa's armrest to lever himself upright. "Sorry I gotta run.

Things to do. Later today I'm taping a promo at WWBC for Monday's show. I guess you heard you and I are going to be working together."

"Hard to believe," I said, accompanying him to the door. I opened it, expecting him to leave. Hoping.

He stopped just short of the threshold.

"For the record, Venici and Bassillio may have put the bullets into your pal, but the goombah who ordered the kill is presently enjoying what I would call a very enviable, very visible life, just a few miles away from this hotel."

The news hit me like a sucker punch. I tried to pretend it had had no effect, but not well enough, apparently.

"Didn't mean to shake your tree," Patton said. "But think about it. You and Lamont played your games with scumbags. Probably thought of yourselves as some kind of urban Robin Hoods. Bullshit like that. Venici was a qualified scumbag, without doubt, and he lived high, but he didn't have the smarts to figure out he was being conned by a real pro like Lamont. That took brains."

"Who killed Paul?"

"A very interesting member of the Italian brotherhood named Giovanni Polvere. A subtle crumb-bum who made it his business to stay off of everybody's radar. Except mine, of course. Shortly after Lamont's death, he went into the wind and reinvented himself. Did a lot better job of it than you. Of course, he had more money than you. And more motivation. I'm not just talking about your pal's murder, or Venici's and Bassillio's. Polvere made some serious enemies here in town. But they're all behind bars now, allowing him to come back with his makeover." He chuckled. "Funny thought. He changed his face and now he's here doing that on a grand scale."

"Stop all this cat-and-mouse bullshit," I said. "What is it you want?"

"Like you, I'm in the information business," Patton said. "But a lot of my work involves providing my information to private parties on a more limited basis."

"Just spell it out," I said.

He pushed the door shut, as if there were paparazzi lurking in the corridor. Maybe there were.

Lowering his voice, he said, "If you've got any interest in knowing what Gio Polvere's calling himself these days, I can provide that for a consultant's fee of just fifty grand."

"Good day, Mr. Patton. You're a little too late and much too expensive."

I reached past him to open the door, but he placed a hand on my arm. "That's your call," he said. "But it'll force me to work the other end of the street."

"If that's a threat, I don't quite get it," I said. "I'm a little out of practice dealing with lowlifes."

Patton stared at me for a beat, then grinned as if humoring me. "You're upset, so I'll ignore the insult. Here's the situation in a nutshell: If you won't take advantage of my services, I'm sure Gio Polvere will, especially after I point out how your connection to the late Paul Lamont might prove a threat to him."

"And why won't he think you're a bigger threat?" I asked. "You're the guy who knows about his past."

"Oh, hell, Blessing, if I haven't learned how to handle situations like that by now, do you think I'd still be around to—"

A sturdy knock on the door not only interrupted Patton, it made him jump.

"Room service," someone announced through the door.

Patton frowned, and his hand moved under his coat before he stepped aside.

"I don't think you'll need that," I said, and opened the door for the attendant to wheel in my breakfast, complete with a yellow tulip stuck in a slender glass vase.

Patton relaxed and let his arm drop.

The attendant looked at both of us and said, "I'm sorry. They said service for one. I can go—"

"No problem," I told him. "This . . . gentleman was just leaving."

Patton lifted the lid on my breakfast. He reached over the buttery omelet, plucked one strip of bacon, and made his exit, nibbling it.

And for the first time, I watched a pig eat bacon. Kind of lost my appetite.

Chapter
SIX

"I've never heard of Gio Polvere, Billy." Henry Julian's deep croak was crisp and clear in my ear. "Which makes me doubt he was a big boy in Chitown. As for the other two punksters, I'm aware of their fate, but I was not responsible for it. Not that I shed any tears for 'em, unnerstand."

My phone call had found him at Glory's Doughnut Shop in Brooklyn. Henry owned the shop and the building in which it stood. His mother, Glory, had turned the place into a local landmark. It was presently run by his sister and her pretty daughter. Since his retirement, Henry spent most of his mornings there, at a table in the rear, dressed in a coat and tie, sipping coffee and catching up on the news of his city and the world.

"Back then, after Paul's funeral," I said, "when I told you I was going to hunt down the men who murdered him, you said you'd taken care of it."

"I beg to differ, young man. I said it had been taken care of."

I closed my eyes, ashamed of the serious mistake I'd just made, accusing him of murder on an open phone line. "My big mouth," I said. "I'm sorry, Henry."

He chuckled. "I'm almos' flattered you'd think my phone might be tapped, Billy. The Feds don't give a damn about this ole man anymore. 'Specially when they got a budget tighter than my socks an' terrorists to deal with. The killin' of that rat Osama didn't make things any easier for 'em. What I'm sayin' is, no sooner I'd found out from a source on the ground that Venici an' the other one had done for Paul, I sent a few of my guys to Chicago to . . . talk to 'em. By the time they got there, the I-ties already were occupyin' the trunk of their sedan. My source informed me they'd been offed in a territorial dispute. Nothin' to do with Paul. So my guys came home. And that was that."

"Sounds like your source was wrong," I said.

"Could be. Polvere is somethin' I'm gonna have to look into."

"Just look, right, Henry?"

"You think what? That I'm gonna send a hit squad out there?"

"Well, Henry, you did send—"

"That was then, Billy. I'm in full retirement now. The most I do is just look into things. Maybe make a few phone calls. Like that.

"Enlighten me more about this ex-cop. But lemme get this gizmo workin' first."

"Gizmo?"

"I got an iPad," Henry said. "Birthday gift from my gran'daughter, Rasheeda. She said my newspapers were too messy. And I got this whatcha-call-it, this app lets me type up notes. Okay, I got it goin'. Give."

As soon as I recovered from the news that Henry had joined the Steve Jobs generation, I told him everything I knew about Pat Patton.

"That his name, huh? Like Dick Tracy's old partner?"

"Beats me," I said. "But this Patton's real first name is Edward or Eddie."

"By any name, soun's like a man needs takin' down a peg. But I'm curious why he's bullshittin' you about Gio Polvere."

"Maybe he's not," I said.

"Think about it, Billy. The man's smart. His story about Polvere is his plan B. He lays it out aforehand in case you say no to the blackmail. He gets you scared of the boogeyman, you'll pay up. An' you won't try to get ahead of the scandal by goin' public yourself."

"But suppose Polvere really did order Paul's death."

"All I'm sayin', Billy, is if this Patton, who don't soun' like a virgin blackmailer, has been sittin' on a secret about a major player for twenty-five years, it's probably because of fear. Highly unlikely he's gonna suddenly get the courage to go chat up a super-dangerous son of a bitch like he says Polvere is."

"Patton doesn't strike me as having a rich imagination."

"That's what needs lookin' into. He was on the job when Paul was murdered. He mighta found out somethin'. But like I said, he didn't do nothin' with it then, and I don't see him doin' anything with it now. Still, I'll look into what he's got."

"Henry . . ."

"Nothin' violent, Billy. I swear. Maybe I can get him to lower that fiddy-gran' tag. We owe it to Paul to find out, right?"

"I wouldn't want—"

"Don't be doubtin' my word, son," he said. "Not a hair will be mussed on Mr. Patton's head. Now, he'll be comin' back at you with a new offer. Fo'ty gran', maybe. Walk away from him. Let me take care of it."

"They may be hiring him for our morning show," I said.

"Well, if that don't beat all? Usin' his piddlin' website is one thing, but a network TV show? Man, that's a free license to blackmail. You better straighten that out with your bosses or he could be puttin' your mug shots on your own show."

"I'm a little less worried about that than I am about the possibility of Polvere being real," I said. "I don't want to have to keep looking over my shoulder."

"Remember what Satchel Paige said?"

"'Don't look back, because something might be gaining on you.'"

"Bum advice. That's precisely when you want to be lookin' back. Even if I'm right about Patton bein' a bullshitter, you be careful in that town. They can say what they want about New York, but the bodies they pull out of the East River usually got their heads still attached."

Good point.

Chapter
SEVEN

I didn't need Henry's final warning to depress me.

I was far from convinced that Patton had been conning me. What if Polvere was real and believed I was a danger to him? How long would I last without having even a clue as to his current identity?

That was a worst-case scenario, of course. And the best case? Patton would sell me out to the supermarket tabloids. All right. Suppose I did wind up on the cover of the *Inquirer*. Well, maybe not the cover. That was reserved for Brad and Angelina and UFOs. On page two, then. How bad would it be? Twenty-five years ago, I paid a price for trying to cheat a dishonest man. It didn't seem like a career killer. Might even give me a little street cred.

Who was I kidding? As a celebrity chef/restaurateur I needed street cred about as much as I needed gingivitis.

What to do?

After about an hour of that, Kiki arrived to plague me with my morning show homework, and Patton, the former Gio Polvere, and the long-deceased Messrs. Venici and Bassillio were pushed to a temporary compartment of my mental vault.

Over a room-service luncheon of cheeseburgers, which, though admittedly delicious, cost nearly as much as a McDonald's franchise, we worked through schedules, correspondence, and publicity handouts for my week's interviewees—among them two city chefs, the newest pubescent singing sensation, and a former *Tribune* reporter who'd written a new biography of the late mayor Richard J. Daley, titled *Da Mare*.

Kiki had brought a copy of the Daley bio. Judging by the humongous size of the tome, the author had done a day-by-day analysis of Daley's seventy-four years.

"I hope he's not expecting me to hold this monster up for the camera," I said.

"It's all a matter of balance," Kiki said. "I've been carrying it in my right hand, and my laptop and everything else in my left. No problem at all."

"Yeah? Well, you work out every day." I lifted the cover of the book, then flipped a few pages. "I'll never get this read by Wednesday."

"Just look at the section with photographs and captions and fake it," she said. "Like you always do."

"That's not true. I usually ask for an audio version and then play it while I sleep."

Somehow I managed to push the book away without giving myself a hernia. "What's the story on the kid singer?" I asked.

"His name's Ellroy Johnson, and he's thirteen."

"A rapper? Rocker?"

"You really should make an effort to stay au courant, Billy," she said. With a sigh, she punched a few keys on her laptop and turned it around to let me see Ellroy Johnson's YouTube video. It had been clipped from last week's *America's Got Much More Talent Than England* (aka *AGM2T2E*), a show on our network, I'm sorry to admit. My interview subject was a seemingly frail little boy, who looked a few years younger than his age. Pasty pale, with slicked-down black hair, wearing a starched white shirt and dark trousers about an inch too long, he marched center stage, stared frozen-faced into the camera, opened his tiny mouth, and . . .

" 'To dream the impossible dream . . . ' " burst forth with vocal timber so full and rich and powerful it overcame the laptop's tinny speakers.

"My God," I said. "Sounds like some insane surgeons swapped out the kid's larynx with Pavarotti's."

"Amazing, no?" Kiki said. "According to his mum, he's been singing like that ever since she took him to the theater to see *Phantom of the Opera*."

"All I got from that show was a fear of being hit by a chandelier."

"Philistine," she said. "Anyway, the boy has a full repertoire of Broadway show tunes that the network is hoping to exploit to the hilt. And here's what some might call the beauty part, Billy: Unless he's singing, he's nonverbal. Like King George VI, only worse."

"Should be a heck of an interview," I said.

"He can always sing it," she said, getting to her feet.

I watched as she closed her laptop and began shuffling papers back into her briefcase. "Eating and running?"

"A very nice gentleman is taking me to the Art Institute."

"Do I know this nice gentleman?" I asked.

"I doubt it. I only just met him."

"At the station?"

"Here, actually."

"In the hotel?"

"The elevator."

"A pickup?"

"No, not a . . . Well, I suppose you might call it that. I'd say it was more a case of two consenting adults flirting a little."

"Who is this bozo?"

"You're beginning to sound like my father, Billy. Not a compliment, by the way."

"We're supposed to be working here," I said, "not cruising the hotel."

She glared at me for a beat. Her angry knit brow and laser eyes were nothing I hadn't experienced before.

"My work is done for the day," she said, her British accent clipped to a razor's edge. Gesturing toward the books and papers with her chin, she added, "Yours is just beginning. Have a lovely evening with *Da Mare*."

As soon as she left, I opened the Daley biography. But I registered only a percentage of what I was reading. Patton kept getting in my head.

By the time Gin McCauley called, I was fifty pages into the book and had barely any knowledge of what I'd read. She informed me that the "crew" was downstairs in the bar "enjoyin' the heck out o' the happy hour," and she hoped I might join them.

I looked at *Da Mare*. *Da Mare* looked back at me.

"We're thinkin' about havin' dinnah at Charlie Trottah's," Gin said.

Visions of the restaurant's grilled turbot and sweet-potato mousse danced in my head.

"You comin', Billy?" she interrupted my reverie.

I was about to say she had me at "happy hour," but I was feeling cautious. "Pat Patton isn't down there, right?"

"Oh, hell, no," she said.

"Then order me a Sapphire martini," I said. "I'll be there before the last drop leaves the shaker."

Patton who?

Chapter
EIGHT

I'd been a pretty good boy that night, drinking and eating in moderation. Moderation being that the wine cellar still had a few bottles left and the walk-in cooler wasn't completely bare. Striving to be an even better boy, I awoke early enough Sunday morning to make the nine-thirty service at the Holy Name Cathedral on State Street.

As you might expect from one of the largest Catholic congregations in the United States, it's something to see, with its marble and bronze, and a sculpture of a surprisingly emaciated Jesus Christ on the cross, suspended from an elaborate 150-foot-high vaulted ceiling. A brochure I picked up said that the cathedral was capable of housing two thousand worshippers, and it seemed to be well on its way to doing it that morning. If they were like me, they were wondering why, considering the surrounding splendor, the wooden pews were so austere. What I'm saying is: Would padded seats be asking too much?

I wouldn't categorize myself as a church-on-Sunday guy, not that there's anything wrong with that. But every now and then I get the urge to rekindle the sentimental memories of attending mass with my parents so long ago. And in times of stress, which, thanks to Patton, I was experiencing, there is something to be said for the serenity of a church service.

That serene feeling lasted for about an hour and fifteen minutes when, leaving the church, I passed a tour group on the steps. The guide was pointing at a cornerstone and saying, "You can still see the bullet hole, marking the spot where Al Capone's men shot down rival gang boss Hymie Weiss back in the Roaring Twenties. Now, you're probably thinking Hymie Weiss doesn't sound very Catholic, but his real name was Earl Wojciechowski, and he was a member of the Catholic Church who may have been attending mass here, hoping for a respite from the violence on the streets of Chicago. . . ."

Me and Hymie.

I spent the rest of the day plowing through *Da Mare*.

Daley's biographer, Willard Mitry, handled the material in the straightforward, just-the-facts style of a seasoned newsman. But there was such an abundance of factual information that I grew a bit groggy separating out the crux.

By page two hundred, barely a fourth of the way into the book, Daley had just started his political career as the manager of the Hamburg Athletic Club, ostensibly a sports and social organization, sponsored in part by the city's Democratic machine. Blinking, I was starting in on a new chapter when the phone rang.

I expected it to be Patton telling me I was a walking dead man.

I waited a few rings, then, with a feeling of what-the-hell, lifted the receiver.

It was Cassandra, calling from the Bistro. "All alone on a Sunday night, Billy? Things a little slow in the Toddling Town?"

"You caught me between toddles," I said. "What's up?"

"The good news or the bad?"

"With you, is there a difference?"

"Blame my parents for giving me this name," Cassandra said. "I'll start with the bad news: Because of all the rain, business was off both last night and today at brunch."

"How bad?"

"Down a third at dinner, maybe a little more at brunch. It's a good thing we're closed on Sunday nights."

"The electricity holding up?"

"So far."

"Is that the good news?"

"No. Charles Limon was here last night with a party of six. He's very anxious to talk with you."

Limon was the stateside representative of RI, Restaurants International, a French conglomerate interested in acquiring 51 percent of Blessing's Bistro. RI's plan was to open a chain of them in Los Angeles, San Francisco, Las Vegas, and other points west and east. Their offer was generous, to say the least. But I wasn't sure I wanted to give up control of my baby. With my television work, the frozen foods, the cookbooks, and the restaurant, I really didn't need the money.

Cassandra, however, seemed to be sold on the idea. This was probably because she assumed that the bigger the Bistro franchise became, the better off she would be as my assistant. I suspected just the opposite, that I would become a figurehead, a Mr. Peanut, as it were, leaving her in an even less enviable position.

"I'll talk to Limon when I get back."

"That's what I told him. He's a charming man. So sophisticated, especially with that premature gray hair and French accent."

"The hair's a dye job, and I understand he's really from Jersey."

"And you call *me* a downer," she said, hanging up.

Back to *Da Mare*. Back to dark thoughts about Patton's threat.

I hoped Willard Mitry wouldn't mind too much if I skimmed his masterpiece a little, as long as I got the title and his name right when we met on the show. I tried speed-reading and skimming for another forty pages, then flipped to the photo section. I had a quick memory flash of Kiki ribbing me about doing that very thing. I hadn't heard from her. I wondered if she was in her room.

I picked up the phone, then put it down again. That was a father's move, and, as she'd made clear, I wasn't her father.

Da Mare. Photo captions. Hitting the high points.

In just a few page flicks I progressed from young baby Richard being held by his mother, Lillian, in 1902 to his marriage to Eleanor "Sis" Guilfoyle in 1936 and being elected to the state senate two years later.

I ordered up another of the hotel's cheeseburgers and a beer, and went back to the photo captions. In 1946, running for Cook County sheriff, he suffered his only political defeat. Nine years later he was elected mayor by only 125,000 votes.

That's when things started getting interesting. His stonewalling of Martin Luther King, Jr., in 1966. And, in 1968, his most ignominious year, his exhorting Chicago police to "shoot to kill any arsonist or anyone with a Molotov cocktail in his hand" after their somewhat more conservative handling of the riots after Dr. King's assassination.

The chickens came home to roost later that year during the Democratic National Convention. Confronted by a mass of protesters clogging the city's streets, the Chicago police turned violent. I glanced at the riot photos and turned the page.

Then I went back to the photos. Blinked and looked again. In one of them, a young uniformed cop was dragging a bleeding hippie by his collar to a police wagon. The hippie's face was covered in blood. He was unconscious. The cop was holding his nightstick over his head and grinning at the camera in a mood that could well be described as sadistic ecstasy.

The decades had made some changes, but I was pretty certain I was looking at a youthful Pat Patton at the beginning of his illustrious career.

I'm not sure when I drifted off.

The hotel phone woke me with a start. I was slumped on the chair with what felt like an anvil crushing my crotch. No anvil. Just *Da Mare*.

I yawned. My neck was stiff and I had that raw feeling in my throat that, I've been told, comes from snoring. The phone rang again.

It was a little past midnight.

Cassandra with more bad news? Kiki in trouble?

As soon as I lifted the receiver I realized it was a mistake.

"Billy," Pat Patton's gravelly voice said, "hope I didn't wake you."

"What do you want?"

"Aw, hell. I did wake you. Well, it's like this, Billy: I thought I'd better give you a heads-up. I mighta . . . misjudged the situation with our mutual friend Polvere a little."

"What are you talking about?"

"Not on the phone. Come here to my place."

"It's late," I said. "I think I'll just go to bed instead."

"Wait, I—"

I counted to ten before releasing the phone plunger and calling the hotel switchboard. "I'd like a wake-up call at five in the morning. And would you hold any calls until then?"

Feeling entirely too smug, I went to bed. There, I was suddenly fully awake to the fact that my silencing of Patton was only temporary. I'd be bumping into him at the show in the morning.

Chapter
NINE

For the next two weeks, our show was going to be broadcast from Millennium Park, a popular public area filled with architectural wonders that had been constructed on the site of railroad tracks and parking areas at a cost of nearly half a billion dollars. As far as I could tell, no one was saying the money had been ill spent. Quite the contrary, the prevailing opinion was that it had been Chicago's most important project since the World's Columbian Exposition of 1893.

Walking through the park at five-thirty a.m., I ordinarily would have been transfixed by its amazing constructions, even in the predawn darkness. But my thoughts were on my inevitable meeting with the monster.

You know the old bromide: Things that worry us the most rarely come to pass? Well, that morning it was true and not true. As I passed the Cloud Gate—110 tons of shiny stainless steel reflecting the lights of our temporary telecasting area—I saw a group of my coworkers huddled around the entrance to the set.

Arnie Epps was looking even more hassled and distraught than usual. He spied me and stepped away from the others. "Damn it, Billy. You're cutting it a little thin, aren't you?"

I looked at my watch. "Nearly half an hour before showtime," I said. "What's the problem?"

"Sorry. I shouldn't be taking it out on you. Last-minute cancellation. I've got nine minutes to fill."

This information was overheard by the show's co-host Lance Tuttle, who shuffled our way. "I could do my version of Ed Murrow's wires-and-lights speech. I know it by heart."

"Not gonna happen, Lance," Arnie said. "We don't do nine-minute speeches on *WUA*. We don't love *Today* or *GMA* that much. Anyway, you must realize the wires-and-lights was anti–TV news."

"Of course. That's what makes it timely," Lance said.

"That may be," Arnie said. "But we don't bite the sharp hook that feeds us."

As I left them to their "discussion," I heard Lance mumble, "Olbermann would do it."

The techs were prepping the lights. The stage-hands were merrily cobbling the set together like little elves. Happy little elves making time and a half. The camera operators were setting up under the watchful eye of Moses Dunham, the line director. None of them seemed to be overly concerned that we'd be on the air in twenty-six minutes.

Trina Lomax was huddled with Gin McCauley. They appeared to be a bit on the uptight side.

"Ladies," I said.

I'd planned on pausing briefly, just to be polite, before heading on to a tiny tent, where Kiki was supposed to be awaiting my arrival with news of my schedule. But Trina stopped me. "Can you stretch your 'meet the crowd' seg another nine minutes?" she asked.

"Assuming there's a crowd to meet," I said.

"We have built it and they will come," she said. Turning to Gin, she added, "That's that. Sorry you wasted time on the prep."

She strode off to put out the next brush fire.

"Pretty grim, huh?" Gin said.

"What's pretty grim?"

"Jesus, Billy. Don't tell me you haven't heard about Patton?"

Patton's not dead. Patton's not dead. Patton's not dead. "What about him?"

"The buggah's dead."

Crap! "What do you . . . ? When? How?"

"A real Mistah Newshound, you are." She took my hand and led me to her tent, where her assistant, a high-energy young man named Guy, was seated at a prefab desk, pounding on a laptop.

"Guy, shugah, wheah's the iPad?"

Without breaking his concentration on his laptop's monitor, he reached down and pulled up a massive leather purse and handed it to her. She found the iPad, turned it on, and in seconds brought what she wanted to its surface.

It was the front page of the *Tribune* website. "Retired Supercop 'Pat' Patton Slain." This was accompanied by a photo of a fortysomething Edward Marshall Patton in his dress blues and a sizable hunk of reportage by a staffer named Farrah Foster.

According to what Ms. Foster had been able to cobble together, the sixty-four-year-old Patton's heart had given out sometime between midnight and four a.m. The location was the three-story, five-apartment building on Cedar Street that had been his home for twenty years.

The condition of the body indicated that he had been brutalized prior to death. His apartment, which occupied the entire upper floor of the building, had been torn apart. A spokesperson for the CPD had issued a statement that robbery appeared to be the motive for the crime, though revenge had not been ruled out. Patton had not been America's sweetheart, exactly. His popular website had consisted primarily of daily video rants. Recent targets had included the former CEO of the *Tribune,* the mayor, the governor, various other local movers and shakers, and the entire Democratic Party, including the illegal-alien Muslim in the White House.

Yesterday, several hours before his death, he'd castigated homicide detectives Hank Bollinger and Ike Ruello, the "dumb-dumb dicks who are screwing the pooch tryin' to get a handle on that hacked-up corpse found on Oak Street Beach. Some guys don't even know what time it is."

"Guess our show is just gonna have to stay liberal-pinko," Gin said.

I mumbled something by rote. My mind was definitely elsewhere than on the effect Patton's death would have on our show. The number of people who wanted to kill the guy could probably fill Wrigley Field, but my money was on the mysterious Giovanni Polvere.

Failing to extort money from me, Patton, that dumb son of a bitch, had made good his threat and gone to Polvere. Only he hadn't been as careful as he'd thought. That was why he'd phoned me last night, and I, in my wisdom, had cut him off before discovering the extent of his folly. It would have been good to know if he'd mentioned me to Polvere. And in what context.

Patton may even have been willing to tell me Polvere's current name. Now he was lying on a metal slab in the morgue. And I was left to wonder if I might soon be on the next slab over.

"Billy," Kiki said, from the entrance, "they're set up for our visitors."

Yeah, so's the morgue.

Chapter
TEN

As much as I love the Big Apple, the Second City looked pretty spectacular that morning as the sunrise made the skyline sparkle under an azure sky. A surprisingly large crowd of early risers was lined up in front of our temporary set, many of them wearing outfits including Cubs uniforms, funny hats, hair dyed the color of orange pop, painted freckles the size of bottle caps. Two men were dressed like homeless. . . . No, actually, they were homeless. And apparently in better spirits than I.

There were banners welcoming the show to Chicago, signs calling attention to local establishments and hometowns and schools and organizations. I spoke to a pleasant young woman who was painted blue in celebration of a blues festival scheduled to be held in two weeks a stone's throw away in Grant Park. A couple of guys—at least I think they were guys—in a cow suit wanted the world to know that it was drink-a-glass-of-milk week. Several cute teens from Wilmette were spreading the word about live performances of Clare Boothe Luce's *The Women* at their school that weekend.

A pleasant young woman dressed in starched white butcher's gear was assuring me that the annual Meatpackers Guild picnic was open to all, when I spied Kiki off camera to my right, pacing impatiently. As soon as the floor manager cut me loose, I headed for her.

"What's up?"

"Nothing we haven't been through before," she said. "Two police detectives want to talk to you."

Right on time. Wonder what kept them?

"About . . . ?"

"They don't confide in me, Billy. All I know is that they chatted Trina up about how the late Pat Patton was going to fit into the show. They've talked with Gin. Now it's your turn."

"Gin was going to interview him. Why me?" As if I didn't suspect.

"I imagine they'll let you know."

She was being even more surly than usual.

"Have fun on your date?" I asked.

"Shut up, Billy," she said.

* * *

Detective Hank Bollinger was big and raw-boned with skin so black it was almost purple. With his premature gray hair buzzed close on the sides and a day's growth of whiskers covering his chin, he reminded me of a salted ripe eggplant. Detective Ike Ruello, was, like his partner, in his early forties. Unlike Bollinger, whose rumpled dark jacket, open-neck blue shirt, and gray slacks looked not only off the rack but also two for the price of one, Ruello's jacket was a well-tailored gray suede, his shirt a black silk, his trousers a crisp charcoal gabardine. Combined with curly black hair on his head and a less curly matching mustache, he cut a figure a bit too fashionable to seem totally loyal to the code.

"I'm a big fan," Ruello said, shaking my hand. "I've tried a lot of the recipes I've seen on your cable show."

Bollinger was evidently not a fan, big or small. He quickly set the professional tone of the meeting in a deep, unwavering voice with all the timber of a bowling ball rolling through a tunnel and all the humor possessed therein. "Good of you to talk with us, Mr. Blessing," he said. *Like I had a choice.*

We were alone in the temporary greenroom. Bollinger and I were seated on campaign chairs. Ruello, possibly to keep the crease in his pants, had decided to remain standing near a silenced TV monitor on which Gin and Lance were vamping until the final credit roll.

Bollinger got out a tiny voice recorder. "You mind?" he asked.

"Not at all."

He clicked the recorder on, mentioned the time,

date, location, and my name, then said to me, "As I'm sure you've heard, we're investigating the murder of retired Chicago police officer Edward Patton. We're here because Officer Patton was supposed to appear on this show this morning. So far, we've talked with your producer, Ms. Lomax, and Ms. McCauley, both of whom have had recent conversations with the deceased. Now we'd like to ask you a few questions."

"Okay," I said. "But before we start, I should tell you that Patton phoned me last night." This was something they either knew or would know as soon as they checked the murdered man's phone record.

"What time was this call?" Bollinger asked.

"He woke me, just after midnight."

"What was the reason?"

It was possible that Patton, being a wily old bastard, had recorded the call. If that was the case, and they knew the gist of our conversation, I was screwed anyway, so I decided I might as well lie. It was a criminal act, I suppose, hiding information crucial to their investigation. But I was convinced that rather than sending them off on the trail of the declared-dead Giovanni Polvere, the truth would only have confused matters by putting me at the top of their suspect list.

"He was nervous about appearing on our show," I said. "I tried to convince him that he'd do fine. He was hoping the appearance might lead to a permanent spot."

"Sounds like you and he were friends?"

"No. We'd only just met on Friday when we were both guests on the Gemma Bright show."

"I see. Then you guys hit it off? Went out on the town, maybe?"

"Nothing like that," I said. "In fact, we didn't even have much of a talk, either then or on the phone last night."

"What about when he was in your hotel room on Saturday?" he asked.

It took everything I'd learned as a young confidence man and an older on-camera host to keep the sinking feeling from my face. How'd they know about Patton's visit? From the chauffeur? Or had Patton kept a log of some kind? Maybe a diary? No. It had to have been the chauffeur. If they had the details of our meeting from a diary I'd be getting the prime-suspect treatment at headquarters.

"Yes, you're right," I said. "He did come to my hotel on Saturday morning. Quite a surprise."

"The reason for his visit?"

"It's the same thing. He was meeting with our producer later and wanted to know what she was like."

"Your producer, Katrina Lomax?"

"Right. Trina."

"What did you tell him?"

I smiled. "Not to call her Katrina. Other than that, to just be himself."

"Be himself, huh? I guess you didn't know Patton very well," Ruello said, earning a scowl from his partner.

"When you and Patton were chewing the fat, did he happen to mention anything about the body that was found Thursday morning?" Bollinger asked.

"We didn't talk about it, but I believe that was why he was on the Gemma Bright show, and I guess he planned on discussing it this morning on our show."

"What'd he say on the Bright show?"

"He had some theory, I think. A hunch."

"Which was what, exactly?"

"I don't know if he ever said. I wasn't all that interested. He was pretty vague with Gemma, and he and I didn't discuss it at all. According to the *Tribune*, you and Detective Ruello are also investigating that death. Is there a connection with the Patton murder?"

Bollinger exchanged a quick glance with Ruello, then was back on me. "When did you arrive in Chicago, Mr. Blessing?"

"Thursday afternoon."

"From New York?"

I nodded.

"When was the last time you were in this city?"

"Three years ago, at roughly this same time. Maybe a month earlier. We take the show on the road every now and then."

Bollinger stood up. "Thanks for your help, Mr. Blessing," he said. "We may be contacting you again. If you think of anything that might help us, please give us a call."

He handed me a white card with an embossed Chicago Police Department shield and his name, phone number, and email address. I put it in my coat pocket. I shook his hand, shook Detective Ruello's hand, and watched them exit the tent.

Then I let out a breath I'd been holding.

My worry had been that they were sadistically letting me natter on about my innocent connection with Patton before hitting me over the head with his file on Billy Blanchard. That clearly hadn't been the case.

But now I had to wonder where that file was.

Still hidden somewhere, on the cusp of being found by the police? Or worse yet, in the hands of the not-quite-deceased Polvere?

"Billy?"

Kiki was standing at the entrance to the tent, holding my cellphone. "Henry Julian," she said.

The old man was calling from his late mother's doughnut shop.

He'd heard the news of Patton's murder and wanted to assure me he'd had nothing to do with it. "I won't say the thought didn't cross my mind, unnerstand," he added. "But like I tole you, I don't operate like that anymore. Seems to me the blackmailer wasn't as smart as he thought himself."

I said I agreed with him.

This was followed by a brief discussion of what the murder might mean to my survival rate. Henry understood, as did I, that unless the file turned up, it probably meant that Mr. X had it. "You should be on your way home, Billy. Chicago's still a tough town. Take more than eighty-ninety years of so-called law enforcement to change that."

I explained that the show must go on. And since it would be here for the rest of this week and the next, so would I.

"Well, then, son, you better keep your eyes wide open and your powder dry."

Chapter
ELEVEN

Lily Conover, my fashionista production partner on *Blessing's in the Kitchen,* our weekly show on the Wine & Dine Network, had landed at O'Hare that morning. When she arrived at my hotel just before three, she was wearing a white blouse under what looked like tailored, formfitting orange bib overalls, cut off a few inches above knee-high white leather boots with high Cuban heels. This was topped off by large round sunglasses with thick white rims and a schoolgirl cap the same color as the overalls on her short-cropped blond hair.

"That outfit could get you shot in this town," I said, as she hailed a cab.

"Oh, please. You're going to talk to me about fashion, Billy? You, who walked around New York City wearing a gingerbread man suit, complete with chocolate buttons."

Following her into the cab, I said, "It's called Halloween on *Wake Up, America!* You might try watching the show sometimes."

"Right," Lily said. "And the show was over at nine, but you were still in the gingerbread suit at noon. I saw you walking down Seventh."

"It was a zipper problem. Anyway—"

She interrupted me to tell the cabbie where we were headed.

It's rare that Lily pays much attention when a restaurateur phones to suggest himself as a guest on our cable show. But this time her interest was piqued, and we were headed to Dann's Sports Den on Clark Street to film a show that would feature its owner, Charlie Dann, the Puff Potato Man.

Dann had been a lineman for the Bears until his knee blew out in a game against Tampa in 1985. That was a great Super Bowl–winning year for the Bears. But a bittersweet one for Dann, who, after a few surgeries, wound up using a crutch for a while and walking with a limp thereafter.

His life in football ended, he and his wife, Gerta, now deceased, opened the eatery, where he used her family recipes to create an eclectic menu that included a unique air-filled crispy french fry that her mother had named the puff potato. It was not to be mistaken for a potato puff, which was heavier and less pastry-like. In any case, it became a staple of both the restaurant and the cocktail lounge, where, at happy hour, it was as popular as the third-martini-free option.

Dann greeted us at the door. He was a big man. Maybe not Refrigerator Perry big but high and wide enough to make me feel low and nearly narrow. In his sixties, he had the dry, wrinkled face and baggy-rimmed but clear eyes of a heavy drinker who'd been off the sauce for a while. He'd minimized the limp over the years but wasn't able to hide it completely.

I knew from the moment we shook and he did not try to pulverize my hand that we would get along fine.

"Your guys got here a while ago," he said to Lily. "They're waiting in the office."

She and Dann had already met. She'd headed to the Den directly from the airport to get the paperwork done and to suss out the possible logistics of the shoot. At that time, she'd also reminded the local two-man crew of the time and place. She's nothing if not efficient.

The Puff Potato Man led us past a long polished bar that looked like it belonged on the set of one of Randolph Scott's better 1950s Westerns. Probably directed by Budd Boetticher. Behind it were a cheerful-seeming red-haired behemoth of a bartender, a huge mirror in an ornate frame, and about a hundred bottles of booze, plain and exotic, along with photos and trophies Dann had picked up during his salad days.

The remaining wall space was taken up by more photos, jerseys under glass, pressed *Chicago Trib* sports pages, and the inevitable giant TV monitors displaying videos of Bears games through the ages, the sound turned down to a whisper.

A couple of graying post–*Mad Men* types in business suits were sipping martinis and debating the relative merits of Walter Payton and Jim McMahon over Brian Urlacher and Devin Hester. One of them paused to question a pudgy young man with hooded eyes and what looked like a homemade crew cut, who was drinking something very brown from a tumbler. He was wearing denim pants, gym sneakers, a yellow T-shirt, and a black satin jacket that had a white onion in the alligator/polo player position over his heart.

He halted in the middle of an energetic response to the query and gawked at us. At me, actually. He seemed on the verge of saying something, but Dann moved us past him quickly.

My host took me through a door at the rear of the lounge into an efficient, clean kitchen, where chefs and staff were getting ready for the evening. Our destination was a small office beyond the kitchen, where the camera, sound, and lights duo Lily had hired awaited us amid more of Dann's football-career memorabilia.

While the sound guy miked Dann and me, Lily outlined her basic plan: The cameraman would pick me up on Clark Street, heading for the Sports Den, and follow me in. Dann would greet me at the entrance to the lounge (avoiding the restaurant, which was, in Lily's professional opinion, "CU," or cinematically underwhelming).

The cameraman would reposition at the rear door of the lounge and tape us as we approached, staying with us while we entered the kitchen area and headed for the office. Then another repositioning to the office door, looking in as Dann and I were seated, he at his desk, with me on the visitor's chair.

They hadn't done much to prepare the office. Just punched up the lighting and changed the position of my chair so that Dann and I would be facing each other.

And everything happened that way.

Then, with the camera and Lily's hawklike eyes on us, we began our interview.

At one point, a pretty waitress arrived with a bowl of puff potatoes, two dipping sauces (one catsup-based and one avocado-based), and a sampling of

Dann's specially brewed pale lager. Both food and drink were pretty darn good.

And so was the interview, if I say so myself.

We went into the kitchen, where Dann took us through the preparation of the puff potato. Though he said he was showing us everything that went into the appetizer, my guess was that he'd probably kept mum on an ingredient or two responsible for his version's unique taste.

We returned to the office for food talk, and I assisted him in blatantly plugging his establishment—we restaurateurs can be clubby—but the part of the interview that turned out the best involved his reminiscences of four years with the Bears.

I told him so once the camera and lights were turned off and the sound guy was removing the mikes and wires from their hiding places on our bodies.

"I love telling the stories," he said. "I better. I been doing it for over twenty years."

"Well, it was a pleasure," I said, as we walked to the lounge.

"You ought to stick around, Billy. Check out our happy hour. In about twenty minutes this place is gonna be packed."

I explained that Lily and the technicians would be staying for a bit. Just to pick up footage of the bar action, focusing on customers eating the puff potatoes. "Unfortunately, I've got to meet with my morning show producer."

"Well, come back anytime."

As we passed the bar, the young guy in the onion jacket hopped from his stool and stuck out his hand. "Hi," he said to me. "I'm Jonny."

I shook his hand. "Glad to meet you, Jonny. I'm Billy."

"I know that. Billy Blessing. *Wake Up, America!* Weekday mornings at seven. *Blessing's in the Kitchen,* Thursdays at nine-thirty p.m., Central Standard Time."

"Billy, this is my . . . my sister's boy, Jonny Baker," Dann said, a bit sheepishly.

"I'm Jonny," the young man repeated. His smile was friendly. His eyes were as guileless as a baby's. "Jonny."

"What's the deal with the pearl onion, Jonny?" I asked.

He frowned and looked where I was pointing. When he saw the embroidered object, his face brightened. He turned around and showed me the back of the oversized jacket. It read: *"The Thief Who Stole Trump Tower,* an Onion City Entertainment."

"You work with the company?" I asked.

"Huh? Oh, yeah. I, ah . . . helped make the sets for the movies. I love movies. And television. Almost as much as the Bears."

Dann gave me a tentative smile. "Jonny helped out with the sets. Nothing to piss off the union."

"I'm a good carpenter. Right, Charlie?"

"Very good."

"I saw you on *Midday with Gemma,* weekdays, noon, Central Standard Time," Jonny said. "We watched because of Carrie."

"Did you like the show?"

"Carrie is beautiful," Jonny said. "And she's nice. Not mean like Madeleine."

"That's enough, Jonny," Charlie Dann said.

"I'm sorry, Charlie," Jonny said.

The young man looked stricken. He took a backward step toward his bar stool.

"It's okay, Jonny," Dann said. "I didn't . . ." He turned to the bartender. "J.R., Jonny can have another cola. In a full glass."

"I heard you talking about the Bears, Jonny," I said. "You sounded like a real fan."

"Yes, I am," Jonny said, smiling again. "Charlie takes me to the games at Soldier's Field."

"Soldier," Dann corrected. "Jonny knows more about the stats than I do."

The boy rewarded him with a proud smile. Then his attention was distracted by the bartender exchanging his small empty tumbler with a full glass of cola.

"So long, Jonny," I said.

"Oh! Yeah. So long."

"C'mon, I'll walk you to the door," Dann said.

Out of the boy's earshot, he said, "Jonny doesn't need a whole lot of supervision. Since my sister passed away, about five years ago, he usually spends time at home with the help or at his dad's office, where he watches TV and his brother Dickie looks in on him from time to time. Today, something came up and Dickie wasn't available."

"What about Jonny's dad?"

"Big Jon? The tycoon?" He grinned as if that was a joke. "He's a little busy to be taking care of the kid. He's in construction and real estate. Maybe you've seen the BDI sign on the building they're putting up across the street. BDI is Baker's Dozen Industries. Jon's doing a lot more hustling these tight money days. But he finds the time for Jonny. He should be here any minute to pick him up."

"Jonny seems to like it here," I said.

"And I like having him around. He's a good kid. Only . . . he's not a kid. He's twenty-six."

"Seems pretty good-natured," I said.

"Yeah. Dickie could use some of that." He frowned. "Sorry. Dickie's just a little too . . . intense. But Jonny, he likes people."

"Except for Madeleine. Whoever she is."

"Madeleine Parnelle. Her husband writes the *Thief Who* books. What I've seen of her, I can't fault Jonny on that one. Mother Teresa woulda been hard-pressed."

We were at the door. A few happy-hour customers were straggling in. They were all in their twenties. They seemed to know Dann, who gave them a wink or a pat on the back.

"The Parnelles eat here often?" I asked.

"Never been in, thank God. Oh, the husband seems okay, if a little distracted, you know what I mean. Like he's got his mind on some other game. The wife makes up for it. She's a real presence. A capital B-I-T-C-H. Treats him like shit, and just about everybody else worse than that. I'd as soon my staff not have to take her kind of crap. Work is hard enough."

"You know the Parnelles from . . . ?"

"I first caught their act at a party at Derek Webber's. You know, the Instapicks guy."

I did know. Webber was one of the current Internet gazillionaires. He chaired an assortment of multinational electronic commerce companies. The biggest was a website called Instapicks that had started out a decade ago as a movie rental-sales operation but now sold everything pertaining to the entertainment world, from MP3s to home theaters ("Why settle for Netflix when you can Instapicks?").

"I wasn't aware Webber lived here in Chicago," I said.

"Oh, yeah." He paused to welcome two striking young female customers.

"Webber's operation is out in Shamberg," he said, when I had his attention again. "But he lives in this mansion on North State Parkway, a block down from the Hefner place. He's the guy behind Onion City Entertainment, producing the *Thief Who* movie. That's what the party was for, to hustle local businessmen to invest in the flicker."

"Did you?"

He smiled. "Not as much as Big Jon, but a couple of pals and I ponied up enough for a point. It won't kill me if the thing tanks. And if it turns out as big as the books, I won't kick myself in the ass for ignoring the opportunity."

I lost him again to a quartet of young men in business suits. I suppose I should have left him to his hosting duties, but I was curious about the CEO of Instapicks and Onion City Entertainment. He struck me as a potential interview subject.

"What kind of guy is Webber?" I asked, when Dann returned.

"A good guy. None of that I-know-more-than-you bullshit you get from some of the new-money boys. Makes you feel he's vitally interested in whatever you're telling him. And I gotta give him props for 'hiring' Jonny."

"How'd that happen?"

"He had a lunch for backers and their families, to show off the studio he'd built out at the Instapicks compound. Jon and I took the boy with, and when Webber made his rounds to welcome each of us, Jonny, in that way of his, said he was a good carpenter and asked if he could help out with the sets. Webber was amused. He said if it was all right with his dad, the job was his.

"I drove him out there and watched while he pounded some nails and got to spend time with the crew and the cast. It was great for him."

"What turned Jonny against Mrs. Parnelle?"

"She saw him standing around, watching the workers, and began shouting that Webber wasn't paying him to dog it. When I tried explaining the situation, the bitch began shouting at me, wanting to know what *I* was doing there. Somebody got Webber, who calmed her down. Then he took Jonny and me to lunch and apologized."

"Webber sounds like an interesting guy," I said.

"If there were more entrepreneurs like him, the country wouldn't be so screwed up," Dann said.

Suddenly his attention was drawn to activity at the entrance. "Well, looky here," he said with a wide grin. "Heeerrrre's Big Jon."

The man who'd just entered was not that big, at least by Dann's pro football standards. He stood six feet. Medium build. Everything about him looked polished—neatly barbered, his face a healthy tan, his smile exposing straight, gleaming teeth. His dark suit was tailored to emphasize broad shoulders and a thin waist. His black shoes were mirror-shiny. I figured him to be in his fifties. What impressed me most was his style—relaxed, confident, ready for anything. A man totally at home in his skin.

The brothers-in-law embraced. When they pulled apart, Jon Baker saw me, and his face lit up. "Chef Billy Blessing, I'll be damned."

He approached with an outstretched hand and gave mine a hearty shake. "I'm Jon Baker, and this is a real pleasure."

"Likewise," I said.

"It's great that you're featuring Charlie on your cable show," he said. "I love the show, by the way. Record it. Watch it. Try the recipes. I love to cook. It's how I unwind."

"Billy's morning show is broadcasting from here this week and next," Dann said.

"Terrific. It's a great city, Billy. I've lived in other parts of the country, but nothing compares."

"You grow up here?"

"Nooo. I'm . . . I was a Malibu Beach boy. I met Donna—my late wife—out there when she was working at Cedar's. She was a Chicagoan through and through, like her big brother Charlie. She hated the West Coast and just about had to put a gun to my head to get me back here, where people have to work for a living. And every day I thank God I listened to her."

The sound of a digital chirp interrupted him. Both he and Charlie checked their phones. It was Jon's. "'Scuse me a minute," he said, and walked away from us.

"The guy's a real dynamo, isn't he?" Dann said. "And the whole BDI thing, this is all since he and Donna and the boys moved here about ten years ago. Out in California he was what they call a 'laid-back dude' who mainly surfed and sunned. Trust-fund baby."

Jon rejoined us, pocketing his phone. "Gotta grab the boy and run. Pleasure meeting you, Billy."

"Same here. Good kid you've got."

"You bet. Two of 'em."

Watching him moving toward his son, Charlie said, "Jon and Donna were braver than I woulda been, having another kid. But Dickie's as sharp as his dad. He graduated from Northwestern, and he's working his way up through BDI."

The bar was going full tilt, and Dann seemed anxious to be about his glad-handing. I thanked him for the interview. He gave me an open invitation for dinner at the restaurant, then limped back into the lounge that was filling with customers, most of whom hadn't been alive when he'd played for the Bears.

Out on Clark Street, the after-work traffic was congealing. Not a cab in sight.

I started walking north, past buildings of yellow brick and concrete. In the next block was a BDI construction site with a backhoe resting idly at the curb beside a huge pile of sand. In just the few days I'd been in town, I'd seen considerable building and rebuilding taking place. What Nelson Algren had once famously labeled the City on the Make was now apparently a city on the makeover. Mainly by BDI.

Because the sand was blocking part of the sidewalk, I waited for a break in the traffic and crossed the two-lane street, walking against the flow. Continuing north, I spotted a small black SUV parked just past the backhoe. The darkened side window was open a crack, and cigarette smoke snaked through it, mixing with the traffic exhaust. While I watched, the SUV backed up and darted out into the traffic, barely missing a dusty sedan driven by a Germanic-looking guy, who began pounding on his horn.

I had no reason to think the driver of the SUV had any business with me. But there's that little twinge you get sometimes from a sixth-sense connection made. Usually it's the feeling that someone's watching you. At that moment, it was Pat Patton's death and my potentially perilous situation.

At the corner, the SUV suddenly attempted a U-turn but was only partially successful. A Lincoln Town Car blocked it. When the Town Car moved on, the Accord behind it stayed where it was and the black SUV made his U.

Coming for me, no doubt.

I ran out into the street, dodged a truck, and continued on past a slow-moving Mercedes sedan to the sidewalk on the other side. Before the SUV's driver could manage a second U-turn, I ran down an alley and hung a right into another alley. Exiting, I continued on a fast walk east and flagged down the first free taxi I saw.

"Hey, I know you, man," the black driver said, as

I pulled the door shut. "You're the morning show dude."

"That's me," I said, and gave him the name of my hotel.

As he pulled away from the curb, I twisted in the seat to look out of the rear window. No black SUV. When I faced forward, the driver was staring at me in his rearview.

"You see anything back there I should know about?" he asked.

"Not a blessed thing," I told him.

Why should both of us be worried?

Chapter TWELVE

"Won't you even consider it, Billy?" Trina Lomax asked.

We were at the tail end of a dinner at Everest in the Chicago Stock Exchange, Trina, Arnie Epps, and myself. I'd been a little surprised to discover I was the only cohost they'd invited. Surprised and wary.

For the better part of an hour and a half, we'd small-talked, observed the view from the fortieth floor, and enjoyed our seven courses that arrived from Chef Jean Joho's educated kitchen with courtesy and efficiency. We were sipping espresso and nibbling on petits fours when Trina finally got around to the purpose of the dinner.

"Gretchen and I feel that the show should feature special coverage of the Chicago PD's investigation of the Pat Patton murder."

My throat closed in on a bite of petit four. Usually happens when a noose tightens. I coughed and grabbed a glass of water. When I could talk, I said, "It's a local murder. Why would—"

"Patton was almost a regular."

"Almost," I said. "He didn't even appear on the show."

"What kept him from it, need I remind you, Billy, is that he was murdered," she said. "It could even *be* the reason he was murdered."

"I get it. You want to use that very dubious possibility to suggest that our show is more relevant than the other morning shows—not to mention edgy and dangerous."

"It is a unique situation," she said. "Not *Today* or *GMA* or *The Early Show* can claim to be that closely tied to a homicide."

"What about you, Arnie, you old hipster?" I asked. "You on board with using a man's violent death to put more eyeballs on the screen?"

Our line producer, who was already looking uneasy with his multicolored Hawaiian shirt nearly hidden by an ancient, shiny blue blazer, winced and stammered. "Well, ah . . . our ratings . . ."

I turned to Trina. "You think the commander will be happy with this kind of exploitation?"

"Commander Di Voss will be happy if his daughter Gretchen is happy. That's why he put her in charge.

I don't understand what's set you off, Billy. We're a current-events show. This is a current event that's every bit as interesting and certainly more newsworthy than some idiocy committed by that *Jersey Shore* crew or Lindsay Lohan's latest legal problems. It's not like we're having Patton's open casket on the show.

"Which reminds me," she said, turning to Arnie, "we should get some footage of the service and the burial."

Back to me. "Anyway, I'm stunned by your reaction, Billy. We were hoping you'd be point man on this."

That possibility was what caused my reaction. There were only a few things I knew as certainty in this life. The one at the top was: The less I had to do with Patton and his murder, the better.

"Won't you even consider it, Billy?"

"Why me?"

"You need to ask? In just three years you've been at the center of two homicidal rampages. You've become the show's murder expert."

Most people don't consider that a badge of honor, but this is television. "You flatter me," I said. "I could challenge your use of the word 'rampages' and explain why being involved in two murder cases does not exactly qualify me as an expert. But I'm too damn tired. So excuse me if I just decline."

Trina's handsome face froze. She was used to getting her way. She was annoyed with me and, I suppose, with herself for assuming this would be an easy sale.

"Will you at least explain your reticence?"

The quick answer to that was "no." But I had to work with these people.

"I've had the misfortune to be involved in two murder investigations," I said. "In spite of what you may think, this was not the kind of publicity I, or any normal person, wants or needs. I'm a chef, not a sleuth. My expertise is in culinary matters, not criminal. And I like it that way. I want customers to come to my restaurant to dine well, not to gawk at the guy who's in the tabloids."

"I don't see how reporting the news—"

"Don't kid a kidder, Trina. When it comes to reporting the news, you've got two anchors and a newswoman on the show. Use one of them for your murder investigation updates. I'll stick to the recipes and the joke of the day."

Trina signaled the waiter for the check. Arnie studied the petits fours crumbles on the serving plate. I sat back in my chair and waited for the venison and wild huckleberries dinner I'd eaten to stop doing the Running Man in my stomach.

Chapter
THIRTEEN

One of the first things you learn about interviewing is that silence can be a useful tool. You ask a question, and the interview subject answers, expecting another question. If you remain silent, the subject often will try to fill in the conversational hole, and in doing so often will provide you with the best quotes of the session.

Since the three of us were old hands at the silence game, the only words spoken on the taxi ride back to the hotel were Arnie's, informing the driver of our destination.

The interlude of thought and introspection calmed things down a bit, and in the hotel's lobby, I thanked Trina for the dinner. She said she'd decided Lance would do the reports on the investigation into Patton's murder. "I'd appreciate your not telling him he was my second choice."

"Of course not," I said.

"I'm going to my room to phone Gretchen," she said. "I don't want to delay the bad news. She'll be as disappointed as I am."

She remained in place, staring at me. Hoping I'd change my mind? When I didn't, she turned on her heel and marched toward the elevator bank, where Arnie waited, peeling off his wilted blazer and exposing one of his trademark Hawaiian shirts, like some six-foot-two mantis shedding a dull layer of skin and emerging as something new and colorful.

I waited to take the next car up.

It's never a good idea to get in Dutch with your producers, but I didn't think Trina could fire me. Even if she did, self-preservation would trump employment.

Or so I told myself. The fact of the matter was, if Gio Polvere, or whoever, had sent the men in the SUV to remove me from planet Earth, I might as well have gone along with Trina's plan. But I preferred to take the optimistic approach. The SUV's inhabitants gave up rather easily. They hadn't been waiting outside the hotel when I hailed a cab to go to Everest. They hadn't been behind us on the drive back to the hotel.

Heading up to my suite, I decided that I'd have to rein in my imagination. As FDR once put it so succinctly, we've nothing to fear. . . .

The red button on the phone in my suite was blinking.

I watched the blinks for what seemed like a full minute, then lifted the receiver.

I was informed: "The following message was left for you at seven-thirteen p.m."

"Chef Blessing, we met a few days ago." The recorded voice was male, nasal, and vaguely familiar. "I'm Larry Kelsto. The comic. I know you're a busy guy, but I'd really appreciate your catching my set tonight at the Komedy Krush on North Wells Street. I'll be on around ten-thirty. I'll leave a pass at the door, and we can have a drink after. I think you'll be interested in hearing my pitch, Chef Blanch . . . ah, sorry, Chef Blessing."

Kelsto's subtlety was something of a surprise. Anyone else hearing the voice mail would write the "Blanch . . ." off as a slip of the tongue. He'd assume Kelsto was selling his comedy talent, not issuing a blackmail threat.

My watch told me I had a little less than an hour to wonder how the little weasel had discovered my real name and, presumably, my checkered past. It had to have come from Patton. Was there a connection? As I recalled, Kelsto had disliked the ex-cop. What was it he'd said? Something about Patton treating his employees badly. But he hadn't worked for Patton himself.

Well, I'd find out more at the Komedy Krush.

Or not.

The club was located in Chicago's Old Town just a few blocks south, in location if not in class, of the legendary home of comedy, The Second City. Its bright orange façade, black awning, and black frame windows presented a year-round Halloween effect that didn't strike me as being particularly humor-appropriate.

"You sure?" the cabbie asked when we pulled up. "If you're looking for laughs, it's too late for Second City, but you got Zanies down the way. Or The Spot—"

"What's wrong with this place? I see people going in."

"Basically, it's the manager, Herman 'the German' Schwartz. He's a . . ." He used a hyphenated word that suggested Herman might have been a bit too fond of his mother.

Hard to tell that from just the look of the man as he stood at the door to his establishment, welcoming customers. He was porcine, in his fifties, wearing a tie-dyed T-shirt and baggy denim pants. White hair coated his cranium, cheeks, and chin, and an emerald-green earring winked merrily from his left lobe. His right arm was decorated with a tattoo of Lenny Bruce caressing a snake.

He seemed pleased to see me. Shook my hand

heartily and led me through the crowd to an area near the bar where the night's comics waited to go onstage. I didn't see Larry Kelsto.

Herman introduced me to the mainly young hopefuls, which included a pretty woman dressed like a cowgirl and a guy with his face painted like a rabid football fan, then finally got around to asking, "Here to sample the best of the hottest new mirthmakers, Billy?"

"Larry Kelsto said he'd be going on at ten-thirty," I said. "It's a little past that."

Herman the German looked pained. "He an old friend of yours, Billy?"

"Not exactly. I just met him a couple of days ago."

"Ah. Okay. Then here's the story on Larry. Emus. The guy's a nudnik. Now, take Sy Stern over there." He pointed to a handsome young guy in a black silk shirt and pressed denims who was holding court with a collection of very pretty women. "Sy's a Jerry Seinfeld waiting to happen. He's got the moves, and he brings the funny. If you're looking for class on your show, Sy's the guy. Lemme get—"

"Hold on. I'm here to see Larry," I said.

"Well, the thing is: Larry's a no-show."

"He's not here?"

"That's what I'm sayin'. See the guy onstage now, the one using a hammer on the Ping-Pong balls and gettin' zero laughs because it wasn't funny when Gallagher did it? I had to send that putz in to fill for Larry tonight."

"He left me a message earlier that he'd be here," I said. "He's probably running late."

"Billy, the one thing Larry never is is late. The

schmuck usually shows up at eight or nine and stays until I kick him out. This is a very unusual occurrence, him not being here."

"You wouldn't have his address?"

He cocked his round head, frowned, and said, "I doubt it, but if . . ."

He was distracted by an occurrence onstage. The comedy hopeful had stopped smashing Ping-Pong balls and was addressing the mainly silent audience. "Why aren't you laughing?" he asked, looking as if he was on the verge of tears. "This stuff is funny."

"Aw, shit," Herman said. "I gotta go give that little pisher the hook before he clears the house. Stay, Billy. I'll send a broad over for your drink order. On the house, of course."

I watched him plow through the tables, step into the spotlight, and take the mike from in front of the wannabe comic. "Time's up," he said to the kid. "You and your crap, off my stage, now."

The audience was suddenly invigorated. Applauding. Facing them, Herman the German blessed his customers with a wide grin, then turned to observe the wretched young man on his hands and knees, picking up his smashed Ping-Pong balls. "Comedy sure is fun, isn't it, Willis?"

That was it for me. I'd get Kelsto's address some other way, tomorrow.

Out on Wells, surprisingly active with Chicago's young night crawlers, I hunted for a taxi, finally found one where Wells collided with Lincoln and Clark.

Halfway to my hotel, the driver, a wiry black man wearing puka shells and a beret, leaned his head back and asked, "Know sumboddy 'n a black RAV4? 'Cause he on our ass."

Looking through the rear window, I saw nothing. "Where?"

"Jus' behin' the bus."

I saw it. The black SUV.

"Wan' me t' lose it, mah bruther?"

There was no way they'd picked me up at the Komedy Krush. That meant they'd probably been following me from the hotel. Following me all day. Doing nothing more than following.

I told him not to bother.

Chapter
FOURTEEN

"You can eat all the soup you want," Adele Ricklas of the Lose-It-Fast Weight-Reduction Clinic was explaining to me and the *Wake Up, America!* audience at six-twenty-four a.m. the following morning. "And you can eat all the fruit. Except for bananas. No bananas on the first day of the diet."

"Why not?" I asked.

Adele Ricklas blinked. She was in her thirties, well groomed, appropriately slim, and perfectly pleasant. But she didn't know the answer. "I . . . Well. It . . . The banana . . . The Cabbage-Soup Diet doesn't work if you eat bananas on the first day."

"But you can eat apples, or strawberries?" I asked, just to keep the ball rolling.

"Oh, absolutely," she said, clearly relieved. "Pears, oranges. Grapes. And on the fourth day of the diet, you can even eat bananas. As many as eight."

It was a rough way to start the day, holding a conversation about the Cabbage-Soup Diet. Anything with cabbage. I'd never really developed a taste for the cultivar, though I had a girlfriend once who claimed that the raw leaves had cured her father's stomach ulcer. I'd never thought about it before, but he was a Son of the Confederacy, and it could have been my relationship with his daughter that had caused the ulcer.

The floor manager was holding up two fingers. Two more long minutes to go.

Just off the set, Kiki shifted her weight impatiently, notepad in hand.

I asked Adele Ricklas if there might be any health problems with a diet that supposedly results in very fast weight loss. She allowed as how it might be a good idea to take a vitamin supplement while slurping toward thinness.

Then she said, "I brought some spicy cabbage soup with me, Chef Blessing, in case you'd like to sample it."

"I'd love to, Adele," I lied, "but, regrettably, it will have to be off camera. Because right now, it's time for the news. Thank you so much for telling us about the Cabbage-Soup Diet."

Our red light clicked off.

I thanked Adele again. Instead of going on her way, she asked, "Aren't you going to try the soup?"

"Once the show is over and I can relax," I said.

She gave me a wan smile and thanked me for "the nice interview."

Watching Ms. Ricklas depart, Kiki said, "You could have tried her soup, Billy."

"Billy no like cabbage in the morning," I said. "Not even at cabbage time, which, in my opinion, is the hour of thirteen."

She showed me her large, round wristwatch. "Speaking of time, you've got six minutes before sitting down with Dr. Hemmick and several dogs to discuss fleas and ticks."

"When did that get added to the list?"

"About a half-hour ago," Kiki replied. "Trina said you'd understand."

I did. Because I'd refused to do the daily on the Patton investigation, she was going to stick me with diet fads and fleas and ticks. Fair enough.

"Lead me to the dogs," I said. "But, at a more decent hour, I want you to call Gemma Bright's office and get Larry Kelsto's phone number and address for me."

"The comic? Why?"

"In case the guy you picked up at the hotel doesn't work out. I thought Larry could fill in."

"Ewww. If you must know, my hotel pickup and I are doing just fine. Seriously, Billy, why do you want Kelsto's information?"

"It's personal," I said.

Seeing her storm off, I realized I'd forgotten to take my tact pills that morning. I suppose if I needed an excuse, I could say that being chased through the streets by a mysterious vehicle tends to put one on edge. On the other hand, there'd been no black SUV on view while I taxied to Millennium Park at five a.m. Hey, even potential cold-blooded killers need their beauty sleep.

Glancing at a monitor, I saw that the show had segued from the news to Gin's interview with the star of *The Thief Who Stole Trump Tower,* my old talk show comrade Carrie Sands. The camera had moved in on the women, holding on a tight two-shot, which, in this hi-def world, could have been brutal. But both Gin and Carrie looked great—clear-eyed and smooth-skinned.

I was concentrating so much on their physical attributes that it took a few seconds for me to get the drift of their conversation, which had veered from the usual "How's the movie shaping up?" to something a bit more interesting.

"A couple?" Carrie was saying in reply to a question I'd missed. "No. But we've become good friends since we began shooting the film."

"How's that friendship working out, with his wife right there coproducing the movie?"

I pulled a director's chair over and sat.

"Well, first," Carrie said coolly but exhibiting remarkable self-control, "Gerard and Madeleine have been separated for nearly two years. And it's not like he and I have been making out on the set. We're not in some kind of passionate affair. Even if we were, I doubt it would have much effect on the way Madeleine Parnelle does business. She's an exceptional woman. Very focused and very professional. She's produced several successful films in France. And, of course, she edits his manuscripts."

"But they are still married," Gin insisted. "Why is that, by the way? Religion? Children? Or is it a financial decision because of the phenomenal success of the books?"

As the camera held relentlessly on Carrie's face, the tension was starting to show in her darting eyes and tightened lips. "That's something you'd have to ask Gerard or Madeleine," she said.

"I'd love to," Gin said. "We're hoping to get both of them on the show."

"It's not the best time for Gerard. He's away, working on book three." Carrie flashed a passive-aggressive smile.

"Will he be coming back before the filming ends?" Gin asked.

"Not unless he's finished writing the book."

And that was the close-down.

I stood, thinking I should stroll over to their set to say hello to Carrie. But Kiki intervened. "Your ticks and fleas await, sire," she said.

Show business is rrrrufff!

Chapter
FIFTEEN

Just before our eleven a.m. staff meeting started, I entered the large tent and rounded the portable conference table (it wouldn't be a real meeting without a conference table) to present Trina with a little blue Tiffany box.

She raised her eyebrows in surprise. "What's this, Billy?"

"A small token of my esteem," I said.

Almost giddily, she undid the bow and opened the box. She removed the top layer of cotton and gawked. "What the hell?"

"Three fleas," I said. "Plucked from my own body after the interview with Dr. Hemmick and his dogs."

She put the top on the box and gave me a wide smile. "Thank you, Billy. Now I owe you a gift. I'll have to think of something equally appropriate."

When the rest of our folks arrived, carrying coffee and edibles—sugar and carbo for the fearless, fruit and yogurt for the health faddists—Trina began her critique of the morning's show. It was, by her standards, moderate criticism. No one cried, except for Lance Tuttle, who was singled out for his flubs in his report on the CPD's progress in finding the person or persons who murdered Pat Patton.

The report was that there was no news to report, but that didn't stop Lance from continuing to refer to the victim as Pete Patton.

After the meeting, free from the constraint of work, I felt it was time to use Larry Kelsto's contact information Kiki had pried from someone on the *Midday with Gemma* staff. When the phone number took me directly to voice mail, I decided to try and catch him at home.

A taxi took me to his address on Eugenie Street, only a few blocks from the Komedy Krush. It was an old clapboard house with flaking gray paint. The rusty waist-high iron gate creaked like the opening of a casket in a horror movie. I walked gingerly along a weed-patched brick pathway and up several wide steps.

The leaf-strewn porch was in the form of an *L*, the short part fronting a jutting section of the house that featured a stained-glass bay window that may not have been cleaned since Da Mare was in office. The longer portion of the porch led me to a dark brown wooden front door decorated with four small glass panels. Beside it was a brass or copper doorbell covered with what looked like several decades' of verdigris.

The doorbell worked, for whatever good that did me. Nobody answered.

Annoyed, I reviewed the bidding.

Kelsto wanted to meet with me, presumably with blackmail on his mind. But he didn't show, surprising not only me but the lovely Herman the German. And now he wasn't answering his phone or his doorbell. Conclusion: The comic just might have made the same mistake as Patton.

I scanned the street. I didn't see the black SUV, nor had I seen it on the taxi drive from my hotel. Common sense told me I should walk a block and a half to Wells Street, flag down a taxi, and forget about Kelsto, who might very well have been inside the run-down clapboard building, drawing flies.

On the other hand, if he were merely out in the city blackmailing somebody else, it was possible that whatever he hoped to peddle to the former Billy Blanchard was inside the house just waiting to be found, taken, and destroyed forever.

I walked down the front steps and followed the brick path to the rear of the house and a patchy yellow grass yard separated from the neighboring properties by a high wood plank fence. A work shed of the same clapboard construction as the house stood near the far end of the fence.

I was not exactly alone in the yard. There were two chrome statues. The complete one was of a knee-high, four-legged animal. Probably a dog, though it didn't have ears, merely a smooth round head and snout. The unfinished work was a slightly oversized, heavily muscled male nude, seated on a matching chrome chair. His right elbow rested on the arm of the chair, his left on his left knee, which was angled to provide an unrestricted view of his supersized chrome plumbing. His right knee—whole right leg, actually—was missing.

Near the shed was a bleached workbench on which rested a welder's mask, thick gloves, and portions of a shiny car bumper that the sculptor probably planned to use for the leg. There was also what appeared to be a piece of machinery—a welder, maybe, or a cutting torch—that didn't strike me as a tool you'd want to leave out in the elements. Its electric cord was still plugged into a socket near the roof-line of the shed that also was host to a bare lightbulb.

I strolled past the incomplete monument to muscular and priapic excess, climbed the rear steps, and tried the back door. Locked.

Frustrated, I sat on the steps and phoned Kelsto.

A sound came from inside the house. People laughing.

It took me a few seconds to realize that Kelsto was

using a laugh track as his cellular's ringtone. It ceased just before the comedian's digital voice asked me to "leave your name, number, and punch line at the sound of the beep. And make it funny."

I wondered if anyone would be moved to comply. I certainly wasn't. Instead, I put away my phone, stood, and headed for the front.

I was still on the side path when I heard the gate creaking open.

Kelsto?

As I recalled, he wore gym shoes. Whoever had arrived was click-clacking across brick and up the wooden front steps.

I hesitated before showing myself.

The doorbell rang. And rang again.

Reaching the front of the house, I saw a woman at the door trying to peer through one of the small glass panels. She had brunette hair and was wearing a black jacket over a black T-shirt, and very tight gray pants tucked into knee-high black boots with two-inch heels. In one hand she held a pair of overlarge sunglasses, in the other a black leather bag only slightly smaller than a suitcase.

"Nobody's home," I said.

She made an "Uhh" sound and spun, backing against the door, clearly startled. I was a little startled myself.

"Hi, Carrie," I said.

"Oh, God." The not-quite-disguised-under-the-brunette-wig Carrie Sands shivered.

"Didn't mean to spook you," I said. "I'm here looking for Kelsto, too."

"This was such a mistake," she said, putting her

glasses back on. They didn't add all that much to her disguise.

She started for the steps.

I beat her to the front gate. "Is it true what they say?" I asked.

That stopped her. "What . . . do they say?" Confusion was edging out annoyance.

"That brunettes have more fun than blondes."

"Oh, God," she said again. Then she did a sort of rag-doll slump, the large bag hitting the sidewalk with a clunk. "Please don't try and be cute." She cocked her head and seemed to be staring at me, though I couldn't actually see her eyes. "What's that little worm have on you?" she asked.

"You first," I said, though I thought I knew what Patton and now Kelsto had on her. On Gemma's show, she'd reacted to a comment the old bastard had made about pole dancers. Having that on a curriculum vitae might seem almost quaint by today's standards, when porno tapes and reality-show bad behavior were stepping stones to fame and fortune. But for someone serious about an acting career . . .

She turned to look at the house. "The front door's locked. Maybe the rear?"

I shook my head.

"And he's definitely not inside?" she asked.

I hesitated, wondering if I should tell her my theory about Larry Kelsto being the late Larry Kelsto.

I didn't get the chance.

She twirled and raced up the front steps to the stained-glass window. I arrived just in time to stop her from swinging her large leather bag into it.

"Damn, girl," I said, forcibly moving her away

from the window. "I don't think you want to do that."

"His . . . stuff could be here," she said, struggling in my arms. "He sure as hell isn't carrying it around with him."

"Do you want to get arrested for breaking and entering?"

She shook her head, and I relaxed my hold on her. I also shifted my position to stand between her and the window. "I heard Kelsto's cellphone ring inside the house," I said. "He's a comedian looking for work. I don't think he'd leave home without the phone."

"Then he's in there. Doing what? Hiding from somebody?"

"That's one possibility. The other is that he's doing a Pat Patton."

"Oh." She winced. "You mean . . . ?"

"Yeah."

"Let's find out," she said, and tried to move around me to the window, readying her bag.

I grabbed her again. "You're a crazy person," I said.

"Let go, damn it," she ordered. "I don't care if Kelsto is dead in there or not. I just want to find the damned folder. Leave me alone."

I pulled her away from the window. "If you're hell-bent on going in, let's be a little more discreet about it."

At the rear of the house, I headed for the shed, hoping to find some sculptor's tool capable of jimmying the back door. Carrie called me back, pointing out a window that was open an inch or two.

"I can pry it up," she said, "if we can figure out a way for me to get up there."

We both looked around the yard for something for her to climb on.

"What about that panther?" she asked.

Funny what odd stuff pops into your head. I suddenly recalled an Ogden Nash poem: ". . . If called by a panther, don't anther."

"I think it's a dog," I told her.

"I don't know. It looks feline to me."

"Whatever it is, it's too heavy for me to drag over here without risking a hernia."

"Well, what, then?"

"I'll boost you up," I said. A mistake. If I'd thought about it, I'd have realized that though she was far from sumo-wrestler size, anything over a hundred pounds of live weight can be tough on the joints.

Using the side of the house to brace my back, I managed somehow to hold her in a linked-hands stirrup. She worked her fingers under the window's lower sash and was able to push it up without driving me into the ground. I was grateful for this, though you would not have known it from the grunting and cursing that escaped my lips.

She slid over the sill like a snake. A sexy snake.

I took a deep breath, cracked my neck, wiggled my shoulders. I decided that if I ever elected to become a second-story man, I'd have to get in better shape.

In a minute or two, Carrie unlocked the back door and asked for her boots, which I'd insisted she take off before her climb. She sat on the stoop to pull them on, presenting a much more pleasing picture of her shapely legs than when she'd been pressing a knee in my face.

She rescued her leather bag from the yard, and we entered the house, stepping into a small storeroom where cleaning equipment lay strewn across the black-and-white checkerboard linoleum, along with assorted dry goods, a majority of which seemed to be plastic jugs full of "powdered protein for maintaining muscle power."

The contents of one of the jugs had been emptied on the floor. Carrie stared at the mess and said, "I passed through the breakfast room and kitchen. It's like this in there, too."

"Maybe we should just . . . split," I suggested.

Ignoring my idea, she hunkered down to examine the powder. "Wonder why they only emptied just the one," she said, rising. "I bet they were interrupted."

I shook my head. "The rest of this stuff is factory-sealed," I said.

"Well . . . anyway, it's possible they didn't find his stash."

Buoyed by this ultra-optimistic hope, she moved on. I was happy to see she carefully avoided stepping in the protein powder, which meant she wasn't a total idiot.

In the kitchen, pots and pans were scattered, and the oven and dishwasher doors were open, as were cabinet drawers. A black plastic garbage bag had been gutted and was emanating an odor of stale cantaloupe mixed with stale coffee grounds. Speaking of stale, the refrigerator-freezer doors were open, with the meat keeper, veggie, and fruit crisper drawers removed and empty. Their contents rested, fully thawed and ripening, on the linoleum.

A plastic icemaker bucket lay beside the apples and oranges. Its contents had melted into a puddle. *Good.* Thawed meat and melted ice cubes suggested that the search had been done a while ago. The searchers were probably long gone. Still, this was not a location where I wanted to linger.

Carrie had moved on to a small dining room with table and chairs that were either antique or Goodwill, a distinction often lost on me. She was standing at a china cabinet. Judging by the paperback books scattered on the floor, it had not housed any china.

She was rooting through papers that the searchers had left on one shelf.

"You might want to be a little careful what you touch," I said.

"Oh." She dropped the pages and stepped back. "Even paper?"

"I think so."

"We don't know for sure that . . . anything bad . . ." She didn't bother finishing the sentence.

"Let's go, Carrie. There's nothing for us here."

"We still have time," she said, and went into the next room. The living room. More aged and weathered furniture that had been shoved to one side so that the dingy rug could be thrown back. Cushions from the couch had been ripped and tossed on the floor, along with several showbiz magazines and issues of *Daily Variety.* Framed prints had been taken from the walls and cut apart. A copy of *The Thief Who Stole Big Ben* was lying beside a Komedy Krush coffee mug that had spilled its contents on the now-bare floor. Near the mug was the plastic back panel to a fairly new thin, medium-size-screen TV that rested on a metal stand.

There were two bedrooms, separated by a single bath on the other side of a hall leading from a kitchen entrance to the front door. The bed in the larger room had been torn apart. More prints had been ripped from its walls. A rough-knit throw rug was balled up in a corner. A small construct-it-yourself bookcase had been tipped over, spilling titles by James Baldwin, Ralph Ellison, Toni Morrison, a poetry collection by N. Scott Momaday, larger volumes on art and sculpture.

There were also weights and barbells. Just a guess: probably not Kelsto's room.

That would be the one with the greasy pizza boxes; bright, too-hip clothes littering the floor; and a collection of video and audiotape recorders, all of them emptied carelessly.

"Damn!" Carrie exclaimed in frustration. She was sitting on the floor, sifting through Kelsto's clothes. "Where the heck are the CDs and DVDs, the computers?"

"Gone with the gypsies," I said. "But there is something I don't see that should be here."

I had her full attention as I took out my phone. I dialed Kelsto's number.

The sound of laughter came from another part of the house.

We tracked it to the far end of the hall. But instead of Kelsto's phone, we found a heating vent near the floor.

I dialed again, and the laughter echoed up through the vent.

The phone was in the basement.

Unfortunately, so was Larry Kelsto.

Chapter
SIXTEEN

The basement was as wrecked as the living room. Moving boxes and old pieces of luggage had been sliced open, their contents spread out on the concrete. But that wasn't what drew our attention. Somebody—Kelsto, presumably—had turned a section of the room into an approximation of the stage at the Komedy Krush. That's where we found his body, seated on a director's chair in front of a fake-brick façade, a few feet from what seemed to be a real standing microphone and a real Minicam attached to a tall tripod. A bright baby spotlight, amateurishly affixed to the basement ceiling, gave us a too-clear picture of his condition.

He was naked except for his candy-cane-striped shorts. His head slumped forward, his dead, glazed, bulging eyes seemingly staring at his bare feet. From wrists to elbows, he was duct-taped to the arms of the chair. A grayish cloth was stuffed in his mouth. Someone had used his body as an ashtray. The burn marks were particularly livid against his pale, dead flesh.

They'd used cigars. The stale smoke smell was not quite overpowered by the combined stench of burned flesh and excrement. There were ashes on the cement floor but no cigar butts. I wondered if it was possible to find DNA on ash. Probably not.

"Gotta get out of here," Carrie said, rushing for the stairs.

I was just as anxious to leave but paused to take a quick scan of the basement. More emptied boxes and tossed books.

And his cellphone. Resting near rumpled pants, shirt, and pink high-top canvas shoes.

Look at it or not?

Not, I decided. Leave it as is for the cops.

Carrie was standing at the top of the stairs, frozen. When she saw me, she put a finger to her lips.

I heard it, too.

Someone on the front porch was humming a tune that sounded like "On the Sunny Side of the Street." There was the distinct click of a key going into the lock.

I pointed to the dining room, and we crept there and continued creeping through the kitchen and storeroom and out the rear door, which I eased shut.

Taking the lead, I moved slowly along the side path.

Whoever had been on the front porch was now inside the house. Judging by the sound of her voice, it was a woman. We were within a few feet of the front gate when she exclaimed, *"Oh, my dear sweet Jesus!"* which meant she'd just seen the mess the house was in.

Wait till she gets a load of Kelsto, I thought.

I stopped Carrie from opening the gate and causing a screeching noise loud enough to wake the . . . bad metaphor.

By lifting the gate on its hinge and moving it very carefully, I was able to open it enough for us to squeeze through.

We were all the way to Wells Street when I realized we'd have to go back.

"Go back? Are you crazy?"

"We . . . didn't clean up," I said. "We left fingerprints."

"Forget it. I'm not going back."

"You and I are on a murdered man's—no, make that on *two* murdered men's—blackmail lists. Maybe there's no evidence of that lying around for the cops to find. And maybe they won't find your prints on the sill of a half-open window. But that's a bet with bad odds."

"How does going back help?"

I explained my plan.

The woman who answered the doorbell at Kelsto's was tall, fit, and in her fifties, skin the color of caramel, hair wiry and black with streaks of gray. She'd exercised caution, keeping the door locked until, peeking out through the tiny glass panes, she was able to verify that I was "the guy from the morning show."

She opened the door.

"Hi," I said. "We're here to see Larry."

"Uh . . . I don't think . . . I clean for Mr. Kelsto and Mr. Parkins. They're not home."

"Well, I'm sure Larry'll be here shortly," I said, stepping into the hall. "He's expecting us."

"Thing is . . . something's not right here," she said, forehead wrinkled in concern. "I come in once a week to clean, and sometimes, if they have themselves a party, it'll be a mess. But this is . . . Something's not right."

She gestured toward the entrance to the living room. Carrie and I looked in on the disorder that hadn't changed in the last few minutes. "Holy mackerel," I said, hoping it sounded more sincere to the housekeeper than it did to me.

"This is just terrible," Carrie said with impressive conviction. But she was a professional liar. She bent down to fondle a few items. "It looks like there's been a robbery."

I touched some stuff, too, making sure the housekeeper noticed. "It does look like a robbery. Maybe the police should be notified."

That panicked the housekeeper. "I don't want any business with the po-leese. 'Sides, could be the boys did this."

"Cut up their cushions and throw pillows? Pried the back off the TV?" Carrie asked.

The housekeeper was blinking now, edging toward the hall. Getting ready to scamper?

I quickly joined her, took her hand, and said, "Any robbers would be long gone by now. And we're here to keep you company. You know my name. I'm Billy. That's Carrie. And you're . . . ?"

"Josepha Davis. Josie."

"Well, Josie, it might be a good idea if you did call the police."

She shook her head and pulled back her hand. "No. No po-leese. I'll just clean best I can, and the boys can do what they want about the po-leese when they get here."

Carrie and I exchanged looks. My great plan wouldn't work unless she called the cops.

"Maybe you should phone the boys, Josie," Carrie said.

The housekeeper was amenable to that. "I'll go get my phone," she said, and left the room.

I nodded to Carrie, and we took off to the kitchen, where she began wiping the window and sill with a silk neckerchief. Using my handkerchief, I lowered the window and locked it. Then I ran to the back door and gave that a hearty wipe-down.

We returned to the living room to await the next event.

It came in the form of Kelsto's laughter ringtone.

A few beats after it stopped, Josie joined us, saying, "I couldn't get through to either of 'em. You say Mr. Kelsto's supposed to be meeting you here?"

"That was the plan when we talked yesterday," I said.

"Then he'll know what to do when he gets here."

Carrie was looking at me anxiously. "He's not answering his phone, huh?" she said.

"No. He left it here," the housekeeper said. "It's got this sound of folks laughing. I could hear it after I dialed him."

"I thought I heard laughter," Carrie said. "But it sounded far off."

"Basement, I think," Josie said.

Carrie and I stared at each other. Josie seemed like

a nice enough person. I didn't feel right about setting her up for the shock of her life. But I supposed she'd eventually have gone down to the basement on her own. In any case, Carrie barely hesitated.

"The basement's a funny place to leave your phone," she said.

"Mr. Kelsto uses the basement to practice his comedy," Josie said. "He probably jus' put it down and forgot it."

Carrie frowned. "I don't know . . . The condition of this room . . . Robbers . . . Larry not being here for our meeting . . . His phone down in the basement . . ."

Josie was frowning, too. "I guess I better . . ." She gave me a pleading look.

"We'll go down with you."

That's me, pillar of compassion.

I positioned myself to block most of Josie's view, but she'd seen enough. "Oh. JesusMaryJoseph," she mumbled. "He's dead, idden he?"

I nodded, and she began to weep.

I helped her back upstairs, straightened a chair in the dining room, and sat her on it. Carrie brought her a glass of water from the kitchen and a towelette to dry her eyes.

She took a long drink of water, almost choked on it, then pushed the glass away. She started to rise. "I got to do . . . call somebody . . . an ambulance . . ."

I put my hand on her shoulder and kept her on the chair.

"You just sit here, Josie," I said. "I'll make the call."

Chapter
SEVENTEEN

Two uniformed CPD officers arrived thirteen minutes after my 911 call.

One of them, a six-two, black-haired, blue-jawed Officer Boyle, herded us into the disrupted living room, while his partner, a shorter, rounder, browner Officer Gilstrap, went downstairs to corroborate our statement about a dead man in the basement.

It was nearly forty minutes, another four beat cops, and a Cook County medical examiner's tech team later when, to my surprise, Detectives Hank Bollinger and Ike Ruello arrived. Since it was doubtful they were the CPD's only homicide dicks, I assumed someone at dispatch had been particularly diligent in connecting Kelsto's demise to their investigation of the Pat Patton murder. I didn't know at the time that there was an obvious connection.

Bollinger gave Carrie a curious look and said, "You usually wear a wig, Ms. Sands?"

"Just when I feel like blending in," she said.

"Might take a little more than that," Ruello said.

Josie began to tell Bollinger about "poor Mr. Kelsto," but he interrupted her. "We're anxious to get your statement, ma'am, all of your statements, but you'll have to give us a few minutes to look around first.

"Please confine your activity to this room until the technicians from the medical examiner's office get their work done. And I'd appreciate it if you hold all your observations, thoughts, and questions until I get back."

He walked to Officer Boyle, who was standing at the entrance to the room, and whispered something in his ear. Then, slipping on blue shoe covers and white latex gloves, he and Ruello went down to the basement to eyeball the corpse.

When they returned, Bollinger asked, "All three of you saw the victim downstairs?"

Carrie and I nodded. Josie made a little moan.

Bollinger asked her if she needed anything. She shook her head from side to side.

He took a breath, then said to Josie, "The technicians are through in the dining room. Officer Boyle's gonna find you a comfortable chair in there and take down your statement. Okay?"

That accomplished, he sent Carrie away with Ruello and then sat down on one of the sliced chairs, facing me. He removed his mini-recorder from his coat pocket and clicked it on. He spoke directly into it, mentioning the date, the time, the address, and his own name. He referenced a case number and followed that with a general description of the semi-destroyed house and the brutalized and tortured corpse of one of its occupants in the basement.

"At the scene are housekeeper Josepha Davis, actress Carrie Sands, and television, ah, performer Billy Blessing, whose statement is as follows:

"Mr. Blessing, would you begin by giving me your full name, your address, and phone number?"

"Local address or home?"

"Both. Also, length of time you've been here in Chicago."

"I already . . . ," I began, and stopped when I saw him frown.

I repeated the information I'd given him yesterday morning.

That done, he asked, "Can you tell me when you arrived at this address today and why?"

It was clear he wanted everything nailed down tight. I provided the scenario that Carrie and I had concocted before returning to the house. Since it was possible for the police to locate the cabdriver who'd dropped me off an hour before I'd phoned in the murder, I told him that Carrie and I had arrived at pretty much the same time a few hours ago and discovered that nobody was home.

"We figured Larry had gotten delayed, and so we decided to take a walk around and see a little of the neighborhood. We came back. He still wasn't here. We drove around a little in her car—it's the violet BMW parked down the street. We came back. This time, the housekeeper answered the bell."

From there, it was simply a matter of describing exactly what had happened, minus our rubbing away our fingerprints.

Of course, Bollinger had a few more questions.

"Why did Mr. Kelsto say he wanted to meet with you?"

"He wasn't specific. He said he had an idea he wanted to bounce off me."

"Couldn't do that on the phone?"

"I suggested that, but he said he'd rather meet."

"You and he were . . . friends?"

"No. I barely knew him. We met a few days ago, backstage at the Gemma Bright show."

"That would be the same show at which you and murder victim Edward Patton met?"

"Yes."

"I've just come from a screening of that show. You and retired officer Patton and the actress accompanying you today, Carrie Sands. Four guests. Two of 'em tortured and killed. The surviving two are right here at the latest crime scene. That's turning into one helluva show. Guess I'm gonna have to give it another look."

It wasn't a question, and I definitely didn't have a response.

"Anything odd happen on that show, something that the cameras didn't catch?"

"Odd? You mean something that would result in two violent deaths? No, nothing that odd. But there was the discussion of the other murder."

"What other murder?"

"The headless corpse found on—"

"That's no longer classified as a homicide," he said flatly.

"I don't under—"

"It is what it is," Bollinger said. "Let's stick to what we've got here. Kelsto didn't appear on the talk show. Any idea why?"

My mind was still on the headless corpse that was no longer considered a homicide. Bollinger had to repeat the question.

"He . . . lost out to the clock," I said. "Happens all the time. I think Patton was a last-minute addition. Gemma wanted his take on the truncated body."

"His take, yeah." Bollinger's grin was not at all pleasant. "You and Kelsto meet before the show or after?"

"During," I said. "We were both waiting to go on."

"And Patton was waiting with you?"

"No. He must have gone directly to the set."

"What about after the show?" he asked. "You notice any contact between Kelsto and Patton?"

"No. I think Larry probably left when he knew they weren't going to use him."

Bollinger thought about that for a few seconds, then asked, "While you and Kelsto were waiting to appear, he say anything about Patton?"

"He didn't seem to be a fan. I think he may have used the word 'asshole.' "

"Not a surprise. But to get back to the here and now, you sure you don't have any idea why Kelsto wanted to see you?"

"I figured it probably had something to do with *Wake Up, America!*"

"That how it usually works? Somebody has an idea for your show, you go halfway across town to see them?"

"No. But I'm a visitor here, with the afternoon off. Larry seemed like a nice enough guy. I figured I'd listen to his pitch."

"What about Ms. Sands?"

"I'd be even more inclined to listen to her pitch," I said.

"I mean, how did she fit into it? Why was she here?"

"She said she'd got a phone call, too."

"She tell you this when you and she were driving around in her car?"

I nodded.

"Please answer the questions. This machine doesn't pick up head movement."

"She mentioned the phone call while we were driving around," I said.

"Were you expecting to meet her here?" he asked.

"No."

He stared at me for a few beats, then asked, "What was Mr. Kelsto's mood when you talked with him?"

"Mood? I don't know. Normal, I guess."

"Would you happen to be acquainted with Mr. Kelsto's roommate, Mr. Parkins?"

"I don't believe I am."

"Wouldn't know where we might find him?"

"No."

"Do you have knowledge of any reason why someone would want to torture and murder Mr. Kelsto?"

"No," I lied.

He made a thing about turning off his machine and putting it into his pocket. "Just between us, brother," he said, "what do you suppose went down here?"

"A break-in. Robbery. Murder. You're the homicide expert."

"Ruello, a fan of yours, says you're something of

an expert, too. Been involved in a couple of homicides."

"No expert. Just unlucky enough to have been in the wrong places at the wrong times."

"And now here you are. Third time's a charm, huh?"

"Like you said."

He brought up his arm, dipped his long brown fingers into his inside coat pocket, and withdrew a glossy photograph. "You ever see this man before?"

The unsmiling black face that stared back at me was a familiar one.

"Yeah. He was at the show, too," I said. "Pat Patton's driver."

"He's also Kelsto's missing roommate, life partner, whatever, Nat Parkins."

Perfect.

Chapter EIGHTEEN

The detectives were finished with us at a little before five.

By then, the media crowd had gathered just outside the Kelsto-Parkins property line. While Bollinger and several uniformed officers escorted Josie to his vehicle, his elegantly dressed partner, Ruello (who, it turned out, hoped to one day open his own restaurant in Chicago), led Carrie and me out through the rear.

Continuing to pepper me with questions about food and drink, he took us across the backyard, past the unfinished sculpture. As we approached a fence exit, I said, "Detective Bollinger mentioned the headless corpse is no longer considered a homicide."

"No. Autopsy said the guy had a bad ticker. Fatal heart attack."

"My God. Then who . . . did that to him?" Carrie asked.

"Happily, that's no longer the problem of the homicide department," he said, rather cheerily. "But corpse mutilation is no little deal. It carries a ten-year felony ticket."

"Corpse mutilation," Carrie repeated, wincing.

The fence exit took us to an alley that led to a street identified as North Sedgwick. There, Carrie and I bid Detective Ruello adieu and made our way to her BMW parked on West Eugenie.

"What kind of world is this?" Carrie asked. "People being tortured. Corpses being mutilated." She adjusted her rearview mirror and added, "Just look at that crowd."

I turned in my bucket seat and observed the media mass nearly a block away. There were several vans almost blocking the street. I supposed one of them might be from our local affiliate, WWBC.

"What do they want?" she asked. "Isn't there enough bad news in the world?"

"Apparently not."

"I guess we should consider ourselves lucky," she said, starting up the BMW and moving it away from the curb. "Maybe they won't even find out we were in the house."

So young. So beautiful. So naïve.

"Maybe," I said, not wishing to dampen her spirits.

As soon as I arrived at the hotel and saw the usually sleepy eyes of the doorman widen on my approach, I realized that once again I'd taken a seat on the murder merry-go-round. In my suite, I discovered that the seat was as hot as a griddle.

The blinking red button on the phone was my first clue. My second was Kiki, in the sitting room, half risen from her chair, looking as though she was about to take flight.

She relaxed at the sight of me and plopped down again, taking a gulp from a water glass containing something that looked like water but probably wasn't.

"You wouldn't happen to have another one of those handy?" I asked.

"Glass?"

"The stuff that's in it."

"Spirits, then." She took a second gulp, winced and coughed, not in a ladylike way.

She weaved a little, moving to the minibar, got out a mini bottle of vodka, cracked the cap, and poured its contents into another water tumbler. Handing it to me, she said, "Another murder, Billy? Really?"

"It's on the news?"

"It's been quite a day for news. First it was the story about that headless corpse being a heart attack victim. Now it's all about you and Carrie Sands discovering the body of the comedian in his basement. On TV. On the Web. On the FM. On that room phone that keeps ringing but that I have stopped answering. And especially on this," she said, picking my smartphone up from the table. I'd left it recharging in the bathroom. That's the problem with allowing your assistant to use your hotel room for business. Nothing, least of all your bathroom, is sacred.

I waited for the harsh liquor to clear my tonsils before asking, "What exactly are they saying?"

"Just what I said. You and the actress found the body of that creepy Larry Kelsto."

"You should speak more kindly of the dead, especially since Larry seemed quite taken with you, as I recall."

That earned me an eye roll.

"How . . . ugly was it?" she asked.

"On a scale of one to ten, about twenty-five. He'd been tortured."

She mock shivered. Or maybe it was genuine. "Why am I not surprised? The other bloke was tortured, too. Patton. Which of us is next? Bad odds, Billy. I told you not to go on that show."

"I don't think people are being murdered because of a TV show. And I certainly don't think *you* have anything to worry about."

"Coo! I'm so relieved," she said sarcastically. She reached out to hand me the smartphone. "Best ring up Gretchen and Trina. They've been pestering me every twenty minutes for the past two hours."

I pushed away the straight vodka and asked if she might find something equally lethal that didn't feel like razor blades sliding down my throat.

"I know how you feel about premixed martinis," she said.

"Beggars can't have standards," I said, rousing my phone from its energy-saving stupor.

Kiki stood, weaving slightly. "Your wish is my command, sire." She staggered to the minibar and pried loose a couple of tiny bottles of premixed martinis. "We who are about to die . . . shall join you in a tot of the juniper."

I watched her unscrew the bottle tops. "If you are about to die, it'll probably be from alcohol poisoning," I said.

"Oh, piffle."

"I've never realized before how British you get when you're shitfaced."

"Shitfaced. Lovely, Billy. So much more colorful than 'pissed.' "

"I'm guessing the reason you're booze-soaked is something more than the fear of being murdered. Romance hit the rocks?"

"Fuck off, Billy," she said haughtily, heading for the loo.

Sounds so much classier when said with a British accent.

I sighed, refocused on the phone, and speed-dialed Gretchen Di Voss, the head of the WBC network. Our arrangement was definitely boss-employee, in spite of a romance that ended a few years ago. Or maybe because of it.

She was still at work in her multi-windowed office overlooking the concrete-and-steel towers of Manhattan. Judging by the chilliness in her voice, she was also mad as hell. "What precisely is your involvement in this club comedian's murder?"

"Yes, I'm fine, Gretch, thanks for asking. And you?"

She did not reply. When I tired of the metallic, echolike broadcasting-from-your-bathroom sound that rushes into your cellphone when no one is talking, I said, "I happened to be in his home when his body was discovered."

"Do you need a lawyer?"

"No. At least not yet."

"According to reports, the man was tortured. I assume the police are linking his death to that of our almost-hired Edward Patton?"

"The lead detective, Bollinger, mentioned something about that," I said.

"Please don't tell me that the comedian is in any way connected to WBC."

I looked at Kiki, who was back, staring at me, fully attentive. Ignoring her drink.

"The comedian—his name was Larry Kelsto, by the way—had been scheduled to appear on the same Gemma Bright show as Patton and me and Carrie Sands. But he was bumped."

"So this Detective Bollinger's assumption is what? That something occurred on Gemma's show that led to murder? That a lunatic is killing everyone who was on the show, and you, the Sands woman, and Gemma are in danger? That either you or Sands *is* the killer?"

Kiki was frowning at me.

"Yes, yes, and doubtful," I replied.

"Do you need protection?"

I considered making a smart-ass riposte about always carrying protection in my wallet but censored myself. "Not at present."

"Well, it's six-twelve your time. Trina will be calling you shortly to let you know when to be at WWBC for a segment on *Hotline Tonight*."

That was a nightly show hosted by Vida Evans from D.C. Vida was a newswoman with whom I'd shared a somewhat fractured relationship during my brief sojourn in L.A.

"Let's talk about this," I said to Gretchen. "I'm not—"

"This is not subject to discussion," she said. "I was disappointed when you refused to be our on-camera reporter on the progress of the Pat Patton murder investigation. I was outright furious that you didn't even have the courtesy to let Trina, or anyone else at the network, know about the second murder, *even though you were on the scene*! So you will be on *Hotline Tonight* or . . . you'll be out of a job."

"Since you asked so sweetly, of course I'll be there," I said to the phone, even though Gretchen had already hung up.

Kiki watched me put the phone to sleep. "You look like you need this," she said, pushing the pre-mixed martini my way.

"No ice?" I complained.

"We proud few prefer not to chill our libations."

I raised the glass in a toast. "To the uncompromised life," I said.

Chapter
NINETEEN

Trina Lomax had cajoled a satisfactory complement of talking heads for the segment.

In addition to yours truly, the others in the hall just outside of WWBC's Studio 3 that night included two acquaintances: Carrie Sands, who glommed on to me as if we'd been friends from grade school, whispering, "Do most of the talking, please!," and Gemma Bright, whose approach was a bit the opposite, clearly not whispering when asking, "What the fuck am I doing here, Billy?" Neither expecting an answer nor getting one.

The strangers were two in number: Lieutenant Maureen Oswald of the CPD Office of News Affairs, a briskly efficient, lean woman with well-groomed reddish-brown hair and a preference for minimal cosmetic enhancement whose active blue eyes suggested both intelligence and a sense of humor, and local private detective, J. B. Kazynski, an amply built dirty blonde in a dark business suit whose arched right eyebrow seemed to suggest a suspicion of events transpiring in the studio, if not life in general.

I was consoling myself with the happy thought that my participation on the show might be minimal with such a full panel when Ms. Kazynski sauntered up, aimed her cocked eyebrow at Carrie, who was on my arm, and said to her in a surprisingly throaty voice, "Think you could go stand on your own two feet somewhere for a few minutes, honey, while I talk to this guy?"

Carrie seemed uncertain as to whether to be annoyed or amused. She chose the latter. Using a breathy voice, she said, "If you need anything, Billy, just whistle," and strolled off, switching her hips.

Ms. Kazynski didn't seem to notice. "Have you read *Hot Corner?*" she asked.

She was referencing one of a series of bestsellers by a Chicago author named Stacy Lynne Chomsky, who had appeared on our show. In the thrillers, a character based on and named for Ms. Kazynski undertakes seemingly mundane investigations that invariably lead to much bigger cases.

I told her that I had read the book. Which I had. At least enough of it to know that her fictional counterpart starts out by searching for an anonymous blogger blackmailing her cousin, a standby pitcher for the Cubs, and winds up taking on the military-industrial complex.

"Yeah, well, Stacy Lynne went a little over the top on that one," she said. "But some of it was straight. That's what I wanted to talk to you about."

"About the book? Why?" I asked, pretending I had no idea why a novel involving a Chicago-based blackmailing blogger could be in the least relevant.

Her cocked eyebrow went up another quarter-inch. "You didn't know the bad guy in the novel was based on that bastard Patton?"

"No. Patton was a blackmailer?"

She smiled, and her eyebrow went up another quarter of an inch. "What do you think?"

"I don't think anything. I barely knew the man."

"Really? If that's true, what the hell was he doing in your hotel room the day before he died?"

I didn't blink. "He wanted to work on our show *Wake Up, America!* He asked me to put in a good word for him."

"Out of the kindness of your heart?"

"Apparently," I said. "How'd you know he came to my room?"

"One of my nephews works in the hotel," she said. "I've got relatives just about everywhere in this town. But getting back to Patton, I'd like to know—"

She was interrupted by the floor manager, a young man dressed in denims, a plaid shirt, and a wireless headset. He didn't look as if he'd started to shave yet. Young and impatient, he herded and hustled all of us into the studio.

"Later," J.B. said, or perhaps warned.

We were in a space about the size of an average walk-in closet. Three manned cameras were positioned a few feet from a curved desk built to seat a news team of three comfortably, not a panel of five. The rest of the studio was taken up by a backdrop of a Chicago nightscape looming behind our chairs, two overhead monitors, miles of coiled and twisted wires and cords, several technicians, the aforementioned teenage floor manager, and Trina, our beloved producer.

It was like the stateroom scene in *A Night at the Opera,* only minus the Marx Brothers. And the humor.

With uncommon seriousness, Trina instructed us on the seating arrangements.

Gemma and I wound up at opposite ends of the table. "We don't want you in the same shot," Trina explained. "This is news. We don't want it to look like a network promo."

Ooooo. Change in policy? Had she watched her own show lately?

She put Carrie next to me, then J. B. Kazynski, and the CPD's Lieutenant Maureen Oswald, all of us touching shoulders like a flying wedge. Except for Gemma, the others were staring at the monitors. I'm not sure what was occupying Gemma's thoughts. I was wondering what the others found so fascinating about monitors registering what in computer language would be called BSD. The blue screen of death.

Shortly before we were set to go live at ten-thirty p.m. our time, eleven-thirty p.m. on the East Coast, the BSD was replaced by a close-up on a polished desk and an empty chair on which Vida Evans would soon be depositing her lovely bottom. Trina gave us a final pep talk, urging us to "just be yourselves, stay attentive, and speak with confidence. And remember, when Vida asks you a question, viewers will hear the question immediately, but there will be a few seconds delay before you hear it here in the studio. You may want to put a thoughtful expression on your face, as if you're pondering the question. Otherwise, it'll look to the viewers as if you're an unresponsive idi—

"What the heck is that?"

Her attention had shifted to a novel titled *Danger Zone* that J.B. had positioned on the table in front of her, cover toward the camera. "It's the new Stacy Lynne Chomsky," she said.

"Please remove it," Trina said. "This is not *The Tonight Show*."

"There are water glasses on the table," J.B. said. "Why not my book?"

"Nobody will think we're pimping water glasses," Trina said, repeating her request that *Danger Zone* be removed.

"The Nazis banned books, too," J.B. mumbled, sliding the novel onto her lap. I guessed it would eventually wind up back on the table.

The floor manager, standing between the dueling cameras, held up a hand showing two fingers. "Two minutes to air," he said.

Vida Evans, all five-foot-ten black-and-beautiful inches of her, settled down in her chair and received her final hair and facial tune-up. "Hello, everyone," she said. "And, Billy, a special hello to you. So nice having you here on *my* show."

A while back, I was asked to cohost *Hotline Tonight,* with Vida participating from the West Coast and I from the East. I'm very happy working in the early morning, having my evenings and nights free. And probably more important, I'd been treated to an unpleasant up-close-and-personal example of Vida's ambitious, one might even say cruelly ambitious, nature. So I turned down the gig. She became the solo host, and the network execs moved her away from her beloved L.A. to D.C. to add to the show's gravitas. That's when those same executives discovered that viewers who wanted gravitas had their fill of it on PBS or *Nightline*.

The ratings were tanking. She was in a city that she hated. And she blamed me.

The floor manager held up one finger. No, not that one. The index.

As that finger disappeared into a fist, *Hotline Tonight*'s symphonic theme began. On the studio monitors, the show's logo popped. When the music faded, an off-camera announcer in D.C. began his earnestly dramatic voice-over: "On *Hotline Tonight* . . . the story of two men"—Pictures of Pat Patton and Larry Kelsto appeared on the screen—"one a former police lieutenant and powerful voice in the city of Chicago, the other a struggling performer in the Windy City's comedy clubs. Both were scheduled to appear on the same popular daytime television show"—Cut to a clip of Patton waving to Gemma's audience—"just days before they were sadistically tortured and murdered"—Cut to another shot, this one of two body bags resting on twin gurneys. Maybe Kelsto and Patton. Probably not.

Cut to an aerial shot of Chicago at night. "Did something occur on the show to cause the murders? Is there a serial killer at large in this great American city?" That drew a groan from CPD Lieutenant Oswald. "If so, where will he or she strike next? Searching for the answers, here's *Hotline Tonight*'s Vida Evans."

Vida, her lovely face as serious as if she'd just seen

her ratings drop even more, welcomed her viewers, gave a brief reprise of what the announcer had just told us, and introduced her "guests." It might have been my imagination, but I think she was gritting her teeth when she mentioned my many accomplishments.

She then said something that had me gritting mine. "I believe you know our own Chef Billy Blessing has become something of an expert on murder. Billy was on the *Midday with Gemma* talk show with the late Pat Patton, and I'm happy to report that he will be guesting on *my* show each night this week reporting on crime in the city of Chicago, with a special emphasis on the Chicago Police Department's investigation into what many are calling the Talk Show Murders."

There's nothing like being dragooned into doing something you've already refused, unless it's being informed of the dragooning on live TV, where all you can do is nod like an idiot. I looked at Trina, standing just behind the floor manager. She was wearing a Cheshire cat grin. "It'll be a joy, as always, to be working with you, Vida," I said, lobbing the conversational ball back to her.

From there, things went pretty much as expected, with Vida trying to pry information from Lieutenant Oswald and having to be satisfied with a very broad overview of what the CPD investigators had learned: basically, that some unknown party or parties had tortured both men until they'd died. The lieutenant would not specify the torture methods or the grisly condition of the corpses, nor would she validate the theory that the midday show was in any way involved or any of the other speculative theories abroad in bloggerland.

Lieutenant Oswald did say that the detectives assigned to the murders were "certainly aware of the fact that both Patton and Kelsto were in this building for *Midday with Gemma*. They're investigating the possibility that the two men may have made contact at that time or that they may have left the studios together. But the feeling is that their connection to the show was coincidental. A careful analysis of the program itself has been made, leading the investigators to conclude that nothing that transpired in the course of the hour led to Lieutenant Patton's murder."

"Really?" Vida asked. "Let's take a look. Right after this commercial."

There was not a lot of chatter during the commercial, nor while we watched a section of the talk show in which Patton and Gemma nattered on about the body on the beach. After the clip, Vida asked, "Lieutenant Oswald, what about Lieutenant Patton's announcement that he was privy to information regarding the corpse?"

Lieutenant Oswald's smile was annoyingly patronizing. "Lieutenant Patton was an outstanding lawman who was not terribly happy in retirement and preferred the world think he was still on the cutting edge of law enforcement. He'd made similar statements about his insider's knowledge before, on television and on the Internet. But they were based mainly on rumor and supposition, not fact. No one took them seriously."

"He claimed to have been right about ninety-four percent of the time."

"Using his own measuring criteria," Lieutenant Oswald parried.

Vida turned to Gemma and asked what she thought about Patton's comment.

"Oh, I believe he knew *some*thing," she said. "I've *never* known him to just make things up."

Taking our cues from Lieutenant Oswald, Carrie and I stonewalled like politicians. We hadn't met either Patton or Kelsto before the day of Gemma's show. We denied seeing any contact between the two men either before or after the telecast. We were surprised to hear from Kelsto but were intrigued by his request for a meeting. That's why we were at his home when the housekeeper discovered his body.

No, we did not know why Larry invited us. We barely knew him. And we knew even less about Edward "Pat" Patton.

"Gemma, what do you think about the theory that a serial killer is working his way through everyone who'd been scheduled to be on your program that day?" Vida asked.

"What a perfectly ridiculous question!" Lieutenant Oswald exclaimed before Gemma even had her mouth open. "This is real life, Ms. Evans, not pulp fiction."

"Including Gemma, five people were scheduled to appear on the show," Vida said. "Two were murdered, apparently by the same hand. Not exactly pulp fiction, is it?"

I felt Carrie's hand grasp my arm. I have to say I was getting spooked myself by the conversation. Being the potential victim of one deranged killer was bad enough. Vida was opening that up to a nation of deranged killers who might want in on the fun.

"Speaking of pulp fiction," I said, derailing the lieutenant's tentative reply to Vida's question, "I think J. B. Kazynski's got a new book she'd like to tell us about."

J.B. didn't waste a second in holding up the copy of her latest Chicagoland caper.

Vida looked frustrated by the interruption. Trina was furious. And J.B.'s motormouthed promo took us to the end of the show.

All in all, that went pretty well.

Chapter
TWENTY

After the telecast, I noticed J.B. lingering near the front door. The private eye had mentioned she'd wanted to talk with me about the murders, and since the word "no" seemed to be among those missing from her lexicon, I knew that meant we'd eventually have that conversation. But not then. Which is why I was still cooling my heels in the studio when Trina ducked her head in and said, "Billy? Good. You haven't left."

I should have opted for the talk with J.B.

Trina led me upstairs in the minimally occupied building. Most of the executive offices were dark, but the conference room had all bulbs aglow, with Lieutenant Maureen Oswald sitting at a sparkling glass table, sipping from a cup of something dark. Judging from her expression, the dark stuff wasn't all that tasty.

"There's a coffee machine just outside the door," Trina said, selecting a chair across from the lieutenant.

"No coffee for me," I said, and Lieutenant Oswald nodded her approval. I selected a chair next to her.

"Re your new assignment, Billy, Maureen has agreed to assist you in every way she can," Trina said.

I smiled at the lieutenant, pretending this was good news.

"I prepare a daily report on department activities," she said. "I'll make sure you get a copy."

"Stale news will be no help, Maureen," Trina said.

"It will be up to date. But I'm not going to kid you, Trina. There won't be any exclusive information. Your merry band will only be here a limited time. The local media are with us always."

"Understood," Trina said. "We'll come up with our own exclusives. Right, Billy?"

"It's what we're known for," I said. "That and the *Carlyle the Walking Penis* sitcom."

The lieutenant raised an eyebrow. "You really have a show called that on your network?"

"It's on right after *Vaginatown*. . . . Joking."

"I'll take your word on that," the lieutenant said, rising. Trina and I both stood, too. "You might want to check with me on the accuracy of whatever 'exclusives' you turn up."

"Absolutely," Trina said, though nobody in the room believed that for a minute.

"Chef Blessing, in reporting on the Patton and Kelsto murders, I hope you're not going to continue to spread any more of that Talk Show Murders nonsense."

"Are you so certain it is nonsense?" Trina asked.

"Pretty much," the lieutenant said. "Good night to you both. Mr. Blessing, you know where to reach me."

Trina and I watched her leave.

"There's definitely something going on, some strong lead they're following," Trina said. "We have to find out what it is by tomorrow night's show."

"I'll get my investigative team on it right away. Wait a minute. I don't have an investigative team. Why not? *Because I'm a chef and a TV show host!*"

I paused to compose myself. "Trina, we both know I'm not a reporter at all. I know my way around a kitchen. I read books. I tell a fair joke, and I can talk to people. Why force me to do something totally alien to my interests?"

"Maybe I see a talent you haven't discovered," she said.

"Really?"

"No. I'm using you because when you got mixed up in those murders on the West Coast, your TVQ score went through the roof. I think that'll happen here, too. And we need something to pull *Hotline* out of its rut."

"If I'm that good, I'm being underpaid. I should call my agent."

"He'll tell you you'll be in a better bargaining position if you do bring in the ratings," she said. "Meanwhile, I don't want to wear you out. You'll only be working the last half-hour of the morning show."

She explained that she'd already notified Arnie that Karma Singleton, our right-wing entertainment reporter, would be hosting the segment featuring the thirteen-year-old basso profundo and some of my other assignments. My interview with the author of *Da Mare* had been postponed a day—which would give me time to finish reading the door-stopper—but I'd still have to chat with the stars of the new WBC reality show *Naked Housewives of Wilmette*.

At least I still got to hang on to a few perks of the job.

Chapter
TWENTY-ONE

It was nearing midnight when I pushed through WWBC's thick glass doors to a crisp, clear starry night, expecting to see the cab I'd ordered. Instead, I found Carrie sitting behind the wheel of her Beamer.

"What's up?" I asked her.

"I've been waiting for you," she said. "I sent your cab away."

"Why would you do that?"

"I was hoping you'd come with me to my place."

"Say again?"

"Oh, God, I guess that sounded weird. I mean, I was

hoping you'd drive with me to where I'm staying. It's on North State Parkway, not that far from your hotel, but we can send for a cab there." She was nattering. Speed-nattering. "It's just that, with everything that's happened, I don't . . . I mean, it won't be that far out of your way, and you're going in that direction anyway, and . . . Please, Billy. I have to park on the street, and there's never an empty space, and I wind up walking blocks and blocks. And it's always dark and really scary even when I don't have a good reason to think somebody might pop out of the shadows and kill me."

I took a closer look at her. "Desperate" was the word that came to mind.

I slid onto the Beamer's leather bucket beside her. "Okay, Cisco, let's went."

She gave me the puzzled look of someone who'd never seen an episode of *The Cisco Kid* when they were growing up. Then she started the engine and we wented.

"All that talk about us being on the killer's list really got to me," she said. "Especially after seeing what they did to that poor man."

She was quiet for a beat, then added, "I'm going to ask Derek to get me a bodyguard."

I assumed that would be Derek Webber, the zillionaire producer of her movie, whom Charlie Dann the Puff Potato Man had mentioned.

"I've heard he's a pretty good guy," I said.

"The best. Really smart. Handsome. Almost Zuckerberg-rich. I'll introduce you tonight. He's usually up late."

"You're staying at his place?"

She smiled. "He and I are sharing a cozy little

four-story, thirty-five-room shack with the film's director, the cinematographer, several other members of the cast, and a full staff."

"Sounds like a sure cure for loneliness."

"I'm surprised you hadn't heard we were all staying at his mansion," she said. "It's usually the second thing any interviewer is curious about."

I was on the verge of asking what the first thing was when I remembered Gin's interview with her on our show. Carrie was having a romance with the author of the *Spy Who* novels, Gerard Parnelle, while Parnelle's wife was sleeping with Derek Webber. The situation struck me as a little too Jackie Collins. Or maybe not enough Jackie Collins.

The "shack" was an elegant red-brick neo-Georgian townhouse fronted by a wall with a wrought-iron gate on North State Parkway. The closest available street parking was a couple of blocks away on Dearborn.

"You're a lovely man, Billy, for indulging my weirdness like this," Carrie said as we walked away from the Beamer. "I guess you think I'm a wimp."

Actually, I was thinking I was the wimp. The neighborhood may have been on the city's ritzy Gold Coast, but that didn't chase the dark shadows away. As we turned the corner on Schiller, heading for State, a metallic red monster of a car zoomed past us, leaving in its wake a dark, very quiet, very sinister block.

"What's that place?" I asked her, indicating a long slab of granite on our right.

"The Chicago Racquet Club," Carrie said. "Derek and Gerard play there . . . played there when Gerard was in town."

"He's off writing a book?"

She nodded. "I really miss him."

"How long before he gets back?"

"He's not coming back. I'm flying to Paris as soon as we wrap."

"When will that be?"

"With luck, another two weeks," she said.

"How often do you talk?"

"I got an email this morning. Gerard says that when we talk it's too distracting. He prefers us to text and email."

Ah, romance in the digital age.

We were halfway down the block, when a man-size hunk of shadow separated from an alcove at the rear of the Racquet Club. As he stepped into a rectangle of light from a club window, I blinked. When I looked again, he was still there, a snarling, six-foot-something baldie black guy wearing a black warm-up outfit and bright orange running shoes.

His hand seemed to be attached to an ugly-looking weapon.

I grabbed Carrie's arm and pulled her down beside a parked car just as I heard several *thunk-thunk-thunk* sounds and pinging noises as the wall behind us developed a line of gouges and chips.

My heart was pounding hard enough to make me wonder if this might be the big coronary. I suppose I even might have wished that to be the case. Beside me, Carrie was shaking like a whipped terrier.

Judging by the padded footsteps on asphalt, our homicidal attacker was crossing the street toward us. Moving slowly. But irrevocably. I use words like that when I'm about to pee in my pants.

Chapter
TWENTY-TWO

I kept my grip on Carrie, and, still squatting, we backward duck-walked away from the approaching footsteps. My plan was simple: Do anything to keep at least one automobile between us and the shooter.

It was a very temporary plan. It relied entirely too much on someone hearing the gunfire and giving enough of a damn to call the cops. The cops would then have to arrive before the shooter stalked us into a position where we would be defenseless. And all of this would have to take place within the next—what?—half-minute?

As if the odds weren't already against us, two more shadowy figures emerged silently from the alley. I assumed they'd come directly at us, leaving us the option of being shot by them or moving into the street, where the orange-shoe gunman couldn't fail to get his job done. Instead, for some unknown reason, presumably stupidity, they took to the street.

That gave us a hairline chance, but we were still contending with three armed killers. I did the only thing I could: I pulled Carrie closer, giving them a smaller target that was mainly me. Any second there'd be another spray of bullets coming our way.

I could feel Carrie's panicked breathing. There was a pounding in my ears I tried to ignore as I strained to hear approaching footsteps.

Instead, I heard what sounded like a garbled word. Were the three of them communicating?

We stayed that way, pressed against the side of a car for what was probably only a minute or two but seemed a lifetime. Then, suddenly, there was the squeal of tires as a vehicle roared down the alley, turned onto Schiller, and charged in our direction.

It braked parallel to the car protecting us. Doors opened.

Carrie trembled against me. I hugged her tighter.

The car doors slammed shut. And the vehicle roared away.

I relaxed my hold on Carrie enough to poke my head over the car's hood. A familiar black SUV was zooming away. Its headlights blazed on just as it made a left turn onto Dearborn.

Edging up to join me, Carrie saw the same thing I did: Schiller Street was now deserted. "What just happened?" she asked.

I shook my head. "The only thing I know for sure is that we're still alive."

"But for how long?" she asked.

Carrie had her own electronic key to the mansion's front door. It took her a few tries, but she finally got it to work just as police sirens sounded. We'd barely made it inside before a prowl car zoomed past, flashing its lights and wailing.

We were in a polished white marble vestibule,

which struck me as looking way too much like a funeral parlor. Carrie sighed and stared at me. "I don't get it. I'm a wreck, and you're as cool as a kumquat."

"Cucumber. Cool as a cucumber. Kumquats make even less sense in similes than they do in salads."

"See, that's what I mean," she said. "You're Mr. Cool. Is this a daily routine for you? Do people shoot at you all the time?"

"Lately, it seems," I said. "But the fact is, I'm not at all cool with it. More like in shock."

"I guess we could both use a stiff drink, or something," she said, leading me down the marble hall to a broad oak door guarded by twin suits of armor.

"All this marble and tin," I said. "Might Mr. Webber be just a touch imperious?"

"Not at all," she said. "Derek's as down-to-earth as an old shoe."

Perhaps one worn by the late Howard Hughes, I thought, as we walked into a space bigger than the average ballroom. I should have said walked down into it, since most of the floor was sunken. The room was dimly lit but not so dim that I failed to see that the ceiling, two stories above us, supported a chandelier that the Phantom of the Opera would have found irresistible. He'd probably have liked the black onyx piano almost as much. Not sure what he'd have thought about the huge paintings by pop artists Robert Rauschenberg and Roy Lichtenstein, among others I did not recognize, that dominated the far wall and seemed to challenge the gentlemen's club leather furnishings and no-nonsense walk-in fireplace and hearth.

Searching for the source of the light, I saw a chrome lamp positioned near the back of a brown leather chair. The chair faced a crowded built-in bookcase that filled one of the mile-high walls. Beside the chair was a small round glass-top table on which rested a book and what appeared to be a cocktail glass, half-filled or half-empty, your choice. A pale, slender arm extended from the chair, its delicate hand finding and lifting the drink.

Carrie walked to the chair, looked at its inhabitant, and said, "Adoree, where is everybody?"

"Ah, they are in the game room, cherie," came the lyrical, accented reply. "We watch your show and then Madeleine goes to work, the boys play their games, and I come in here to read."

Carrie saw me heading their way and said, "Billy, do you know Adoree Oden? Adoree, Billy Blessing."

As I rounded the chair and came face-to-face with the woman seated on it, I think I froze. I'm not sure, because I'd more or less lost track of everything except Mademoiselle Adoree Oden. She looked up at me and smiled. "*Enchanté*," she said.

There are brunettes and brunettes, enough varieties that the word doesn't mean much anymore. All of them have a certain appeal, except perhaps the ones who are about as brunette as Carrie under the dye and as to temperament as solid as marzipan. There is the modified-Afro brunette who's tall and toned and serious, who spends her prework hours at yoga and her after-work hours with similarly minded friends, parsing the latest Palin pruncio or discussing the condition in Darfur and giving both topics equal time. There's the willowy brunette who poses rather than talks because she really doesn't have much to say, and the tiny, gamine brunette who chatters like a magpie and makes about as much sense.

There is the beautiful but oh-so-bored brunette who might have stepped from the pages of *Vogue* and who looks at you as if you've just crawled out of a used copy of *Hustler*. And the ultra-hip brunette who's into cloud computing and urbanomics and knows the best place in town to dine on Korean tacos. She's fun for a while, until you try to slow her down long enough for a normal conversation and she suggests you both take a power walk instead.

There's the Dragon Lady brunette who seems mysterious with more than a hint of danger attached, but rescue her from a dull party and you'll discover she's living in Queens with a husband, two kids, and a mother-in-law. There's the bubbly brunette, as effervescent and sexy as Halle Berry, who picks you up in a bar and invites you to dinner and back to her hotel room, where you will probably awake the next morning missing a kidney.

There's the wise-and-knowing brunette, with a touch of gray in her hair, whose disposition is as calm as a country pond and whose understanding of the human condition is so complete she can spot your failings ten minutes after you've met and won't hesitate to offer her expert advice on self-improvement. And there's the zaftig brunette with a full-throated laugh and a grand sense of humor who seems so friendly and charming when you first meet but after a couple of vodka Red Bulls turns frantic and starts tossing crockery.

Adoree Oden was none of these. At least, I hoped to God she wasn't. She seemed beautiful and smart and sophisticated and even-tempered . . . and did I mention beautiful? Skin the color of caramel, eyes a luminescent lime, lips of cherry red. Hey, food is my life, okay?

"But this is a coincidence," she said. She showed me the book she'd been reading. *Wake Up to Murder* by yours truly. Her backup novel rested on the table beside her cocktail: Raymond Chandler's *The Long Goodbye*. Her literary preferences cinched the deal. She and I were soul mates.

I would have mentioned this to her, but, as I said, I was too damned agog.

"Is something the matter?" she asked, in her utterly charming French accent (which I will not begin to attempt to duplicate in print).

Carrie was giving me an amused look. She said to the goddess, "C'mon, Adoree, you must've looked in a mirror today. Billy's just a little poleaxed."

"*Qu'est-ce que* 'poleaxed'?"

"Awed by your . . . presence," I managed to get out.

"Ah, well, then"—she placed my book on top of Chandler's, stood, and took my hand in hers—"I have to say I am a bit poleaxed myself."

My hand felt as if it were on fire.

"I may call you Billy?"

"You may call me anything your heart desires."

"I was very impressed by your sangfroid on the television when being questioned by the hostess, who seemed so hostile in her unattractive Fendi blouse. I asked Derek if he had the book you mentioned." She indicated the copy of *Wake Up to Murder*. "You see, I am quite enamored of . . ."

"Yes?"

" . . . the noir. I have only just started your book, but I know I will enjoy it."

"Ah, if you two will excuse me," Carrie said, "I have to talk to Derek about something."

"But of course," Adoree said, moving even closer to me. "We will join you. I am sure Billy did not come here tonight to spend his time with me."

True, but that's before I knew she was there. "*Now,*" I felt like shouting, "*My time is yours!*"

But that may have sounded a bit desperate. So I remained mum and gratefully allowed her to take my arm and, pressing it against her silken body, lead me into Derek Webber's game room.

Calling it a man cave would not be doing it justice. Superman's Fortress of Solitude didn't come close. The room was a mash-up of boardwalk arcade, shipboard casino, and Best Buy showroom. It was stocked with several dozen standing machines, from the primitive Pac-Man era to the latest Skee Ball X-Treme, slots, video poker, pinball, a wall taken over by active midsize flat-screen monitors, all gizmos flashing lights and emitting slightly muted electronic bongs and beeps.

There was a long white enamel table on which six computer monitors rested, five of them displaying alternate Windows and Mac desktop logos. The sixth was being used by an attractive woman in her late twenties or early thirties with short henna-red hair, an ample bosom barely contained by a black-and-silver halter, and long, shapely legs extending from black shorts. A ring glittered from the big toe of her bare left foot.

She didn't seem to be aware of the noise, the flashing lights, or us.

Carrie moved past her without pausing, heading for the other side of the room, where six men were seated at a green felt table, engaged in a refreshingly electronic-free, real-life game of old-fashioned poker. With one exception, they were pre–middle age, not quite clean shaven, and enjoying themselves, probably because, judging by the beer cans and booze bottles, they were at least slightly in the tank.

The exception, age-wise, was a dour gent with blond, almost white, hair and one of those mustache-less beards that outlined his pink face with a frosty band running from sideburn to sideburn. He was at least a decade older than the thirtysomethings.

When Carrie called out, "Derek, we need to talk," I expected him to reply. But it was one of the others who raised his arm and urged her to come closer for an embrace. A handsome guy with an easy smile who reminded me of a young Gregory Peck. He was wearing a pale yellow silk shirt that probably cost more than its Asian seamstress made in a lifetime, well-used denim jeans with a worn spot at the right knee, and white running shoes trimmed in red.

"You know I love to talk, Carrisima," he said, drawing her toward him.

As he did, he seemed to sober and immediately removed his arm from Carrie's waist. He cast a sheepish glance at the henna-haired woman, who, to his apparent dismay, was staring at him without expression.

As he broke eye contact with her, he looked our way, squinted, frowned, and then his face relaxed in a broad smile. He closed his cards into a neat packet and got to his feet. He was about my size in height and maybe a little more than half my size in girth. "Chef Blessing? This is great. I was hoping to get the chance to meet you while you were here in Chi-town."

He came forward, cards in his left hand, his right extended. Against my desire, Adoree freed mine so I could shake it. "This is great," he said. "I take it you and Addie are . . . friends?"

"This lovely man and I just met," she said. "He came with Carrie."

"Really?" Webber gave the word a musical three-syllable pronunciation. He turned to the blond actress with a curious yet oddly pleased expression. "I gather from the TV show that you two spent the day together at what turned out to be a murder scene. Bummer for romance."

"Billy and I are friends," Carrie said, using a corrective tone. "He was kind enough to keep me company on the drive here from the station."

Webber turned to me. He seemed a little deflated that his star and I weren't ready for our tabloid romance. I wondered why.

"We paused the game to watch you and Carrie," he said. "That lady in D.C., what's her name? Vida? She's got a real chip on her shoulder pad for you, Billy. Am I right?"

I shrugged.

"Well, anyway, you didn't let her get to you. And we were ecstatic that Carrie was able to plug our little movie project. Speaking of which, the beautiful lady at the computer is my coproducer, Madeleine Parnelle."

The henna redhead gave me a noncommittal nod and continued to glare at Webber, who was pretending not to notice. "Gerard just emailed her the rough draft of his next chart-busting opus, and she's a bit anxious to check it out. She's vetted all his books. Some say she does more than that."

I understood he was saying that Madeleine Parnelle might even be as responsible as her husband for the success of the novels. But since he, Webber, was hitting the sack with Madeleine, that made his comment something of a double entendre, not that anyone but I seemed to notice or care. Evidently, they were more sophisticated than I. And in my unsophisticated way, I wondered if the affair might be running out of steam. That could explain why the idea of my matching up with Carrie appealed to Webber. If she were changing partners, maybe Parnelle might consider reclaiming his wife's attentions.

Webber interrupted my speculation by asking, "Did Addie tell you the part she's playing in the film?"

"I am Madame Acardine, the monstrous, how do you say, mean girl of the piece?" Adoree said, trying to look sinister but only making herself more adorable.

"That must take quite a lot of acting," I said.

"Adoree's a wonderful actress," Carrie said. "She was nominated three times for the César." The French Academy Award.

"Always the bridesmaid," Adoree said.

"Never the bride?" I asked.

"Not so far." She held up her left hand and wiggled a naked wedding-ring finger.

"Hard to believe," I said.

"Meet some other members of the crew, Billy," Webber said, indicating the poker players. "The Frenchman with the white powder on his mustache is our director, Austin Deware. Austin directed the *en Français* version of the book that made a ton of loot and won a million awards and turned him into an international A-lister. We fully expect him to top himself with the American version."

"It weel be my *Shinatowne*," Deware slurrily proclaimed. He could have still been in his twenties, pudgy with a soft pale face he was hoping to toughen with a Fu Manchu mustache that actually did seem to be hosting a few dots of white powder. Probably not dandruff.

Webber continued his intros. To Deware's right was the room's elder presence, Lars Bergamot, the film's cinematographer. To his right was a ferret-faced black man named Harp Didio, *The Thief Who*'s assistant director, a misleading title, since the AD actually assists the producer. The almost too-handsome blond hiding his eyes behind aviator sunglasses was a current television heartthrob, Sandford Hawes. According to Webber, he was the romantic lead, an incompetent insurance investigator who ultimately wins the antisocial heart of the hard-boiled girl thief.

The final card player was Webber's business partner, Alan Luchek. "Alan is the bad cop at Onion City Entertainment," he said. "I handle creative, he handles the biz, and he's more ruthless than a Somali pirate."

Luchek certainly didn't look the role. He had the freckled face of a teenager and a mop of red hair that, unlike Webber's perfectly molded coif, seemed to have been clipped by a distracted country barber. Opie as bad cop? A stretch, but he did have the majority of the games' poker chips stacked in front of him.

"P-pleased to meet you, Chef B-B-Blessing," he said, making that bad-cop image even more fanciful.

"We might as well call the game for tonight, huh?" Sandford Hawes suggested. "I know we're off tomorrow, but I can still use the z's."

"No!" Webber said, walking back to his chair. "Not with the hand I'm holding."

"There's something I have to talk to you about, Derek," Carrie said.

"Sure," he replied. "What's on your mind?"

"It's . . . personal."

Webber wasn't obvious about it, but he gave Madeleine Parnelle a quick glance before replying to Carrie. "Okay. Let's take it into the living room. Billy can play my hand for me."

"Actually, I'd like Billy to join us," Carrie said.

Webber got that amused grin on his puss again and said, "Fine. Ah, Addie? Know anything about poker?"

"My papa was a croupier at Cercle Clichy Montmartre in Paris," she said. "I began playing the game at the age of nine."

"You learn something new every day," Webber said, handing her the cards.

I watched her walk gracefully to the table and take a seat. She turned and winked at me, assuming quite correctly that I'd been following her every move.

"You coming, Billy?" Carrie asked.

Sadly, yes.

Back among the big pop-art paintings, I said, "So this is what you call your living room, Derek?"

"Living room, party room, screening room, library." He turned to Carrie and said, "What's up, babe? You've got my full attention."

"Billy and I were shot at tonight."

His eyebrows went up. "Shot. Like, bang-bang?"

"Like that," she said.

"Where the hell were you, for Chri' Pete? In some South Side dive?"

"Around the corner, on Schiller," she said.

"No shit?" He looked from Carrie to me, not really expecting me to contradict her. "This is, what? That thing they were saying on the tube? Some crazy asshole killing everybody who was on that talk show?"

"Maybe," I said.

Gone was the convivial host, replaced by the guy his associates saw during business hours. "Give me the full play-by-play," he said. "No. Wait. Let me get Alan in here."

The company bad cop ambled in, carrying a bottle of Mountain Dew. He suggested we move to a gathering of leather chairs on the far side of the recessed area. He perched on the arm of his chair and said, "Rek m-m-mentioned a shooting?"

While Carrie gave us an accurate description of what had transpired on Schiller Street, Alan Luchek listened carefully, his boyish head cocked to one side, eyes intent on the actress. When she'd finished, he asked me if I had anything to add.

I told them about seeing the other two figures heading toward the shooter. I held back on seeing the black SUV's departure or that it had followed me in the past. I told myself it was because I wanted to minimize my participation in whatever was going on.

Luchek was frowning. "I thought the TV show tonight was just b-b-blowing wind. A k-k-killer b-b-bumping off guests on a talk show sounded a little *Murder, She Wrote* to me. Somebody b-b-beating up on Patton? No b-b-big surprise. The other guy, I dunno. Maybe he saw something. B-b-but a hit squad going after you guys, this is serious shit."

"I guess we should call the police," Carrie said.

"Whoa," Luchek said, clutching his heart. "The insurance on the f-f-film is costing an arm and a leg as is."

"Maybe we should see where we are before letting the world know we've got a potential problem," Webber said. "Okay?"

"Okay," she said, only half convinced.

"You were driving?" Webber asked.

She nodded.

"Notice any cars following you?"

"I don't—" Carrie began.

"Maybe," I said, and told them about the black SUV and that I'd seen it before, following me.

"Th-th-that suggests you were the t-t-target," Luchek said.

He seemed relieved.

Glad one of us was.

Chapter
TWENTY-THREE

"It didn't worry you, Billy?" Webber asked. "Having somebody on your ass?"

"I wasn't sure they were following me. They weren't there earlier today, I don't think."

"Well, they made up for that tonight," Webber said.

"It doesn't matter who they were following," Carrie said. "If Billy hadn't pulled me out of the way, we'd both be dead."

Webber moved closer to Carrie and put his arm around her. "Don't worry, Carrisima. We're not going to take any chances with your life. We're gonna get you some protection."

"B-B-Bucky," Luchek suggested.

"Perfect," Webber agreed.

"You're talking about a bodyguard, right?" Carrie asked.

"The ultimate bodyguard with the perfect name. Bucky Hurtz," Webber said. "Three hundred and ten pounds of muscle, bone, and sinew. But he's also street-smart, neat, clean, and polite. Some say he killed a guy by accident during a mixed martial arts match when he was attending Northwestern. Others claim he was the only survivor of a mercenary squad in Afghanistan. Folk songs have been written about Bucky Hurtz."

"It's late. I'll c-c-call him in the morning," Luchek said, and took a hit of Mountain Dew.

"What about Billy?" Carrie asked. "He really needs a bodyguard."

The two men looked at me, then at each other. I made it easy for them. "WBC will pop for security."

That was probably true, assuming I presented them with the problem, which I wasn't quite sure I wanted to do.

Webber insisted on driving me to my hotel.

Being chauffeured by a billionaire in one of his three Ferraris was such a trip that in spite of my concern that the black SUV was lurking somewhere unseen, I was feeling obnoxiously superior.

Then Webber started talking about the murders and my mood flattened like a chicken paillard. "Any idea what the hell happened on that talk show to put you and my star in jeopardy?" he asked.

"Not a clue."

"It's got to be something involving Patton," he said. "The guy was a murder waiting to happen."

"What makes you say that?"

He executed a fancy turn before replying.

"He wasn't a very nice man."

"You knew him?"

He made one of those fake smiles, as natural as the grin of a skeleton. "Worse than that, I tried to do business with him. Onion City started out producing reality series. *The Desperate DARs of Savannah, Bartenders: Life Behind the Whiskey Curtain*. A few others. Patton pitched a true-crime series, based on CPD files and a diary he kept the whole time he was on the force. He wanted to call the show *The Overworld*. Every week would be another example of how the criminal underworld families of the thirties, forties, fifties, and sixties directly influenced today's major movers and shakers."

"Sounds like an interesting idea," I said.

"That's what Alan and I thought. Frankly, I've got a thing about the city's gangland history. So we sat down with the guy and his lawyer and hammered out the deal. We all shook hands. But we couldn't get Patton's signature on the agreement. He kept giving us excuses. He wanted to get the concept approved by his buddy, Chief of Police Oz Dillman. Or his attorney felt the need to clear a few names, just to make sure no jailhouse lawyer could make trouble. A week before our first network pitch, Patton decided to walk away."

"Give a reason?" I asked.

"Not to us. Not then. A couple weeks later, the son of a bitch wrote on his blog that he pulled out because he discovered Onion City had roots in organized crime, or as it is known hereabouts, the Outfit."

I opened my mouth and then shut it. No sense asking a dumb question.

"Of course it was bullshit," Webber said. "But that didn't stop the FBI from putting us through the wringer for months. They wound up 'discovering' what everybody knew, that Onion City was an outgrowth of a little online service called Instapicks, which had its roots in my family's garage, not in any Outfit boardroom. Getting that clean bill of health cost a lot of time and money, Billy. Thank you so much, Patton. May your dark soul rot in hell."

"What was his point?"

"Beats me. At first I expected that shyster of his to tell us his client would make the whole thing go away for some ridiculous fee. When that didn't happen, I wondered if they might not have sold the fucking series themselves directly to NBC or HBO."

"Is it possible he really believed you were tied to organized crime?" I asked.

"I don't know where he would have gotten that idea. Anyway, even though he had this super-cop rep, I've talked to people who say he looked the other way every now and then if the price was right. In other words, he wasn't the kind of guy to be offended by the prospect of spending Mob money."

Patton's real reason for walking away from their deal was a puzzler, but it wasn't my puzzler. "What can you tell me about Patton's lawyer?" I asked.

"Huh?" Webber asked as his mind shifted gears. "His lawyer? A little—no, make that a big—weasel named James Clement Yountz. Of the firm Garaday, Hilton, Pendrake, and Yountz. On Boul' Mich. Not exactly a shady operation, but they have their share of bent-nose clients, and this is Chicago."

"The city that works?" I said.

"The city that works you over."

"You're not a Chicago boy?"

He smiled. "Close enough. About fifteen miles to the north. Winnetka. Alan's from the land of the big wind, too. We were high school buddies. New Trier. Go Trevians!"

"Your family still there?" I asked.

We were nearing my hotel. He maneuvered into the right lane.

"Nope. My dad's . . . gone. Mom lives in Miami with a retired city judge. Nice guy, I guess. Heidi, my younger sister, is in L.A., working for a talent agency. And my older sister, Roz, is in Weston, Connecticut, married to an ad exec. Got a couple of kids. She opted for the housewife bit over a career. Says she's happy."

"You happy?" I asked.

"I don't give it much thought. I guess that means I am. You strike me as a happy guy, Billy. You a family man?"

We were at the hotel parking circle, where about a dozen cars were blocking all three lanes, either awaiting passengers or disgorging them. "No family," I said. "Not married. Never have been."

"Ever wonder what it might be like?" he asked.

"Not a day goes by," I said. "What about you?"

"Down one. But I'm not totally against another try. Just have to see what the future brings."

A lane opened up, and he pulled the Ferrari into it. Several valets rushed us. It was that kind of sports car.

"I'm having a little party tomorrow night at Restaurant Pastiche. Mainly business. Some media. People with money in the movie. But it should be fun. Drop by."

One of the valets had my door open. "I'll be tied up with the *Hotline* show until eleven."

"We'll still be partying."

Stepping out of the vehicle, I said, "Will Adoree be there?"

"Sure," he said. "Addie's a knockout, isn't she? And, being French, that makes her a little different from the American actresses I've . . . dated. But she *is* an actress. That means she's more than a woman and can make you feel less than a man."

I guess I frowned, because he added, "Hey, scratch that, huh? I'm . . . not exactly an expert on romance. Go for it, if that's what you want."

He held out his hand, and I slapped it.

I watched the Ferrari drive away and decided I agreed with Charlie Dann, the Puff Potato man, that Derek Webber was one of the good guys.

Chapter
TWENTY-FOUR

"Do you realize the time, Billy?" Cassandra Shaw, the manager of my Manhattan restaurant, said between yawns.

"I'm sorry. Your message said to call you as soon as I got in."

"I left that message at . . . Oh, well, fuck it, I'm awake now. A.W. is awake. Perhaps I should go downstairs and ring all of my neighbors' door buzzers and we can all be awake."

I looked at my watch. "It's only two-twenty-five there."

"I had a very long day, Billy, handling my job and yours at the Bistro."

"I wouldn't have called, except that you sounded pretty desperate."

"You really have to turn your phone on," she said. We'd had this conversation before. The problem, as she well knew, was that I have to deactivate the phone whenever I go on the air, and, no matter how hard I try, I can never remember to reactivate it when the show is over. I'd been greeted by the voice mail she left at the hotel, to wit: "Billy, where the hell are you? This fucking restaurant is about to self-destruct."

"What's happening to my restaurant, Cassandra?"

"Oh, Billy," she said and moaned. This was not like her. She was as tough as she was competent. "It's a mess. We had another blackout about an hour before the first serving."

"Great. We should put the electrician on staff," I said.

"He found one problem. But evidently not *the* problem. Anyway, the customers seemed amused by the prospect of dining by candlelight. The electrician restored the power, but by then we were running an hour or so late. I told the waiters to offer drinks or appetizers on the house."

"Good."

"So what with keeping everybody happy and answering dumb questions from the staff and cracking the whip on the electrician—who was charging us double for emergency service even though he'd obviously screwed up on Friday—and trying to calm down Maurice, who, it turns out, really doesn't like the dark, I was ready to blow my own fuse." Maurice Terrebone is our usually unflappable kitchen supervisor.

"So you took care of everything?" I asked.

She hesitated before replying, which was yet another worrisome thing. Cassandra is just about the most outspoken person I know. Finally, she said, "I don't think the power outages were accidental."

"Say what?"

"I think somebody's trying to put us out of business."

Considering that just hours before someone had tried to put *me* out of business, I was inclined to accept her theory. Still, I felt it deserved a devil's advocacy. "Three blackouts do not automatically add up to a case of sabotage," I said.

"It's not just the blackouts, Billy. Yesterday we had a Ladies in Real Estate luncheon in the big private room. According to the servers, the guest speaker had just been introduced when a couple of gray rats crashed the party. The ladies were not pleased."

"Rats? This is damned serious," I said.

"Oh, really, Billy? Let me tell you what serious is: It's spending an early part of the dinner hour trying to keep our customers oblivious to the fact that in the kitchen, inspectors from the Department of Health and Hygiene are being threatened by a chef wielding a butcher's knife."

I groaned. "The real estate ladies called the health department?"

"One of their husbands worked at the health department. Judging by the speed with which the investigators descended on us, he worked very high up in the health department. They went over the building from cellar to attic, which is why they were still at work when the dinner crowd arrived."

"But they didn't close us down?"

"No. As you may recall, we'd had an inspection a little over a month ago," she said. "No sign of vermin then. And they could find no sign of them now, other than the two corpses flattened by Silvio the busboy. We still have our A rating."

"They uncovered no point of entry?"

"Not even any feces, other than some droppings in the private room. I think the rats were planted, and I think someone has been doing something to our electrical system."

"Okay. What do you suggest?"

"We need professional help," she said.

"Do we know anybody that does that kind of guard work?" I asked, mindful of the fact that her fiancé, A. W. Johansen, was the East Coast rep for an international security company.

"What about A.W.?" she asked, indignantly.

"Good idea. Hire him. But make it a barter deal if you can."

"What do you mean?" she asked.

"I mean barter. He keeps the restaurant secure, and in return he gets an open food-and-drink tab. Of course, there's the conjugal use of my manager."

"Asshole," she said, and hung up on me.

True. But a funny asshole. No?

* * *

Having amused myself, I checked my watch. A quarter to two. I called the desk and asked for a six-forty-five wake-up. Because of my new schedule, I wouldn't be needed until seven-thirty. My plan was to read *Da Mare* for a while and then grab at least a four-hour snooze.

Using both hands, I picked up a copy of the massive book and toted it into the bedroom, where, properly pajamaed, comfortably ensconced in crisp, clean sheets and a thin coverlet, I began the usually satisfying process known as reading yourself to sleep.

The chirping hotel phone woke me from a nightmare in which I was lying in a graveyard with a cement headstone on my chest. In the real world, it was two-thirty a.m. and the headstone was my copy of *Da Mare*, which promptly slid onto the floor as I reached for the phone.

"Turn on the TV, Billy," a female voice ordered.

"Carrie?"

"Channel eight."

Still a little out of it, I shifted the phone to my left hand and used my right to grab the clicker. "What . . . ?" was all I managed to get out before the flat screen on the dresser shelf activated with a blinking invitation to watch the hotel's movies on demand.

"Quickly," Carrie said. "Damn. Too late."

I continued to struggle with the clicker, finally working my way to channel 8. Spencer Tracy was talking to Jimmy Stewart about a rubber plantation in *Malaya*. "I don't get it," I said. "Why am I looking at an old black-and-white movie?"

"I called you about the news break," she said. "You missed it."

"Missed what?"

"The guy who tried to shoot us."

"What about him?"

"He's dead. It was just on the news."

"Yeah?" I was wide awake now, flipping through channels.

"He was wanted by the police," she said. "His name was Aldanzo, something like that."

"I've got the story," I said. "Channel nineteen. A mug shot . . . definitely our baldie."

The news reader was in the middle of his report. " . . . of Amos Alanz was found in an empty lot in the 3100 block of West Lake Street. His neck was broken. According to CPD officer George Palaki, there is a strong possibility that the death was gang-related."

"I just found the channel," Carrie said. "Did he say 'gang-related'? My God, is a gang out to get us?"

"It was the dead guy who was out to get us," I said.

"I'm sorry I woke you," she said, leading me to think I'd sounded more annoyed than I was.

"It's fine," I said. "I don't take pleasure in anybody's death, but if somebody had to be murdered, I'm glad it was him."

"Why was he murdered, do you think?"

"Maybe because he shot a building instead of us." I yawned. "You always stay up this late?"

"No. But I can sleep in. And it's morning in Paris, and I was hoping Gerard might . . . It's not important."

"Call him."

"I don't want to disturb him. His email yesterday said he's meeting with his publisher today. And

Madeleine sent him notes on the rough draft. I'm sure he'll write me as soon as he can. Billy, it's really selfish of me to keep you talking. You have to get up so early in the morning."

"I'm glad you called," I said. "But I'd better grab a few z's before sunup."

We said our good nights. I replaced the receiver, clicked off the TV and the lights. If I had even a hint of curiosity about Amos Alanz's murder, I didn't let it keep me up. I was asleep before my head hit the pillow. And unlike the late, unlamented Mr. Alanz, I would still be getting up in a few hours.

Chapter
TWENTY-FIVE

The only thing worse than going on camera after four and a half hours of sleep and a pre-breakfast consisting of two cups of black coffee, two jelly doughnuts, and a Slim Jim is doing all that and then having to interview Elvita Dawes Hart. Ms. Hart was the spokesperson for the WBC reality series *Naked Housewives of Wilmette*. I guess you'd say she was the Barbara Walters of the show, though, at roughly eight-seventeen in the a.m., thankfully more or less clothed.

In her fifties, with hair the unnatural color of pitch; a face that bore the traces of Botox, a tanning parlor, and some nipping and tucking; and a body that had probably gone from voluptuous to overflowing without her noticing, Ms. Hart was not exactly the best advertisement for her show. Which may be why she'd brought along Lurleen Applegate, a petite platinum blonde wearing a thong and what looked to me like a Day-Glo tether reining in her surprisingly robust chest.

"Alas, Lurleen is about as naked as this network allows," Ms. Hart said, "but during our stage performances we really let the dogs out, so to speak."

"Good to know," I said. "Maybe you could tell our viewers some of the other differences between the TV and stage shows."

"Oh, it's like apples and grapefruit, Billy," Lurleen said, moving closer until her bare thigh brushed against me. "Here's the thing. We're not nudists. But we believe that a certain amount of nudity releases us from our inhibitions."

"That's right," Ms. Hart added. "When we and our guests discuss a topic—like our country's dependency on oil from the Middle East—we get a much freer-flowing conversation if we're down to thongs and pasties. Or, in the case of the guests, who are all male, by the way, jockeys or briefs."

"I bet we have a sling just your size," Lurleen said. She smelled of vetiver oil.

I stayed game, finished up the interview, bid the housewives a forever farewell, and departed for the tent I was using as a dressing room/office. Kiki was seated at a makeshift desk. She was not alone. J. B. Kazynski, lady private eye, was occupying a campaign chair, talking on her phone.

She was dressed in what I assumed to be her working outfit, a dark gray suede jacket over an antique Cubs T-shirt, tight denims, and leather boots. She stood and held up her free hand with index finger raised, an indication, I assumed, that she would be only a minute.

I didn't care if she took ten.

"What's next on my schedule?" I asked Kiki.

"You've a meeting at eleven with Lieutenant Oswald, who's supposed to have some new information on the monster's murder."

"That 'monster' stuff may be a little harsh, now that the man's deceased," I said.

"Po-*ta*-toes, po-*tot*-oes," she said. "Here's where you'll find the lieutenant."

She handed me a yellow note, which I stuck in my pocket.

"Stay as sweet as you are," I said, and headed out.

"Hold it!" J.B. yelled, fumbling her phone shut. "We've gotta talk."

"About what?"

"A shooting last night."

"A shooting?" Kiki asked. "Who got shot?"

J.B. was staring at me. She raised her eyebrows in an "It's your call" gesture.

"C'mon," I told her. "I'll buy you breakfast."

"Damn it, Billy, who got shot?" Kiki yelled after us.

The restaurant I'd picked was called Heaven on Seven. There are other Heaven on Sevens in and around the city, but this is the original, located on the seventh floor of the Garland Building on Wabash, offering breakfasts and lunches strongly influenced by chef/owner Jimmy Bannos's tour of duty in the kitchens of such New Orleans legends as Paul Prudhomme and Emeril Lagasse. Jimmy had been on our morning show several times, demonstrating his specialties of the season.

The last time I'd been in Chicago, the place had been closed for kitchen renovation, so it was one of the pleasures I'd promised myself this trip. I hoped J.B.'s presence wouldn't interfere.

Sitting under a George Rodrigue Blue Dog painting, she gave me a bored look and said, "I already had breakfast with my landlord, Mr. Kazanachas."

"Let me guess," I said. "Mr. Kazanachas is a retired elderly gentleman, wise beyond even his advanced years, who watches over you as if you were his daughter."

"You know him?"

"No, but it seems quite a few of you hard-boiled gal gumshoes have father-figure landlords."

"Yeah? Well, it makes sense. Our lives are lonely enough. It's good to have somebody we can rely on and talk to."

"And it helps the exposition," I said. "Well, if you've already had breakfast . . ." I signaled to the waitress.

When she arrived, I said, "The lady will have . . . what? A cup of coffee?"

"Well, yeah. But I also want an order of bananas Foster French toast. No, make that pecan French toast." She stared at me defiantly. "If that's all right."

"Fine," I said, and ordered poached eggs on crab cakes with creole sauce.

"I have a very active metabolism," J.B. said, when the waitress had gone. "Mr. Kazanachas's breakfasts are pretty basic."

"I think your metabolism will love the French toast here," I said. "Okay, you called this meeting."

"I'd like to know about what happened last night after that dog-and-pony TV show."

"Could you be a little more specific?"

"Last night you and the blond boopsie actress almost caught your lunch on the way to Derek Webber's mini-mansion. Am I right?"

I kept my face professionally blank.

"I wouldn't call Derek's mansion mini," I said.

"C'mon, Billy, give. What's going on? How does the joke go? Getting involved in one murder could be bad luck. Getting involved in two murders is just plain careless."

I thought she was referencing not a joke but Oscar Wilde's famous quote, "To lose one parent may be regarded as a misfortune; to lose both looks like carelessness." But I didn't think it was my job to enlighten her. Nor would she have appreciated it.

"What two murders?" I asked.

"Well, three, if we count Pat Patton," she said. "But that would be something of a stretch. I mean, Patton and Larry Kelsto seem to have been killed by the same guy, but you more or less discovered Kelsto's body and you weren't that connected to Patton. Or were you?"

"Patton is becoming the Kevin Bacon of corpses," I said. "Everybody's connected to him, including you.

So if we don't count him, who's the other murder victim?"

"Amos Alanz."

"Who he?"

She gave me a look of profound disappointment. "Is this the way it's gonna be? Alanz is the dirtbag hit man who shot up a section of Schiller last night in an apparent effort to put bullet holes in you and the Sands woman. And then, in the early morning hours, he turned up dead in an empty lot on the South Side with his head twisted around farther than the kid in *The Exorcist*."

"What makes you think Carrie and I were involved?"

"He tried to shoot you, but you got away. You went to Webber's, where the actress is staying."

"This is common knowledge?"

She gave me another disappointed look. "Of course not. The media reported the shooting on Schiller and the fact that Alanz's body was found. But as far as I can tell, the cops are clueless. They don't know about you and the actress. And they haven't tied the shooting on Schiller to Alanz."

"How'd you find out?" I asked.

"It's what I do, Billy."

"And you're interested because . . . ?"

She didn't immediately answer. Eventually, she said, "If Alanz was trying to kill the boopsie, then it's part of something I've been hired to investigate."

"Tell me about that," I said.

"Maybe later," she said.

And our food arrived.

* * *

The eggs and crab cakes were exceptional, almost to the point where I was able to enjoy them without wondering what the hell J.B. was up to. To look at her, she was just a young woman attacking French toast with a dedication beyond mere hunger.

"That . . . was . . . fantastic," she said, when she'd worked her way through the carbo and syrup mound down to empty plate.

"It's supposed to be," I said.

She gave me a long look. "I'm hoping you can do more than give good breakfast."

"Depends on what you're after."

We both waited while the waitress refilled our coffees and removed the dishes. Then: "How well do you know the Onion City guys?" she asked.

"About as well as I know you."

"Yeah?" she said, as if she didn't quite believe me. "Well, here's the situation. My nephew, Louie Zielinski, was one of the original computer geniuses Derek Webber hired for Instapicks. A couple years ago, he got married. His wife, Vicky, was an ASA, an assistant state's attorney, for Cook County. A real shrew, you ask me. Louie's this sweet guy, who melts into a puddle at the first hint of confrontation. A year ago, he let Vicky browbeat him into quitting and cashing in his Instapicks stock. That gave them the financial independence to do something she wanted to do: teach."

"You faulting her for that?" I asked.

"Let me finish. She got jobs for both of them at the University of Wisconsin—she's at the law school, he's teaching advanced classes in computer science—and everything has been copacetic . . . until several months ago, when the never satisfied little Vicky began getting on Louie's case again."

I sipped my coffee and wondered what Cousin Louie's situation had to do with Onion City or me.

"The thing is," J.B. said, "Vicky may be a shrew, but she's a shrew with an uncompromising honesty. And she's worried about their nest egg."

"She saw Pat Patton's blog about Onion City being financed by the Outfit," I said.

"Close enough. She saw a reference to it in the school newspaper. Then she looked up the blog. She began quizzing Louie about Instapicks. Now, I can tell you this about my cousin: Joey Doves Aiuppa and Wings Carlisi could've been cooking garlic pasta sauce in the next office at Instapicks and he'd never have smelled a thing."

"I'm still trying—"

"If the Instapicks cash is black money, Vicky wants my cousin to give back the fortune he'd made legitimately from selling his shares in the company."

"Wow. She shouldn't be teaching, she should be running the FBI."

"She's honest, but not to a fault," J.B. said. "She digs their present way of life. So she convinced Louie to part with some of that possibly tainted cash to put me to work checking out Patton's claim. And that's how I've been spending my time."

"What have you found out?"

"That Patton was a loudmouthed, vindictive old coot who was not adverse to stretching the truth when it came to people he disliked. And he disliked a lot of people."

"Derek Webber?"

"You tell me," she said. "You have any idea why Patton would have disliked Webber enough to make up a lie about him?"

"As I said, I barely know Webber. What about attacking the problem from the other end? You've been on this for a while. You find anything to substantiate Patton's claim?"

She shook her head. "Just the opposite. Webber's start-up money came from a relatively small inheritance, when his father died. He and his buddy Alan Luchek worked on Instapicks in his garage."

"No family connection to organized crime?"

"None I could find."

"What about Luchek's parents?"

"Salt of the earth."

"So if you haven't uncovered any basis for the claim of a reputed liar, and your client would no doubt be happy to hear the money is legit, why not close the case?"

"Because neither me nor my biographer roll that way."

"I don't understand," I said.

"You told me you read all my books," she said.

Did I tell her that? Bad me.

"If you had," she continued, "you'd know that I always start out trying to help my friends or relatives with a specific problem that eventually broadens into an investigation of something very big, something that has international repercussions. In *Deadly Mission*, for example, the mugging of my cousin, who happens to be a nun, led to my uncovering a bogus Catholic mission in Bogotá that was illegally importing cartel drugs and exporting American currency. In *Fatal Courtship,* the youngest sister of my best friend at Oriole Park Elementary disappeared from a tennis court two days before her wedding. At first I figured she'd had second thoughts about marriage and done a fade. But then I started getting death threats, and some guy wearing a Dr. Phil mask worked me over using a baseball bat—"

"A baseball bat? Really?"

"Well, in the book, it was a baseball bat. In reality, he was just a bald-headed asshole with a 'stache who slapped me in the face once or twice after I kneed him in the sweetbreads. But my point is this: I started out looking for a missing girl, and before it was all over, I had to take on the sex slave trade operating from this country to Bangkok."

"In the book, you did this," I said.

"Well, in real life, too. Kind of. I mean, the missing girl wasn't in Bangkok. She was working at a gentlemen's club in Joliet. But Stacy Lynne, who's like my biographer, said we had artistic license to change it to Bangkok, which is way hotter."

"Of course it is, but the average temperature of Bangkok compared to Chicago aside," I said, "where do you or Stacy Lynne see your Onion City investigation taking you?"

"To something funky going down on the Internet. Maybe involving Net neutrality. Or an evil genius like the late Osama getting a hacker to take over a social network to rile up people in some Middle Eastern country so he can install his man as their leader."

"That sounds like another winner," I said, waving my credit card at the waitress.

"You're not leaving?"

"Too many things to do, too little time . . . ," I said to her, mentally adding for my own benefit, *to waste on bullshit like this*.

"But I've a lot more to ask you."

Watching the waitress take the card to the cashier, I said, "You got all I have. Picked me clean."

"What about Alanz? Was he trying to kill you or the actress?"

"I really don't know," I said. "I was too busy trying to hide. And what does that have to do with your investigation?"

"Did Alanz say anything?"

"Kinda hard to hear anybody say anything over the gunfire!"

"Why didn't he kill you?"

The waitress had returned in time to hear J.B.'s question. She looked a little apprehensive as she handed me the credit slip to sign. I gave her a full 25 percent tip, and she scurried off.

"You didn't answer the question," J.B. said.

"I honestly don't know." I stood and headed for the elevator. She was at my heels.

"Maybe he wasn't really trying to kill either of you."

"Maybe." It was a possibility I'd been considering.

The elevator arrived just as we did.

"Any reason why somebody would send you a scare message that strong?" she asked as we descended.

I shook my head.

"Could it be Sands he was trying to scare?"

"I don't have a clue. And I think we've just about covered the subject."

"We've just started," she said.

We stepped from the Garland Building. There was the smell of ironworks on the air, harsh and near toxic. I saw a taxi cruising toward us on Wabash and waved him down.

"You have a car?" I asked J.B.

"Over by the park. Need a lift somewhere?"

"No," I said, and got into the cab, pulling the door shut behind me. "Just wanted to make sure you won't be following me. Have a nice day."

The driver wanted to know my destination. I suggested he head out and I'd tell him on the way.

As we departed, I looked back at J.B. She was pointing her phone in our direction. Taking a picture of the taxi. She'd be checking the driver's schedule to see where he'd dropped me.

I wondered what she really was investigating and why she was spending so much time and effort on poor, innocent little me.

Chapter
TWENTY-SIX

If J.B. had bothered to inquire, she'd have discovered that the cab deposited me at 3510 South Michigan Avenue. That's the address of Chicago police headquarters, where Lieutenant Maureen Oswald was expecting me in approximately twelve minutes. Kiki had said the lieutenant promised to impart new information. About Larry Kelsto's murder? Or Pat Patton's? Or both? Or neither? Or . . . the hell with it. I'd know in just a few minutes.

Or not.

The man who cut me off as I approached the building's glass doors was dressed like a Wisconsin farmhand who'd just arrived in the big city. He was wearing a red plaid shirt tucked into faded blue denims. He stood at a little over six feet in worn brown work boots. His blond hair hadn't been combed that morning, maybe never, and stuck up in corn-silk tufts. He had a half-grin on his square-chinned, dopey, beardless face. "You're him, right?" he asked.

"Everybody's somebody," I said, and attempted to walk around him.

He sidestepped, staying in my way. "I mean, you're the guy on the morning show? Blessing?"

"Yeah," I said. "I'd love to chat, but I've got to get to a meeting."

"No, you don't." That came from someone standing directly behind me.

He was a few inches shorter than his coworker, older by a decade, and, I suppose, women might have found him ruggedly handsome with his three-day growth of beard. He was wearing dark aviator sunglasses, a brown leather bombardier jacket, fashionably weathered, khaki slacks, and white tennis shoes. His right hand was in the pocket of his jacket along with something that gave him a lopsided look.

I had the feeling I'd seen him somewhere before, but I couldn't place the location.

"See that silver van parked at the curb, friend?" he said. "The three of us are going to stroll to it and go for a little ride."

"Really? In front of police headquarters you're doing this?" I asked.

He scanned the area casually, noting the civilians and cops entering and exiting the building. "I don't see anything here to stop you from taking a bullet," he said.

"Good point."

We headed for what I assumed was the silver van. It was silverish. And van-ish.

Country Boy opened the side door, exposing middle and rear seats.

"In," the handsome bombardier ordered.

The middle row consisted of two separate buckets. Bombardier prodded me toward the far seat, and he took the one beside me, removing his hand from his pocket and pointing his gun at my groin. I wondered if he targeted that area on all of his kidnaps or if he suspected it might be my particular Achilles heel.

Country Boy shut the door and circled the van, sliding behind the wheel in front.

We sat like that for a minute or two while Country Boy puttered around. Finally, Bombardier said, "Anytime you're ready, Ace."

"I keep pressin' the button, but it won't start, C-man."

"Turn the key."

"Cars don't have keys no more, C-man. They got buttons you press."

"Then press it."

"It ain't doing nuthin'."

"You fucking with me?"

"No. Maybe the battery wore out. It jus' won't start." Country Boy slid down on his seat and began to inspect the underside of the dashboard. "Gaw damn," he said. "The wires are all just hangin' down like they been yanked out."

Suddenly, Bombardier jerked upright beside me. He slowly lifted the gun until it was a few inches from his right ear, aimed at the van's ceiling. Long black fingers appeared from somewhere behind us and plucked the weapon from his unresisting hand. The barrel of another gun was pressing against Bombardier's neck.

I turned my head very slowly and saw a very black face surrounded by dreadlocks. It rewarded me with a big, gold-toothed grin. Without losing it, he drew back the hand holding C-man's gun and slammed it hard against the back of the hard case's skull.

When C-man grunted and tumbled forward off

the seat, Ace suddenly became aware that all was not right in the rear of the van. He turned, and his eyes bulged. Almost as much as the zoot-suited wolves in Tex Avery cartoons when they see a pretty girl. All that was missing was the "boi-yoi-yong" sound effect.

Natty Dread was already on the move. In one fluid motion, he gracefully shoved the seat carrying the unconscious C-man forward far enough for him to use his gun to flatten some of Country Boy's straw hair. Country Boy bounced against the left door and slid under the steering wheel.

"Mek haste, bredda," the very black man said to me in a pleasant Jamaican singsong, "a fore jancro ketch us heah."

He tossed C-man's gun onto the front seat and tucked his into the pocket of his dark gray warm-up jacket. "Why you still sitting? Leggo."

I heard the tap of a horn to our left. A big white Cadillac Escalade had pulled up beside us.

"Naa mek mi vex, mon," Dreadlocks said. "Yu doan wanna romp wit me." He was no longer smiling. He reached into his pocket, presumably for the gun. "Us step out yah," he ordered.

I definitely did not want to romp with him. Which is why I stepped out.

Kidnapped twice. Right in front of Chicago police headquarters.

Had to be some kind of record. Hello, Chicago, Hello.

Chapter
TWENTY-SEVEN

"Me name be Trejean," my Jamaican captor informed me when we were ensconced on the rich leather mid-vehicle seat in the white Escalade. He gestured to our driver. "Dat lily-brown Portugee behin' de wheel be Hiho."

The white biker type seated beside Hiho introduced himself through a yellow beard. "I'm Dal, the brains of this crew."

"Dal be a jesta, a samfi man," Trejean said. "We put up wit his foolery 'cause he be fambly."

The three of them were young, probably still in their twenties. As seemingly different as their modes of dress. Under his gray jacket, Trejean wore a black tee and narrow black trousers. From what I could see of Hiho, he preferred a hipster narrow-brim purple hat, a pale rose silk shirt, and suspenders matching the color of the hat. Dal opted for a leather wifebeater that left his heavily larded, muscular arms on display in all their naked glory. There was a tattoo of a pretty bespectacled woman near his left shoulder that looked suspiciously like Sarah Palin.

"Where we headed?" I asked.

"You'll find out soon enough," Dal the jester said. I turned for a final woeful look at the rapidly diminishing police headquarters building where Lieutenant Oswald was no doubt assuming I'd blown her off. I saw that the silverish van of my primary kidnappers, having loitered much too long in the passenger zone, finally was attracting the scrutiny of two uniformed officers.

Great work, guys. Keep that traffic flowing.

"All fruits ripe," Trejean said. At least that's what it sounded like. He had positioned himself with his back to the left side of the big SUV, facing me. "Yu nuh easy," he said.

"I don't understand," I said.

"Jamaican jibber-jabber," Dal explained. "Tre thinks you look worried. Shit, man, you've got nothing to worry about. We're protecting your ass."

"Is that what just happened?"

"What else? Those boys were bad hombres. They were going to . . ." Dal pointed a thumb-and-finger gun at me and made the appropriate bang-bang noise.

"And you boys?"

"You've just been rescued by the A-Team," Dal said.

Hiho giggled. "Love it when plan come together," he said, the first peep out of him. A TV fan. Maybe I was wrong, but I didn't think Hannibal Smith ever giggled when he recited that line.

"Not that I'm ungrateful," I said, "but why rescue me?"

"Info above our pay grade," Dal said. "We're told to keep you alive, that's what we do."

Trejean chuckled. "Dal bad bwoy. Las' night, snap that hot-steppa's neck."

"Hot-steppa?"

"In Jamaican lingo, a hot steppa is a criminal hot-stepping from the cops," Dal explained. "He's talking about the wrong-o who tried to light up you and the blond lady last night on the Near North. We took care of him."

"Bad bwoy, Dal," Trejean said, as if it amused him.

"Tre's ribbin' me because we weren't supposed to get fatal on him until we found out who hired him. But the guy just wouldn't cooperate—"

"He tess Dal."

"Yeah. He tested me, all right. I may not look it, but I'm pretty even-tempered. That prick head-butted me. Made me see red, and I took that hard head and twisted it. A little too much."

"A fuckery, dat," Trejean said dismissively. "Car odah so bad, made us gwine adoor."

"Ruined my ride," Hiho said.

"My bad," Dal said. "See, when his neck popped, the guy voided himself, front and back. Left the car smelling like a French pissoir."

"Worse," Hiho said.

"We had to dump that set of wheels."

"That would've been a black SUV?" I asked.

"Yess. Black Beauty," the newly chatty Hiho said. "Noble goddamn machine. A real machine. Not like this . . . this pale white marshmallow."

"Hiho's not a big fan of luxury," Dal said. "He believes in what my mom used to call a spartan lifestyle."

"The purple hat had me fooled," I said.

"You don't like my hat? Fuck you, Mister *GQ*."

"Actually, Hiho," Dal said, "it's not a great color for a man of your complexion."

"Fuck you, too, smartypants."

Great, I was now in an episode of *Project Runway*. As amusing as my kidnappers were, I decided the wise thing would be for me to get my Sherlock Holmes on and start observing.

We'd been traveling west on Madison for a while, but Hiho had made a few turns and now we were passing a tall red-brick building with giant O's filling its display windows. Oprah Country. The next block was completely given over to the talk show queen's Harpo Studios.

"You being in TV," Dal said, "I guess you know her, huh?"

"We met once or twice," I said.

"What's she like?"

"The meetings were brief. She seemed pretty much like on the show."

"They say studio haunted by woman they call the Gray Lady," Hiho said. "Place built on a morgue fulla dead bodies."

"Shut up, dat," Trejean said, obviously no fan of ghost stories.

"Wasn't a morgue, exactly," Dal said. "Used to be an armory. Back in the early 1900s a big ship capsized on the lake and they stored some of the victims there. I think that's how it went."

"Dal got de ed-u-cay-shun," Trejean said.

Hiho took a few more turns and we were in a Starbucks/hair salon/boutique fashions commercial area.

He maneuvered the white Escalade down a narrow drive between a three-story yellow plaster building with a green awning and a white wooden two-story that, according to a shiny brass plate, housed THE LEGAL COUNCIL. I made a mental bet with myself that our destination would not be a building in which anything even remotely "legal" would transpire. And I was right.

Hiho parked near the loading area of the yellow building. He and Trejean remained with the Escalade while Dal walked me toward closed double doors in comradely fashion, his big, moist arm heavy on my shoulders.

A sign beside the doors read: UBORA EMPLOYEES ONLY. PATRONS PLEASE USE THE MAIN ENTRY.

"It's okay," Dal said, opening the door. "You're with me."

"What's Ubora?" I asked.

Dal smiled. "The sign out front says it's an international gallery of fine art. Me, I don't even care much for comic books."

We entered a large shipping area. Sawdust and plastic Bubble Wrap formed little and big mounds on the floor beside various basic tools, thin barewood crates, and heavy cardboard boxes. With a soft vocal—Norah Jones, I think—playing through the speakers, three sullen males and two sullen females, all of them brown-skinned, young, and wearing green T-shirts under red bib overalls, were taking their own sweet time carefully crating a stack of oil paintings. They gave us the brief glances that our importance to their lives required, then returned to their tasks.

The paintings they wrapped so listlessly were news magazine–size and outlined by identical gold-leaf rococo frames. Each was a portrait of a different rabbi.

"What's that all about?" I asked.

"The rabbis?" he said with a shrug. "It's the art world. Go figure."

After three flights up in the service elevator we arrived at a tastefully appointed reception area with indirect lighting that, combined with the powder-blue walls, gave the room the color of the sky in Dehiwala Town, Sri Lanka, at sundown. As best I could remember.

The couches and chairs were of soft white leather. Sand dunes?

A baby spot cut through the Sri Lanka–ish glow like a giant, well-aimed moonbeam calling attention to a very blond woman seated at the reception desk. She was something to see, perched ramrod stiff on her chair, looking pale and lovely in a soft yellow dress with a scoop neck. She reminded me of Tippi Hedren in Alfred Hitchcock's *The Birds,* minus the neurosis. Her only visible flaw was the ugly sliver of black plastic stuck in her right ear.

"Hi, Sugar Tits," Dal said. "Buzz the boss that I'm here to deliver the male."

"Is that a new gold tooth, Dal?" she asked. "Oh, no, I see. It's just leftover lunch." She pressed a button on the console resting on the desk. After a few beats, her lips moved, and I guessed she was saying something into her earphone, but I couldn't hear a peep.

She pressed another button, and the door to the left behind her swung open. Dal winked at me and used his left hand in a sweeping gesture to suggest I enter in front of him.

Time to head down the rabbit hole. Whoever was waiting on the other side, I doubted it'd be Elmer Fudd.

Chapter
TWENTY-EIGHT

After the reception area (and receptionist), the room we entered was something of a letdown. It was windowless, its soft light coming from two antique lamps. One with a filigree shade was perched on a carved, round wooden table with a marble top in the corner of the room to my right; the other, resting on a square table in the opposite corner, boasted a beaded rose shade. The walls were a restful ivory, except for four paintings that appeared to be, on first glance, primitive depictions of rural black Americana.

Two overlapping Oriental rugs partially covered a dark wood floor. There were several carved wood parlor armchairs in varying solid hues and, against one wall, a large hand-painted leather trunk decorated with metal studs. As I mentioned, I'm no expert on antiques, but my guess was that the furniture was Victorian.

A delicate glass-topped coffee table stood in for a formal desk. On it rested a cordless phone, a fluted glass half filled with what looked like champagne, and the inevitable iPad. Behind the table was the one touch of vibrant color in the room, an orange velvet love seat. Empty at the moment.

As the rest of the room seemed to be.

I turned to Dal, who was standing to my right. "What now?" I asked.

"Now we meet, sir." The voice came from my left.

He was standing near the wall beside the open door, a dark black man approximately five and a half feet tall, very thin and very fit. He was wearing an immaculate three-piece white suit, a crisp powder-blue shirt, and a black tie with a large knot. His scalp was covered by a meringue of neat white hair. He sported a matching mustache. If he'd been wearing glasses with a thicker frame and a goatee, he'd have resembled a skinny black Colonel Sanders.

The white hair was the only sign of advanced years. His face was unlined, and half-lidded eyes behind rimless glasses gave him the look of a relaxed, self-satisfied man.

"My name is Mantata, Chef Blessing," he said, extending a manicured hand, which I shook. He smelled of mimosa—the flower, not the cocktail. "It's a pleasure to finally meet you."

Ordinarily I'd have replied in kind, but I wasn't sure that politesse was required or expected when one was kidnapped.

My silence didn't seem to faze him. He gestured toward one of the chairs facing the coffee table and said, "Make yourself comfortable, please."

I sat and watched as he unbuttoned his jacket and adjusted the crease in his trousers before lowering himself onto the love seat. He was quite a gent.

"Would it be too informal if I called you Billy?"

"Not at all. And I'll call you . . . Mantata?"

"It's the only name I use," he said. "As you may know, in Swahili it means 'troublemaker.' Alas, I am now several decades past the time when that sobriquet applied."

"I don't think I'll buy that."

He smiled and turned to Dal, who'd remained standing. "Would you ask Roxanne to get off her delightful derriere and fetch something for our guest to drink? A flute of Roederer, perhaps?"

"No, thanks," I said.

"Some fizz water, then?" He indicated his glass. "I use it as a digestive. Or we have tea."

"Tea would be fine."

"Bravo. Tell Roxanne it's teatime, Dal. Oh, but before you do that . . . a brief report, please, on the events at police headquarters."

Dal dutifully complied.

"You made note of their license plates?"

"Illinois, but they'd smeared mud over the numbers."

Mantata sighed. "What's your afternoon like, Billy?"

Since I'd more or less given up on freedom temporarily, the question caught me by surprise. Other than the meeting I'd missed with Lieutenant Oswald, I was drawing a blank. I got out my phone and tapped it to life. Four messages waiting. The numbers I recognized belonged to the Bistro, ergo Cassandra; Kiki; and Arnie Epps. That left "Private Caller." More mystery. I ignored it and the three others and scrolled across various screens until I arrived at my daily schedule. There was nothing but the *Hotline* show much later that night.

"I've a meeting at three," I lied. I'm not sure why.

"Where?"

"WWBC."

"Ah, then, Dal, perhaps you'd better visit Fredrika," Mantata said.

"Oh, Christ," Dal said. "Not again."

"As fond as I am of your biker-trash persona, I think we'll dispense with it for a bit. Go to Freddie and be back here at two-thirty. That will give Billy plenty of time to make his meeting."

Dal looked crestfallen. "Fredrika, really?"

Mantata seemed to enjoy the big man's despair. "And don't forget our tea."

He waited until his employee dragged himself from the room.

"Who's Fredrika?" I asked.

"You'll see," he said. "What do you think of Dal?"

"Think of him?"

"Did he mention he'd attended Duke University?"

"Not even a hint," I said.

"He's a Dalrymple. Of the South Carolina Dalrymples. The family is richer than Croesus. And very social."

"They all dress like badass bikers?"

He chuckled. "Hardly. Only our Dal fell from grace."

"What happened?"

"The old story. Boy meets girl. Girl is a rebellious drug-addicted crazy who draws him into her web. Boy loses mind, loses girl, and embraces a debauched and ruinous lifestyle, thinking someday he'll get her back."

"Self-criticism?" I said.

He frowned. "Explain."

"Didn't you just say working for you was part of a debauched and ruinous lifestyle?"

"I hope you're being facetious. Dal was living on the edge, trafficking in meth and using as much as he sold. Riding with rowdies. That's the ruinous lifestyle. Working for me has put him on the road to salvation. He's been clean for nearly two years."

"He killed a man last night," I said.

"Baby steps," Mantata said. "And, speaking of the man he killed . . ."

He interrupted himself when his blond receptionist entered. She carried a silver tray containing a teapot, delicate China cups, silver spoons, a tiny cream pitcher, a bowl of sugar, and a plate with little cookies. As she bent to place the tray on the coffee table beside the iPad, Mantata's eyes never left her cleavage.

"Would you pour for us, Roxanne, dear?"

"Of course."

Bending again, she filled our cups, straightened, smiled sweetly, did a sharp about-face, and left, closing the door behind her.

"She is a jewel," Mantata said.

"A jewel? She's the whole tiara."

That seemed to please him. He dropped two sugar cubes into his tea, stirred, sipped, then added another cube. "As I was saying, the man who incurred Dal's wrath last night was apparently trying to assassinate you and a lovely young actress."

"What am I doing here, Mantata?"

"Staying alive. No small achievement, since someone obviously wants you dead. You mistakenly think the someone is a man named Gio Polvere."

"How would you know that?"

"My old friend Henry Julian asked me to keep an eye on you. He told me you think Polvere was some sort of Mob mastermind who is now living here in Chicago, prospering under an assumed name. That's quite a theory."

"It's Pat Patton's theory, not mine," I said. "He passed it on the day before somebody killed him, which, to my mind, lends it a certain authenticity."

He studied me for a beat, then nodded. He placed his teacup on the table and leaned back against his sofa. "What exactly did Patton tell you about Polvere?" he asked.

"Not much. That he was a crime figure in the eighties who was responsible for the murder of my foster father—"

"Paul Lamont," Mantata said. "I liked Paul. He was a charming rogue who lived by a moral code more stringent than mine. He died by it, too."

"You know something about his death?"

"Nothing specific. Most con men are perfectly happy to pluck low-lying fruit. Paul eschewed the naïve in favor of the fat and the greedy. That made his game a much more perilous one. The year he died, he came here seeking a specific kind of mark—a mean-spirited, stupid, and, of course, obnoxiously rich member of the Outfit who would be in no position to go running to the cops or to let his associates know he'd been played. If *Webster's* carried a picture of that particular definition, it would resemble Louis 'Baby Shoes' Venici."

"Not Gio Polvere?"

"Well, there's the rub. In those days, Venici was the poster boy of organized crime as far as the media were concerned. He loved publicity. If I'd even heard the name Polvere back then, it didn't register."

"Patton said Polvere had Venici killed. Is that possible?"

"Doubtful. At the time, Venici was under the wing of Joe Nagall. If Baby Shoes wasn't acting on his own, it would have been Nagall calling the tune. Frankly, I wasn't much interested in what the I-ties were doing as long as they left me alone. My business on the South Side was untouchable, if I may use that word, as per a deal I brokered back in the sixties with Momo Giancano. He went to bat for me with Mob consig-lieri Ricca and Accardo. Our arrangement remained in effect until my retirement."

"You're retired?"

"Don't I look retired?" He leaned back against the love seat and made like a crocodile, only showing fewer teeth. "He was a good friend, Momo. But there was talk of him turning state's evidence, and one of his associates shot him several times in the back and head while he was at the stove in his home, preparing peppers and onions."

"If we could stick to Polvere," I said.

"Of course. Sorry for the digression. Polvere. This is what I have, Billy." He leaned forward and picked up the iPad. He began running his digits over its surface, expanding and retracting images, like a child working with finger paint. Eventually he found what he wanted and turned the gizmo toward me.

It was a page from the *Chicago Tribune,* Wednesday, June 15, 1987. The obituaries. Second from the top of the third column was: "CEO Dies in Fire. Giovanni Pietro Polvere." Under that was a brief synopsis of a short life prepared by the *Tribune* staff and wire reports. Date and place of birth unknown. In 1981, he was elected to the board of North Side Amusement Co. In 1984, he became a board member of Near North Disposal Services. Both companies were subsidiaries of Windy City Industrials, where he was listed as CFO in the company's 1987 prospectus.

According to the notice, faulty wiring in Polvere's home caused the fire that resulted in his death on the night of June 10, 1987. He lived alone. He was not married. There were no known surviving family members. Services were held at Saint Joan of Arc Church in Evanston. It was suggested that donations to the parish be made in lieu of flowers.

There was no accompanying picture of Polvere.

"I've heard of staying on the down low, but this is ridiculous," I said. "No date or place of birth. No record of school or military service or work history other than a couple of career milestones in the eighties. And then he died."

"How did the Bard put it? 'Nothing in his life became him like the leaving it.' "

"I suppose Windy City Industrials is a Mob operation?"

"It was. Until 1995, when it shuttered after the Justice Department indicted most of its executives under the RICO Act."

"Don't you find it significant that Polvere died only months after Paul was murdered along with his two killers?"

"Perhaps. But that's irrelevant to the current situation, since, being dead, he's probably not the man trying to kill you."

I was suddenly very hungry. I popped one of the little crumbly, buttery, sugary tea cookies into my mouth. I followed that with another and washed it down with tea that was only lukewarm. "Every mystery novel I've ever read," I said, "if somebody dies in a fire, they always turn up in the last chapter alive with a gun in their hand."

"In real life, it's very difficult to stage a fire that the investigators won't label arson."

"Unless Polvere had help from someone in a position to make sure his death wouldn't be questioned," I said.

Mantata stared at me for a beat. "Someone like a high-ranking cop, you mean?"

"Exactly," I said. "Someone like Pat Patton."

Chapter TWENTY-NINE

Mantata and I had lunch at a neighborhood Cuban restaurant—chicken and white rice for him, shrimp and yellow rice for me. While he and I wolfed down the delicious food, Hiho and Trejean kept watch seated near the front door. I didn't think it was only me they were mother-hen-ing. Mantata must've created an impressive list of enemies over the years.

Before leaving his office, he'd promised to put his researchers to work on the fire that took Polvere's life and his subsequent funeral. "I'd suggest a little midnight grave digging," he'd said, "if we had any DNA to match against whatever might be left in the coffin."

During lunch we dropped the talk of internment for something a bit more appetizing—the food and how much we were enjoying it. Then it was back to Ubora, where Mantata informed me that he had business to conduct. He suggested I enjoy the art until Dal returned. Dal was to be my personal bodyguard for the duration of my Chicago visit.

"Can't Hiho just drive me back to my hotel?" I asked. "Dal can pick me up there."

"I'd prefer you wait."

So I did.

*　*　*

The beautiful Roxanne directed me to a small empty office, where I got out my phone and began a series of callbacks.

Cassandra informed me that thus far in the day, my restaurant had remained problem-free from rodents and Con Edison. Her fiancé, A. W. Johansen, had assigned an Intertek Security operative to work undercover as a Bistro waitress. She'd begin that night. All seemed right in that corner of my world.

Kiki's news was not as comforting. Trina had been fuming about my missed meeting with Lieutenant Oswald. No big surprise. Lily Conover had left word that she was back in Manhattan. She was supervising the editing of the show with Charlie Dann the Puff Potato Man and was a little disappointed in the sound quality but thought it would suffice. She thought we should devote a show to Chicago pizza, since everyone seemed to concur that it was the best in the free world. I asked Kiki to pass along my approval.

"Why did you miss the meeting, by the way?" Kiki asked.

"Personal business."

"In the middle of the day? Oh, God, Billy, say you're not doing the deed with that private-eye person."

"I'll keep you posted," I said, and clicked off.

Next up, Arnie Epps, who also wanted to know why I'd missed the meeting.

"Overslept," I told him.

"At eleven o'clock?"

"It's the wacky schedule Trina has me on. Our show in the morning and *Hotline* at night. I've got to catch a few winks when I can."

"Yeah. About *Hotline*. They won't be needing you tonight."

It was good news but also a bit insulting. "Really? Who bumped me? Some Hollywood B-lister go off his or her nut on the road to rehab?"

"No." He hesitated, then said, "There's been a development in the Patton murder investigation, and when you didn't show up, Lieutenant Oswald called Trina to say she was going to release it to the media. Trina talked her into breaking it on Gemma's show. It won't rate more than a brief mention on *Hotline*."

"What's the development?"

"An arrest warrant has been issued for Patton's chauffeur, Nat Parkins."

"New evidence?"

"Nobody mentioned any. Parkins was working for Patton and bunking with the dead comic. And he ran."

"That's old news," I said. "Did the lieutenant have anything more to say about it with Gemma?"

"Not really. They spent most of the interview talking about policewomen's uniforms."

"There's got to be more to the story. Let me see what I can find out, and if it's substantial, rebook me on *Hotline*."

"Uh, that's not gonna happen," Arnie said. "Tonight's show is a special about the mishegoss in the Middle East."

"In other words, all the talk about my missed

meeting being the reason I was bumped was just guilt-tripping bullshit."

"Well, you know Trina. And you did miss the meeting."

I pressed the red button on my phone, ending the conversation.

The last number on my call log was unfamiliar, and the caller had not left a message. I dialed the number. Ring, ring, ring. No answer. And no transfer to voice mail. Maybe it was my new dream girl, Adoree Oden, and she'd turned off her phone when shooting on the film began.

I withdrew from this fantasy with the happy thought that, no longer tethered to *Hotline,* I could get to Derek Webber's party at a more reasonable hour.

In higher spirits, I headed back to Roxanne and inquired if Dal had returned.

Not yet. She suggested I tour the gallery.

I'd made it through the modern-art room and the Impressionists and was sharing the graphic-art section with a bunch of high-schoolers when a hint of Aramis cologne told me that a new comic connoisseur had entered the room. He was a big man in a beautifully tailored tan suede jacket, white silk shirt open at the neck, and cocoa slacks. His short streaked brown hair was combed straight back. His beard was neatly shaped.

Dal grinned and said, "What do you think?"

"You look like a million bucks."

"I look like my father," he said.

He turned his head in the direction of the teens, whose chatter and laughter I'd tuned out. In just three strides, he joined them, twisting the wrist of one of the boys and shaking an object from his hand. It bounced quietly on the carpet. A box cutter.

The boy's friends nearly stampeded me on their rush from the room, the gallery, the building. The trapped kid was in a panic, trying to twist free from Dal's grip.

"What kind of an asshole risks jail for this crap?" Dal asked the kid.

He released the boy and watched, bemused, as the underage art thief followed his friends. He bent down and picked up the cutter. Then he looked at the art that the kid was getting ready to liberate. It was an oil painting of television's Buffy the Vampire Slayer, signed by the actress.

"Boy's going to have a bare wall near his bed," I said.

Dal shook his head in wonder. "The price tag on this is nearly two thou. He's risking a serious grand-larceny rap for a TV pinup? Kids today have no sense."

We walked to the front of the gallery, where a young black man in black chino pants and a dark green sweater with black piping stood near the door. Dal handed him the box cutter.

"From those punks just run outta here?" the black man asked.

"Right," Dal said. "Oakley, you might want to walk through the place every now and then, see what folks are up to."

"Don't tell me my business. I stay by the front door, they can't leave with nuthin'."

Dal shrugged. "Your call."

He joined me, mumbling under his breath, "Asshole. Painting would have gone right past him, under the kid's shirt, tucked in his pants. But that's his problemo, not mine."

He adjusted his coat, straightened the collar of his shirt, and said, "Presentable enough for you? Mantata says I'll be sticking with you for a while."

"You look fine. Fredrika clearly must be the makeover queen of Chicago."

"Naw. She's just a good barber. Hairstylist, actually. I had these threads hanging in my closet. It's what I wear when I'm not working. You know, when I go out nights, hitting the traps. The boss didn't think the biker vibe would go down well with your showbiz crowd."

"Now we'll never know," I said.

He consulted the gold-banded watch on his wrist. "We'd better head out to your meeting at WWBC."

I'd forgotten the fib I'd told Mantata. "It's been canceled," I said.

"You mean I got a haircut and dressed up for nothing?"

"We'll be going to a dinner party later. Right now, we may as well head to my hotel."

"Yeah, about the hotel, what's your setup there? Suite?"

I nodded.

"So I can tuck you in at night and come back for you in the morning, the very early morning. Or I can bunk on the couch in your suite. I've got a bag in the car."

"We'll see how it goes," I said.

As we moved toward the gallery's rear exit, I asked, "Shouldn't we tell Mantata we're leaving?"

"He's tied up with some shark," Dal said. "Roxanne will tell him."

"Shark?"

"Lawyer. I hate the bastards. This one was particularly slimy. Name of Yountz."

"He Mantata's attorney?" I asked.

"I don't think so. I've never seen him before. You know him?"

I shook my head. I didn't know him, but I knew of him. And I wondered what the late Pat Patton's lawyer and Mantata had to talk about. Call it a hunch, but I doubted it was about art.

Chapter THIRTY

The car Dal used was a sporty little maroon two-seater he identified for me as a Nissan Z. As we approached the hotel in it, instead of turning into the drive leading to the front doors, he gunned the car and drove past.

"Circling for a better landing?" I asked.

"You didn't see the blue-and-whites?"

"The cop cars? Yeah."

"I prefer not to go running into buildings where the cops are doing their thing," he said.

"You wanted for anything?" I asked, almost biting my tongue when I remembered he'd just killed a guy the night before.

"Nothing specific I know of," he said. "But with all the new electronic and digital goodies they've got, you never know what little surprises they're ready to spring."

"Well, it's a cinch they're not looking for you in my hotel," I said.

"Maybe they're looking for you," he said.

I told him I thought that was unlikely and convinced him to take us back.

But as we were walking across the lobby, a familiar voice called my name.

The rumpled detective Hank Bollinger was walking our way. He started to say something to me, stopped, and gave Dal the stink eye. "Do I know you?"

Dal was probably cursing me under his breath, but he looked blissfully innocent. "I don't believe we've met," he replied.

"Oh, this is Detective Hank Bollinger, CPD," I said.

"I'm Henry Hart Dalrymple," Dal said, extending his hand, which Bollinger shook awkwardly. "A pleasure, detective."

Puzzled but disarmed, Bollinger turned to me. "I understand most of your group is staying here?"

"The *Wake Up, America!* crew? Right. What's going on?"

Bollinger hesitated before answering, then said, "Pat Patton's chauffeur was spotted in the hotel."

"Isn't there a warrant for his arrest?"

"Yeah."

"You really think he killed Patton and Larry Kelsto?"

"It's not what I think, Mr. Blessing. It's what the evidence tells us."

"What evidence?"

Bollinger ignored the questions. "I don't suppose you have any idea why Parkins might have come here?"

I shook my head.

The detective stared at me for a beat, then turned to Dal. He frowned, nodded, and made an awkward retreat.

"That was fun," Dal said, when they'd left. His eyes flicked from the departing detective toward the two uniformed cops near the front desk. "It'd be nice if we could get out of everybody's line of sight. Like in your room."

"Sure," I said, walking him toward the elevators. "But there's no reason to be nervous."

"Speak for yourself. You're probably not carrying an illegal concealed weapon."

Now I was nervous, too.

The door to my suite seemed to be stuck.

I put all my weight behind it and pushed through into the suite. That's when I discovered the problem with the door. Somebody had tried to slide a manila envelope under it.

The package rested on the carpet. I bent to pick it up, but Dal stopped me. I'm not sure when he drew his gun, but it was in his hand. Silently, he moved past me into the suite. He gestured that I was to return to the hall. I did that, and he closed the door quietly in my face.

The next few minutes seemed like an hour. Finally, he opened the door and motioned for me to come in, handing me the envelope. "I don't think anybody entered the suite," he said, "unless it wasn't you eating those chocolate doughnuts in bed."

"My pre-breakfast," I said, indignantly.

"Then not even housekeeping has been here. Let's see what you've got."

I looked down at the envelope in my hand. It was heavily taped.

Dal raised his right pant leg, whipped a knife from its scabbard. "Allow me," he said.

He took the envelope, inserted the tip of the knife smoothly through the tape holding down the flap, and made a very neat incision. "Just like cutting through a layer of flesh," he said.

Was he kidding?

The envelope contained only one item, a copy of a film script. *The Thief Who Stole Trump Tower.*

"Disappointed," Dal said. "I was expecting something a little more mysterious."

"Me, too," I said, carrying it to the sofa.

"Okay if I use the head?" Dal asked. "Cops make me nervous, and nerves make me need to—"

"Be my guest," I said.

I searched the envelope for a note. Nothing.

I fanned the pages of the script. Nothing dropped out.

It was just a plain copy of the original. No cover. One hundred and ten pages, collected by two brass brads. First page contained the title, the screenwriting info, "by Madeleine Parnelle, adapted from the novel, *Le Voleur Qui a Vole la Tour Eiffel,* by Gerard Parnelle," and, at the far-right bottom, the name and Winnetka address of the Onion City production company.

The script might have been nothing more than morning show business, something Trina or Arnie wanted me to look at prior to an upcoming interview. I phoned Kiki to see if she knew anything about it.

She didn't.

"Maybe the actress dropped it off," she said.

"Actress? You mean Carrie Sands?"

"How many actresses in this city do you know, Billy? That's who I mean. She probably thought you'd want a copy, since everybody is so bloody interested in the bloody movie."

"Wow. Two bloodys in one sentence. What's up?"

"Oh, it's just . . . Everybody has an angle," she said.

"I'm not sure Mother Teresa—"

"This isn't funny, Billy."

"What isn't?"

"You meet a bloke. And you seem to hit it off. And then . . . bam, he's just another hustling wanker."

I assumed she was referencing the guy she'd met in the hotel. "Want to talk about it?" I asked.

"No, I do not. I want to sit here and stew and condemn him to the fiery furnace of hell."

"That bad, huh?"

"Lord's truth, Billy, I'm getting too old for this."

My phone suddenly made the unpleasant noise that accompanies a second caller.

I checked the log and saw that it was a private number, possibly the same one that had called before.

"Kiki, I've got another call waiting," I said.

"Oh, take it. Don't mind me. I'm just feeling sorry for myself, like a bloody idiot."

"I'll get right back to you," I said, and took the other call.

"Bill Blessing."

"You get the script?" It was a male voice with a hollow sound, as if the caller was in a tunnel.

Dal entered the room, saw me on the phone, and raised his eyebrows bemusedly.

"I got it," I said into the phone. "Who are you?"

"I . . . Nat Parkins. Look, I'm in deep shit, or I wouldn't be doing this. But I need money to get out of town. I either get it from you or from the others."

"What others?"

"The people in Patton's red files. The ones he was blackmailing."

"How many were on his list?"

"In total? Shit, I don't know. Boxes full, going back thirty-forty years. We left nearly all of 'em. I guess the cops could have 'em now. Larry said we should just take the ones that are active. Four of them."

"When exactly did you and Larry take the files?"

"When? Oh, I see what you're getting at. I didn't kill the old man. He was hard to put up with and gave me a lot of shit, but he paid me every week. And I'm sure as hell not into torture or murder. He was already dead when Larry and I got there."

"When was that?"

"I don't know exactly. Around one-thirty in the morning. Look, you want your file or not? Fifty Benjamins and it's yours. If not, there are two other calls I got to make."

"You said you had four files."

"Yeah. But there's one of 'em I'm sure as hell not callin'. Way I see it, he had the old man and Larry killed."

"Who's that?"

"Maybe I'll tell you. When I see the green."

"What's the movie script you left got to do with anything?" I asked.

"You don't know?"

"No. Why should I?"

"The old man, Patton, had it in your file. I figured it'd prove to you I had the shit."

"Oh, I believe you've got it," I said.

"Good. Then we have a deal? Your file for five grand?"

I wanted all the files.

"Where and when do we meet?" I asked.

"There's a place near the L tracks on East Forty-seventh, Nero's Wonder Lounge. Meet you there in an hour and a half. Bring the green. And come alone."

"I have a driver," I said. "He'll be with me."

Dal had taken a chair across from me, listening to my end of the conversation. He smiled.

"He stays in the car," Nat said, and hung up.

When I'd brought Dal up to speed, he said, "Just

as well I stay in the car. In that neighborhood, it'd be gone in less than sixty seconds."

Chapter
THIRTY-ONE

Dal was right about the neighborhood. Not exactly upscale. And me with a pack of hundred-dollar bills still in their Bank of America wrapper forming a bulge under my coat pocket.

Nero's Wonder Lounge was in the shadow of the L tracks, sharing the area with a beauty shop that specialized in "hair braiding," a Western Union office that was proud of its ability to cash checks, a sandwich joint featuring hoagies and Philly steaks, a pawnshop, and, across the street, a drugstore that looked like it did most of its drug business on the sidewalk.

"Oh, yeah," Dal said, looking around, "I'm definitely staying in the car." He slid the gun from its holster and placed it on the rubber mat near his right boot.

I started to get out, but he stopped me. "Hold on, Billy. You really want to carry five grand in cash into that bar?"

"I don't know of any other way of getting the files."

"How about you tell him to go fuck himself and I

go around this crap hole to the rear door and grab him when he comes out?"

"The money seems less labor-intensive."

"You understand that when they catch him—and they will—they'll ask where he got it. And he'll give you up, and you'll be arrested as an accessory after the fact."

"I'd still be better off than if we used your plan. At least now, when they pick him up, he'll still be in one piece."

"We make a citizen's arrest," he said. "It's the smart play."

"Let me just pay the two dollars," I said.

"Your call." He reached across me to pop open the glove compartment.

I was trying to think of a way to politely refuse the gun he was going to offer when he held out something that wasn't any kind of weapon I knew. It looked like a plastic whistle on a white cord.

"What's this?" I asked, taking it and dangling it by the cord.

"Air horn, Billy. Keep it handy. First sign of trouble, give just a light blow. It'll blast out a one-hundred-twenty-decibel honk that'll scare the shit out of anybody not expecting it. And since it can be heard for nearly a mile, I'll be in there in seconds."

I thanked him, got out of the car, slipped the air horn into my coat pocket, and walked toward Nero's Wonder Lounge, where the deep-smoked windows were so dark and grimy there was no way of telling what I'd find inside.

No surprise: What I found was more dark and grimy. Judging by the music, the jukebox was locked in the pre-rap heyday of Motown. The smell was stale booze and cooking grease and disinfectant. There was a long bar, where several old-timers sipped from straws stuck in a communal barrel. In another section of the large room, a weary caramel-colored woman wearing a soiled apron stood behind a glass partition, stirring what looked like a large pot of . . . something, maybe chili, maybe meatballs and tomato sauce. She looked like she was in her sixties. The stuff in the pot looked older.

Of the twenty-five or thirty tables in the room, five were occupied by solo men. A sleeping man at one. Eating and drinking men at three. And at a table at the back of the room near the window, a glaring man, waiting for me.

He stood, walked to the window, and looked through a small clear section of the smoked glass. Then he sat back down at the table.

Nat Parkins wasn't nearly as put together as he'd been when last I saw him. His slick hair was downright nappy, and that neat line of mustache had been removed. Great disguise. His eyes were bloodshot, and his clothes—a dark T-shirt and khaki pants—had that lived-in-for-three-days look. The smell coming off him was stronger than the eau de grease. But he was still big and powerful. And dangerous.

"You look a little run-down, Nat," I said, taking a chair.

"I wonder why. That guy standing by the Z-car supposed to be your driver? He doesn't look like a driver. He looks like muscle."

"He's my driver."

"You got the money?"

The only things on the table were a bottle of beer, a spiral notebook, a pencil, and his big hands. "I don't see any red files," I said.

"Show me the loot and I'll tell you where to get your file."

My file. What about the others? And I didn't like the "where to get" part.

"Gee, Nat, you see any dandruff in my hair?"

"Dandruff? Hell, you don't even have any hair."

"I don't have any hayseeds sticking out of my ears, either. So don't expect me to give you any—"

He held up a hand and pointed behind me. The woman I'd seen ladling the food was shuffling our way. "Git you somethin', honey?" she asked me. "Hey, don't I knows you?"

"You don't know nuthin'," Nat told her. "My homie here wants a brew in a bottle with the cap still on."

The woman shrugged off this implied critique of her draft beer. " 'Nuther for you?"

"I'm good."

She shuffled off, muttering.

Nat leaned toward me, keeping his voice low. "I'm not playing you. If I had the files with me, what's to stop that big blond dude out there from just takin' 'em? You give me the money and I tell you where they are. They're easy to get to."

"That's not going to happen," I said, standing. "Don't call me again unless you decide to show up with the files."

"Hold on. Sit yourself. Let's see if we can't work this out."

I sat back down.

"Twenty-five hundred," he said.

I shook my head. "Not twenty-five cents, unless I see the folders."

He slumped. "Fuck this," he said. "I don't know what I'm doing. This isn't my scene. A week ago I was living a normal life. I had a job. I was starting to sell my sculptures. Larry wasn't the easiest guy to live with, but we got along okay.

"Then that stupid old man had to get greedy, and the shit hasn't stopped raining down on my head."

"Could be worse. Look at the old man and Larry."

"I definitely don't want to join that club," he said.

"Is that why you ran?"

"Yeah, I figured a big homicidal dog was hunting my black ass. Now the cops are, too. I've gotta put miles between me and Chicago."

"The cops have any reason to think you did it, other than the fact you took off?"

"Yeah. They musta found my shoes with Pat's blood on 'em."

"That'd be a clue, all right."

"I told you I was there after he was dead," he said defensively. "Like a fucking idiot I stepped in his blood." He said it louder than he'd planned, and he scanned the room to make sure nobody was tuning us in.

"Why'd you go there that night?"

"Pat phoned me a little after midnight. Caught me at a comedy club in the neighborhood where Larry works out his material. He said he was worried. Somebody had threatened him, and he didn't want to be alone."

"He tell you who threatened him?"

"Nah. But it wasn't anything new, him getting threats. And I was a little wasted, because when Larry performs, booze is free. Anyway, I told Pat I'd come. But Larry was just starting his last set. And when that was over, he was wired, as usual, and wanted to go somewhere and eat and talk. Before that, I phoned the old man to see if he still wanted company."

"What time is this?"

"A little after one. Pat's phone rang a bunch of times, and I figured he'd gone to sleep. So I hung up. But I was a little worried. He'd been acting kinda strange. On Saturday, he even got out his old Police Special and cleaned it up. This was after he went off by himself for a couple hours. That was weird, too. He hates to drive.

"All that on top of the call when I was at the club, I thought I better check up on him before Larry and I had our late-night pizza."

He paused while the waitress presented me with a bottle of Bud, capped. "Got ya the premium stuff," she said before shuffling off.

I didn't bother uncapping it. I wasn't thirsty. "So you and Larry went to Patton's sometime after one?" I prompted.

"Yeah. In Larry's car. Took us another twenty minutes to find a place to park in that neighborhood. Shit, I just realized something."

He straightened in his chair. "There was a Range Rover pullin' out, leavin' almost enough space for two cars. That was just down the street from Patton's. It coulda been the bastards who killed him, leavin' the scene."

"How many men?"

"Two. One tall, one closer to the ground and thick. I didn't get much of a look. Trees make it a little dark around there."

"They were in a Range Rover?"

"Big fucking machine. Metallic red."

"Killers would probably be driving something a little less conspicuous," I said. Then it occurred to me that a big metallic red car had roared past Carrie and me just before our confrontation with the hit man.

"I guess it coulda been horndogs who'd been cruising the bars on Rush. Come to think of it, one of 'em was wearing a team jacket. Couldn't see the name on it."

"So you parked and went up to Patton's apartment," I said.

"Yeah. As soon as we cleared the stairs, I saw the door to his place was open and knew that couldn't be good."

"Had it been pried open?"

"You think I bothered to check the door? I was too busy looking at how messed up the living room was. I mean, it had been seriously trashed, but it was like whoever had taken the books off the shelves and cut up the cushions and the rug had done it carefully."

"Didn't want to wake the neighbors."

"Maybe. Anyway, the old man—Jesus, they'd shoved his socks in his mouth, then cut and roasted him. And the smell . . . I still get a whiff of it every now and then. Larry and I see all this and we head for the door. But Larry stops and says, 'No.' He's incredibly cool. He asks me if I've got any idea what the killers were trying to torture out of Patton.

"I tell him the old man kept some money at the

apartment, but that's sure to be gone. Larry asks if
there's anything else. And I remembered that on Saturday, before we went to your hotel room, Pat goes
into the crapper and comes out with this little plastic
bag. It's drippin' wet. He gets a key out of it. Then we
drive to a storage place on Clark. He goes in and
comes out with two red folders. One of 'em looks
empty, the other's got papers. From there we head to
a Minuteman copy shop on North Clybourn.

"So I tell Larry all this, and he makes a beeline to
the crapper. The medicine cabinet and linen closet are
hanging open. The floor is a pile of tossed towels with
the top of the toilet tank resting on the pile. Larry
stares into the open tank, sticks his hand down in it,
and starts unscrewin' the brass float ball. He pulls
that apart, and inside is the plastic bag and the key.

"We get some flashlights and go to the storage
place and pop the lock. Spend hours searching
through all the crap Patton had in there. His old cop
outfits, caps. Trophies. Personal papers. Love letters
some broads sent him back in the seventies. Turns out
the guy even got married back then. Don't know
what happened to his old lady. Probably walked out
on him."

"Tell me about the files."

"That's what the place mainly was: files. But the
current four—the ones we grabbed—were right on
top."

"What were some of the names on them?"

"Besides you? Well, there was . . . Naw. Not without some green changing hands."

I considered offering him some of the five thousand for the name of the man he thought killed Pat-

ton and Kelsto. But pulling out a wad of bills and peeling off a few didn't strike me as a smart move, even if we weren't in a pit like Nero's.

"Finish your story first. What'd you and Larry do after you had the files?"

"Went back to our place. It's like three-thirty, four in the morning. Larry's so wired he stays up, readin' through all the files. I was so wiped that even with the image of Pat's body in my head, I crashed hard. Wasn't till morning I saw the blood on the edge of my shoe. I've watched enough TV to know you can't just clean that stuff off. So I hid the shoes in the shed at our place.

"I barely got 'em hid before the cops showed." He lifted his beer bottle and was annoyed to find it empty.

I moved my bottle across the table.

He twisted off the cap. "I don't like staying in one place too long," he said. "Are we making a deal here, or what?"

"That depends on whether you can convince me to trust you. What brought the cops to your house?"

He shrugged. "They found out somehow I worked for Pat. Nothing more. They threw questions at me for a couple hours and split."

"They ask you if you murdered Patton?"

"That was question number one," he said. "The next: Where was I between midnight and five a.m.? I had to bring Larry into it, to back up my alibi that we'd gone to bed at twelve-thirty and stayed there till morning."

"Did they tell you your rights?"

"No. I didn't get the sense they thought I was involved. Not then."

"What other questions did they ask?"

"The usual. Did I know anybody who'd want to kill the old man? Hell, it was easier to give 'em the names of people who didn't."

"Was it around then you mentioned that Patton visited my hotel room?"

He opened his mouth, possibly to deny it, then nodded. "Yeah, I told 'em that."

"Did you tell 'em why he came to see me?"

"No. 'Cause I didn't know. I only figured that out later, when I looked at your red file. The clippings tell the story. Only thing I couldn't figure, and still can't, was why he'd stuck that movie script in your file. I know he didn't have one in the folder he took to your hotel room."

"What exactly is in my folder?" I asked.

"Just some newspaper clips, copies of your police record, and some guy's death certificate."

"You tell the cops about any other trips you and Patton made?"

"They just wanted to know the recent ones."

"What else did you tell them?"

"I told them about him driving off somewhere on his own after he'd seen you. I told 'em I didn't know where, which was the truth at the time. I told them about him getting out the gun and that he was worried when he called Sunday night."

"Where'd he drive, Nat?"

He shook his head. Held up a hand and rubbed his fingers against his thumb in a give-me-the-money gesture.

"He called it an errand. Said I should go hang somewhere for a couple of hours, he had an errand to run by himself. But he'd be back in time for some business he had at a TV station. I don't know what happened out there, but when he left me he was a happy camper. When he got back, not so happy at all."

"What else did the cops ask you?"

"Nothing special."

"Maybe about the headless body on the beach?"

His face broke out in a partial smile, the first since I sat down with him. "Yeah. They wanted to know if Pat said anything to me about it."

"Had he?"

"Hell, yeah. That was pretty much what he was talking about the last few days. How the cops were fucking up. And how he was smart enough to know how it connected to some other crime."

"He mention what crime?"

"No."

"Did he say anything about the headless guy dying of natural causes?"

"No. He—"

Someone shouted "Hey!" outside the bar.

Parkins ran to the clear pane and looked out. "Shit!" he said. "That's the one."

I moved to the clear pane, too.

A big red vehicle was parked near the front door. It looked like the same one I'd seen that night on the way to Webber's home.

There was the sound of gunfire and shattering glass.

I dropped to the not exactly clean floor. I turned to check Parkins's condition, and discovered he was among the missing. The bar's rear door was swinging shut.

I got up and ran to the door.

All I saw in the paper-and-trash-strewn alley was a row of overflowing garbage cans and living proof that you can draw more flies to garbage than you can to honey.

Chapter
THIRTY-TWO

When I returned, Dal was in the bar, looking for me. He didn't seem to realize that everybody else in the room was looking at him.

"Billy," he yelled. "Gotta boogie."

I looked at our table, wondering if Nat had left his notebook. It and the pencil were gone.

We boogied.

The maroon Nissan Z had a line of bullet holes along its left side, leading to a hanging piece of wire where the extended mirror had been blown away.

By the time I made it to the passenger seat, Dal had the engine revving. "Let's see how lucky we are," he said, and steered us away from the curb.

"The question is," he continued, as he drove us away, "did that asshole hit any vital parts?"

I assumed he meant parts of the car.

"What happened?"

"These two very white guys drove up. Don't know if you've noticed, but there aren't a lot of white guys around here. The driver didn't bother to park. Just hovered. The other guy hops out. Twenties. Thin, six-foot-plus, black hair, dark suit, white business shirt. No tie. Average-looking, but there's a very intense vibe coming off him.

"He's heading for the bar. I figure I'd better slow him down. I get out of the car and shout at him. He responds by pulling a Glock G32 from under his jacket, and I dive inside the car just before he stitches up the open door. I return fire while he's running back to the Range Rover. He dives in, and they're gone."

"It was a metallic red Range Rover," I said.

"Yeah. You saw that? It makes even less sense. Who goes to a shoot-out in a red Range Rover?"

"The same guys who tortured and killed Pat Patton," I said. "Very stupid or very confident."

"I vote for very crazy," Dal said. He had his phone out.

I heard him ask to be put through to Mantata. While he summarized the shoot-out at Nero's, having nothing better to do, I searched the streets we were passing for the red Range Rover. In a city boasting more than three million cars, the result was no more than expected.

Dal finished his conversation as we crossed the Kennedy Expressway, traveling west. "The man's not happy," he said.

Our destination was Zeke's Auto Repair on North Milwaukee. To my surprise, Zeke was a female. Literally if not ostensibly. A woman-of-the-plains type—ageless, big, muscular, straight gray hair tied in a ponytail, wearing baggy, oil-spotted Levi's and an *Orange County Choppers* T-shirt. She gave me a quick, curt nod, had a raucous laugh at Dal's "purty clothes," and barely spent a minute looking at the damage to the car.

"Hell, Dal, this is all Bondo bullshit," she said. "Rattlin' cages again, huh?"

"Something like that," he said. "You know anybody drives a metallic red Range Rover?"

"Nah. My customers all got good taste. 'Cept you. You like these foreign crapwagons. Be ready for ya tamarra. Take the Camaro." She pointed to a yellow two-door with twin thick black stripes down the center of the hood.

"It looks like a fucking bumble bee," Dal said. "What about the Mustang?"

Zeke turned to the mechanics working on cars in the shop. "Bessie, Dal here wants to borry ya new 'tang," she shouted.

A tiny woman rolled out from under a Buick. She was young and had oil smudges on her attractive pug face. "Dal can go fuck himself," she said, and rolled back under the car.

Zeke gave Dal a helpless shrug. "What can I say? A woman scorned. Key's in the Camaro. And pick up ya damn Nissan early tamarra. Cars that ain't homegrown give the shop a bad name."

"Colorful character," I said, as we drove east.

"Huh? Oh. Zeke, yeah. Character."

"Something on your mind?" I asked.

"I'm a little surprised at Bessie's attitude. I thought

we were . . . okay. I guess I did stand her up last time. But she knows the nature of my job with Mantata. Brush fires spring up, putting 'em out takes precedence over a roll in the sack. I explained all that to her."

"In those words?"

He didn't answer, which I took to be a positive response.

"This car rides fine," he said.

"Where's it taking us?"

"Ubora. Mantata wants to talk with you about the shoot-up."

"Me? I didn't even see it."

"I think it's got less to do with the shooting than what would have happened if the guy had made it inside the bar with his Glock."

"Nat Parkins was out of there so fast," I said, "I doubt the killer would have had the chance to shoot him."

"Well, that's the thing Mantata wants to talk about. He's thinking maybe Parkins wasn't the target."

Me? The target? Now there's a happy thought.

Chapter THIRTY-THREE

To take my mind off how close I'd come to experiencing multiple bullet wounds again, I phoned Kiki for news of the day.

"Trina says that since you're not doing *Hotline!* she expects you to do the first hour of the show tomorrow, and Arnie has scheduled your interview with the *Da Mare* author for six-twenty a.m."

"What else?"

I heard paper crinkling on the other end. "J. B. Kazynski called and left her number. Please tell me that it's only business."

"Not even that," I said. "Next."

"Lily C. called from New York. After cursing you for not turning your phone on, she said to tell you she fixed the sound on the Puff Potato Man show. She thinks the show is better than the one scheduled for Friday, and since this is a sweeps week, she'd like to switch the play dates."

"I can't remember which show was scheduled for Friday."

"The, ah"—more paper crinkling—"the organic milk controversy."

"Oh, hell, yes. Tell her to change it," I said.

"Derek Webber's office called," she said, "to remind you about a dinner party tonight at Pastiche. Eight p.m. I looked up the place, Billy. On the Chicago River. Very swank. It was designed to look like a restaurant in Paris on the banks of the Seine."

"Which one? The River Case? La Plage? Le Petit Poucet? Riviere?"

"If they're on the Seine, just like one of them."

"That must be why they named it Pastiche," I said.

"Sometimes I hate you."

I put my phone away and turned to Dal, who was steering the car with thumb and forefinger. "You ever hear of Restaurant Pastiche?"

"Oh, yeah. Very new. Very French. Very good. Yachts floating by on the river. The lights of the city on the water. If you and your companion aren't bumping uglies twenty minutes after dessert, you did something wrong."

"You and I are having dinner there tonight," I told him.

"In that case, ignore what I just said."

Mantata seemed on edge.

"Sit down, gentlemen," he said.

I took the chair near his desk. Dal chose the couch, as if purposely distancing himself from the discussion.

"The episode at the lounge is vexing," the elegant elderly black man said. "But before we get into the gunmen in the red vehicle, Billy, please enlighten me on your conversation with"—he consulted the iPad on the coffee table—"with Nat Parkins."

I gave him a pretty accurate summation, during which he seemed to relax.

"So we're certain he did not murder his employer and his roommate?"

I nodded. "From what he told me, I'm convinced that the men in the red Range Rover committed those crimes."

"Yes. About that vehicle . . . A Range Rover, painted a color that the company calls Rimini Red, was discovered abandoned less than an hour ago on South Shields Avenue, scant blocks away from the lounge. It had been on the stolen list since Monday morning. Its license plates belonged to another vehicle entirely. Would it surprise you to know that its owner was Onion City Entertainment?"

"They reported it stolen on Monday?" I asked.

"Yes. They claimed it probably had been taken from the premises the previous night. The same night Pat Patton was tortured and murdered."

"This isn't good news," I said. "Especially since I'm supposed to go to a dinner the CEO of Onion City is hosting tonight."

Mantata asked where the dinner was being held.

I told him, and he replied, "I doubt anything untoward would transpire in such a public place," he said. "And . . . you will be there, too, Dal?"

Dal nodded.

"You both should pad up, just to play safe."

Dal looked at me. "Size-forty-two chest?"

"Yeah. But I hope this won't make me look like

the Michelin Man." I was hoping to hook up with Adoree.

"What good is stylin' if you're dyin'?" Dal said.

"You're sure you've never seen the gunman before?" Mantata asked him.

"I'd have remembered."

Mantata pursed his lips. "An import? And the driver is a blank, so—"

"Not exactly," I interrupted. "Nat told me one of the guys he saw getting into the Range Rover near Patton's home was short and thick. That's got to be the driver."

"Or the driver could've been one of the guys tried to kidnap Billy," Dal said.

"Perhaps," Mantata said. "But . . . ."

He looked up as Roxanne entered the room. "Sorry to interrupt, but Emma just called," she said. "The only prints on the Range Rover were from locals who were in the midst of vandalizing it when the patrolmen drove up. They scattered. Possibly because of them, the vehicle's interior was clean except for a piece of rumpled paper under the passenger seat. She's sending you a photo."

"Excellent," Mantata said, blessing her with a smile.

We all watched her exit.

"Who's Emma?" I asked.

"One of my few remaining loyalists among the blue line," Mantata replied. "The point I was trying to make before . . ."

Again he paused as a tiny bong sounded on his iPad and an image popped on the screen. He picked up the device, his forehead creasing as he studied its surface. Eventually, he turned it around for us to see.

"Gibberish or significant?" he asked.

Dal duck-waddled toward the small screen, squinting.

It was a sheet of paper. At its top was the Onion City logo, an inch-high onion containing a dark cityscape outline, like a snow paperweight housing a Christmas tree. Someone had scribbled "Starbucks" in almost childlike printing, then drawn several dark pencil slashes through the word. This was followed by the similarly printed names "Phipps, Williams, Scott, Cobb, Watts, Jackson, Neal, and Sorey." After that final letter *y*, the writer had dragged the pencil down the page almost to the bottom.

"Those mad-as-hell lines drawn through 'Starbucks,'" Dal said, "were either made by a guy who works for Mr. Coffee or who drinks too damn much of the stuff."

I shrugged. "I guess I vote for gibberish," I said.

"There is at least one substantial bit of information," Mantata said. "The company logo."

"It was a company car," I said. "Any employee could have dropped that paper before the car was stolen."

Mantata lowered the iPad to the coffee table. "Speculating on a paper that may have been dropped by one of the killers has its merits," he said, "but pawns are merely pawns. We need to get a line on the king. To that end, I've spent several hours today perusing the Internet bloviations of the late Pat Patton."

"And . . . ?" I said.

"The good news is I don't think my IQ was lowered to any degree. The bad news, the man's archives are a rubbish heap of misinformation, innuendo, outright lies, and obfuscation. But there was one thing that bears further investigation."

"Do I have to ask?"

"Not that long ago, Patton and Onion City were in negotiation on a television project."

"I know about that," I said. And I summarized what Webber had told me about the negotiations and how, at the last minute, Patton had refused to sign the contract, claiming he did not want to do business with organized crime.

"Webber told you this?" Mantata seemed quite surprised. He paused for thought, then nodded. "It was clever of him. The information is out there on the Web, where you could have found it at any time. Better that you hear it from him, thereby establishing his openness and honesty while at the same time casting doubt on the legitimacy of Patton's claim."

"You seem convinced that Webber is behind all this," I said.

"Definitely leaning in that direction."

"In 1987, when Paul was murdered," I said, "Webber would have been a little kid."

"You should accept the probability that your perilous situation may have nothing to do with Paul's death," Mantata said.

"But that's my only connection to this whole mess."

"Incorrect," he said. "You're connected to Patton."

"I'll give you that. So what?" I couldn't see his point, and that was upgrading my annoyance to anger.

"I know it's hard for you, but you must look at this objectively, Billy. According to what Nat Parkins told you, Patton was in possession of four active red files, each containing blackmail-worthy material. Pat Patton was murdered. Parkins and Larry Kelsto became possessors of the red files. Kelsto was murdered, and Parkins, who has the files, is afraid for his life. I think we're in agreement that whoever possesses the red files is a potential murder victim. Isn't it possible— no, make that probable—that the man behind the killings thinks you have the files or have knowledge of what's in them?"

"At last we agree," I said. "I'm fairly certain one of those files will tell me the current identity of Giovanni Polvere."

"Your head is as hard as onyx," Mantata said. "Please at least entertain the possibility that Patton was lying to you, trying to extort money from you with his Polvere fiction. On the other hand, he went on record identifying Webber's company as being linked to the Outfit. I'd put my bet on Webber being the Mr. X looking for his red file."

I had two problems with Mantata's smug conclusion. I was convinced Patton had not been pulling my chain about Polvere. And I liked Derek Webber.

I turned to Dal. "The night the hit man shot at Carrie Sands and myself," I said. "You were following us, right?"

Dal nodded.

"Was the red car following us, too?"

He hesitated, then said, "Yeah. We spotted the Rover parked at the TV station with its engine running. When you and the actress drove off, the Rover followed you, and we followed it. But we lost sight of it when you two were parking your car. We were hunting for a place where we could observe you without being noticed when Trejean saw the Range Rover dropping the crazy bastard off and driving away."

"Why did they drop him off, I wonder?" Mantata said. "Wouldn't it have been simpler to do a drive-by?"

"Some hit men have their own method—," Dal began.

Mantata cut him off. "When they were waiting for you, Billy, they had no way of knowing you'd be accompanying Ms. Sands. That posed a problem. She's the star of Webber's movie. Her death would be too costly a price to pay. They didn't want to risk a drive-by. They wanted the killer to be able to dispatch you without harming the lady. You did say the initial shots he fired went over your head?"

I nodded. "But what the heck was his exit plan?" I asked. "The guy shoots me and he's stuck with my body and Carrie. And no ride. Why did the red car drive off?"

"Good question," Mantata said.

"Maybe they dropped him off, saw us, and panicked," Dal said.

"Perhaps," Mantata allowed. "It is a puzzle. Thinking outside the box, we might even speculate that Webber got Ms. Sands to lure you to that spot."

"Now she's part of this murder cabal, too? That's a little too cynical for me. And too unbelievable. I know how frightened she was."

"Need I remind you, Billy, she's an actress."

I shook my head. "You're wrong about her. Wrong about Webber."

He gave me a stern look. "Billy, because of our mutual friend, I'm doing my best to keep you alive. If you resent my help, there are other, considerably more profitable ways Dal and I could be spending our time."

"I appreciate your help, Mantata. And Dal's, certainly."

"Good. Be careful tonight. By tomorrow, I should be in a better position to suggest our next move."

"Why then?" I asked.

"By then I will have accumulated more data."

On the way to my hotel, I asked Dal, "Was it my imagination, or did Mantata seem a little more obnoxious than usual?"

He smiled. "He's always a little hardheaded and high-handed. Comes with old age, I think. But there's something else, too. When I first started working for him, there were twenty of us in the crew and, what with his . . . businesses, mainly on the South Side, we were hustling all the time. Wasn't that long ago. Then things changed. The gangs took over. Black gangs, white gangs, Latino, Asian. Over a hundred of 'em by now, each claiming a bigger slice of turf. One night, for no particular reason we know of, somebody blew up a car with five of our guys inside. Mantata pulled the plug on everything. Now he's down to a few primarily aboveboard operations, mainly in Bronzetown. And the gallery, which is where he spends most of his time.

"You've met the only crew that's left. There are four other guys we use when we need them, which isn't very often anymore. But basically it's me, the crazy Jamaican Trejean, and the even crazier Hiho. What we usually do is collect and deposit the cash from Mantata's coffee shops and bakeries and barbershops and pool halls. We solve small problems. And we keep the old man company.

"What I'm getting at: It's been pretty boring for us, and especially for Mantata. Then you come along, and it's almost like old times. Except now we're the good guys. Mantata used to see himself as a black Professor Moriarty. You bring out the Sherlock Holmes in him. I think he digs it."

"What did you study at Duke? Psychology?"

"Hell, no," he said. "It was Duke, not Harvard. My major was coeds, my minor chemical enhancement."

Ah, the halls of higher learning.

Chapter
THIRTY-FOUR

"Where are you, Billy?" my restaurant hostess-manager, Cassandra, wanted to know.

"In my hotel room, getting ready for dinner."

"I hear a man singing."

Dal was in the suite's sitting room, singing along with a contestant on *The Voice*.

"Just a friend," I said, not wanting to get into the whole thing with her. "He's staying with me for a few days."

"In your hotel room?"

"Can't a couple of guys hang out in a hotel in their bathrobes without narrow minds jumping to conclusions?"

She was silent for a beat, then decided to change the subject. "We identified the little bastard who's been causing the trouble. A busboy named Phillipe, who's been working here for less than a month. The undercover security lady saw him setting some roaches loose in the main dining room just before lunch."

"Crap! What'd you do?"

"We got rid of the roaches. Most of them, anyway. It was a little tricky, since we didn't want Phillipe to know he'd been observed."

"Why didn't we?"

"Because as any expert in security knows, you don't chop off the finger while the hand is still at large. Or something like that."

"Your boyfriend tell you that?"

"Uh-huh."

"Other than Phillipe and his roaches, everything okay?"

"Better than that. We're just about at full capacity in the main room, and three of the private rooms are busy. How's Chicago?"

"It's got Marshall Field and Soldier Field, and it's on a nice lake, but," I began to sing, " ' . . . It hasn't got the hansoms in the park, it hasn't got a skyline after dark. That's why New York's my home sweet home.' With apologies to the late Sammy Davis."

"You and your hotel friend should do a duet," she said, and clicked off.

At ten to eight, Dal stood in the doorway to the bedroom, resplendent in black blazer, dark gray turtleneck, and lighter gray slacks. There was no evidence of his gun or Kevlar vest.

"You're looking good," he said.

"I look like Bibendum, the Michelin Man. And I feel like I'm wearing a corset."

"You'll get used to it," he said.

I still hadn't by the time we reached Pastiche.

It was in a modern tri-level building located on the Chicago River, near the Merchandise Mart. A semi-officious maître d' informed us, in a French accent that sounded almost comical, that the Onion City party was being held down the stairs to our right.

The stairwell led to a just-above-river-level indoor-outdoor dining area, where a lovely young brunette seated at a table introduced herself as Jo Sennett, Derek's social secretary. She welcomed me and asked Dal for his name, which she checked off her list. "The bar is to the left, but guests are gathering on the terrace," she said. "Have fun."

"Fun," Dal muttered. "Billy, if the women guests all look like her, you're going to have to keep reminding me why we're here."

"I don't know about you, Dal, but that is why I'm here."

The restaurant's efficient layout, furniture, and especially the white cushioned chairs on the terrace made it easy to recognize which French Seine-side establishment had been its inspiration: Riviere. I hoped that the menu would be as successfully reproduced.

We were neither the first nor the last to arrive. There were about fifty people milling on the large terrace, with room for another twenty or twenty-five. I recognized a few of the cast and crew members I'd met at Webber's mansion sprinkled in among those present. Near the boat dock, the marsupial-like assistant director, Harp Didio, was chatting up three young executive types. Webber's partner, Alan Luchek, his red hair temporarily tamed by more than a dab of mousse, shifted his weight from foot to foot anxiously while struggling through a conversation with an elderly, obviously affluent couple.

Thief's director, Austin Deware, was at a table, doing shooters with several young men and women who might have been film students. Nearby, at another table, the actor Sandford Hawes, dark Ray-Bans lending their air of mystery to his absurdly handsome face, was holding court with an array of women, young, old, and in between.

A waiter arrived, bearing a tray containing bite-sized grilled somethings, accessible by toothpick. I tried a sample.

"Well?" Dal asked.

"Grilled calamari," I said. Instead of mentioning that the calamari was soaked in lemon butter, garlic, basil, and tomato, I merely added, "Delicious. Try 'em."

He took two, and I continued to scan the crowd for Adoree. I didn't see her, but I spied Madeleine Parnelle engaging several executive types in conversation. She was wearing a midnight-blue dress with sparkles and a neckline nearly down to her navel. Her head was adorned by a matching version of an African skullcap.

Panning right, I locked eyes with Carrie, who was at the far edge of the terrace. She turned to a tall, professorial gentleman, said something to him, then began working her way through the crowd toward us.

Following just behind her, looking a little apprehensive, was J. B. Kazynski.

"Billy, I'm so glad you're here," Carrie said.

"And in such sleazy company," J.B. added. She was glaring at Dal, who was wincing and looking ill at ease.

"Dal, this is Carrie Sands," I said.

"A pleasure," he said, turning from J.B. with relief. He shifted his face into what I suspected was his ruggedly appealing Daniel Craig grin. "Henry Hart Dalrymple, at your service, ma'am."

"Jesus Christ!" J.B. grumbled. "Excuse me while I puke."

"I take it you and Dal are not strangers," I said.

"J.B. tried to kill me a while back," Dal said.

"It was just a warning shot. If I'd wanted to kill you, you'd be dead."

Carrie was looking at them both, her eyes open

wider than Little Orphan Annie's but with more pupil.

"Dal's my bodyguard," I told her.

"Uh . . . J.B.'s mine."

"What happened to the legendary Bucky?" I asked.

Dal and J.B. stopped their sniping to ask in unison, "Bucky Hurtz?"

"Y-yes," Carrie said. "I think Derek and Alan talked to him, but he said he'd retired."

"Bucky retired?" Dal said, as if he couldn't believe it.

"He was the champ," J.B. said. "Remember when the Imperial Insane Vice Lords marked Senator Rockville's family . . . ?"

"As soon as the senator hired Bucky, he grabbed one of the Lords—" Dal said.

"Not just one of the Lords," J.B. interrupted. "He grabbed Li'l Hay-sus and nailed him to a tree."

"Crucifixion-style," Dal said.

They both laughed.

J.B. turned to me suddenly and said, "Could we talk for a minute, just the two of us?"

I nodded and, with Carrie and Dal watching us with curiosity, followed her to a less populated section of the restaurant's interior.

"What's with you and Dal?" she asked, keeping her voice low.

"Friend of a friend put us in touch."

"He's a sociopath."

"Nobody's perfect," I said, and started to walk away.

"Wait! That's not why I wanted to talk."

I didn't think it was. I stood there, looking at her, waiting for her to ask me not to repeat anything she'd told me about her investigation of our host and his company.

It was evidently hard for her to ask a favor. She'd tried to make it a quid-pro-quo situation by telling me something she didn't think I knew about Dal. That hadn't worked, and now she was trying her best to come up with a spin that would make her seem less needy.

"I'm in a position to find out who tried to kill you and Carrie," she said. "Don't screw it up."

"How could I do that?" I asked, with fake innocence.

"By telling Webber what I stupidly told you about my nephew," she whispered through clenched teeth.

"Oh, I see. You want me to keep your secret? All you have to do is ask."

"It's as much for your benefit as—"

"All you have to do is ask," I repeated.

"Okay. Will you?"

"Sure," I said. "Can we go back to the party now?"

When we returned, Carrie was laughing at something Dal had said.

"What's so funny?" J.B. asked defensively, as if she assumed they'd been talking about her.

"Dal was telling me about the time Bucky rescued several young undocumented Asian women from a house of prostitution in Joliet," Carrie said.

"Yeah," J.B. said. "He got 'em out in the confusion he caused by dumping a garbage can full of sewer rats into the reception area."

Regardless of the reason, the use of rats to clean house was a little too close to home for me to be amused. But it definitely raised J.B.'s spirits. She felt she had to top it with another merry tale of the legendary Bucky Hurtz.

While our keepers amused themselves, I suggested to Carrie that we slip away to the bar for cocktails. This resulted in a mojito for her and a Sapphire martini for myself. I tapped my glass against hers and said, "To a long life."

"Amen."

"Last night, when you asked me to drive to Derek's with you, was that your idea?"

"What do you mean?" She seemed genuinely puzzled. I immediately regretted giving Mantata's unpleasant suggestion even a second's thought.

"I don't even know what I mean," I said. "It's been a long day. How was yours?"

"Not bad. We filmed some exteriors at Trump Tower."

On the deck, our bodyguards were laughing again.

"How'd you hook up with J.B.?" I asked.

"After Bucky said no, Alan remembered seeing her on the show with us and called her service. She said she was busy but finally agreed to farm out the job she'd been doing and come aboard. I'm glad. I doubt I'd feel as comfortable with Bucky, as legendary as he may be. And J.B. seems very professional."

I'd say, I thought to myself. J.B.'s nephew and his wife were paying her to find out the source of Onion City's financing, and now Onion City was a client, too, which put her in a position to complete the first job. Brilliant.

"I got a nice long email from Gerard today," Carrie said. "He misses me, and he thinks he'll be finished with the corrections to the final draft by the time I meet him in Paris."

A Frenchman who prefers email to the sound of his lover's voice? I wondered if good old Gerard might be working on something in Paris besides his mystery novel. By hooking up with Webber, Madeleine Parnelle had given her husband a reason to romance a younger woman. But maybe the guy didn't need a reason. Maybe he was just a self-gratifying son of a bitch who now had found somebody more to his liking than Carrie. I sipped my martini, scanned the crowd, and tried to keep my speculations about Gerard Parnelle to myself.

"I know what's on your mind," Carrie said.

"Really?" I said, hoping she was wrong.

"You're wondering where Adoree is."

"Am I that obvious?"

"She's on Derek's yacht with some of the investors. They'll be here any minute."

"That's what this blowout is all about, right?" I asked. "Feting the moneymen?"

"And the media. There's a private dining room upstairs where they've set up lights and cameras. Before too long, Sandford and I and Austin and Adoree are gonna be escorted up there for interviews. With the usual crowd—*ET, Insider, Extra, Access Hollywood,* E! channel."

"Anybody from *Wake Up?*"

"You mean besides you?"

Was that why I'd been invited? *Maybe,* I thought.

But roughly ten minutes later, when camera crews appeared and the crowd out on the deck started to gather at the rail to welcome Derek the yachtsman and his passengers, I realized this was merely going to be a social night for me. Sharing the cruise with Cap'n Derek, the lovely Adoree, and an assorted collection of white men with expensive haircuts in business gray suits was the morning show's willowy flame-tressed conservative entertainment reporter, Karma Singleton.

Karma was draped against Derek close enough to leave an indentation of her right breast on his blazer. Our host seemed to be enjoying himself, in his yachtsman outfit of midnight-blue blazer, white turtleneck, white slacks, and—wait for it—skipper's cap. Thurston Howell III would've approved.

He raised a megaphone to his lips and called out, "Ahoy, Pastiche. We are preparing to come ashore from the good ship *Duchess the Fourth.*"

"Derek has three other yachts?" I asked, as we walked out on the terrace to join the festivities.

"I don't think so," Carrie said. "Oh, you mean *Duchess the Fourth.* No, that's just . . . Al Capone's yacht was named *Duchess the Third.* Derek's a big gangster buff. His pet project, which he's been working on forever, is a television series about organized crime in Chicago. I guess there was a show like that a long time ago, but he says that one was more about the police."

As the yacht bumped the dock, Karma and Derek were pushed together even closer.

"Who's the redhead bimbo doing the vertical

grind with Webber?" J.B. asked, as we joined her and Dal.

"Karma Singleton," I said. "I work with her. She's the show's entertainment reporter."

"Looks to me like the only thing she's entertaining is a ride on the hobby horse."

"Doesn't make her a bad girl," Dal said.

"Tell that to Lady Parnelle, who's looking daggers at Webber," J.B. said. "Speaking of karma."

Madeleine was at the terrace rail, definitely not in high party spirits.

"Poor Derek," Carrie said.

"That romance wilting a little?" I asked her.

She sighed. "I think so. And it used to be so happy at the castle."

As soon as Webber set foot on the terrace, la Parnelle was at his side, saying something to him through clenched teeth. He smiled at her as if she was complimenting him on his cap, a passive-aggressive move that seemed to push her anger past the verbal stage. When her mouth clamped shut, he left her and began pressing the flesh and welcoming his guests.

A tall, handsome gent moved Adoree off to another section of the terrace, where they met with a group of middle-aged couples. I wondered if she knew I was at the dinner. Or if she cared.

"Billy, what are you doing here?"

It was Karma, approaching quickly and with purpose.

"Hi, Ka—"

"This is my beat, Billy," she hissed. "They shouldn't have sent you."

"Nobody sent me," I said. "I'm here as a guest."

"Oh." She stared at me, apparently trying to decide if I was telling her the truth. "Guest of whom?"

"Not that it's any of your business, but Derek invited me."

"Oh," she said again.

Then, as if the mention of his name had drawn him to us, Derek was there, pumping my hand and saying, "Glad you came, Billy. I see you know Karm—. Of course you do. You guys work together."

"More or less," I said.

"And who's this guy?" he said, referencing Dal. "He looks like that Irish actor Donal Logue."

After I introduced them, Dal told Derek, "Not Irish and not an actor. I'm in security."

"Oh." Derek looked from Dal to the bodyguard he'd hired, J.B., then to me. "I get it," he said. "But I think we're pretty safe here."

"Unless you consider all those skyscrapers across the river as potential cover for a sniper," J.B. said. "With all those windows, they could be looking down at us right now through a scope on an AW-fifty."

"That's what I've always loved about you, J.B.," Dal said. "Your positive outlook."

She turned to me and suddenly stuck her forefinger into my chest. "And whose positive idea was it to put Billy in this lumpy Kevlar vest?"

"Excuse me, kids," Webber said, "but I'd better get the ball rolling here."

"Why don't I join you?" Karma said, grabbing his arm, not waiting for an answer.

"I know Madeleine," Carrie said. "Your red-headed friend is in more danger than we are."

I looked at the buildings J.B. had mentioned. And

the windows. And I wondered if that was true. The vest offered some comfort, but in every movie I'd ever seen on the subject, a red laser dot appeared on the victim's forehead just before the sniper invariably went for the head shot.

Chapter
THIRTY-FIVE

When Carrie went off to her media interviews, with J.B. hovering after, I suggested to Dal that we move inside the building.

"Don't let what J.B. said get under your skin, Billy. We're not exactly in Afghanistan."

"Of course not," I said. "I just want to get another martini."

Part of that was the truth. I needed a little liquid fortitude if I was going to be having dinner in the open under God, the stars, and any possible number of snipers.

"If you're worried," Dal continued, as we waited for the bartender to do his thing, "we can eat in here."

I was definitely worried, but not enough to spend the rest of my time in Chicago hiding. Still, when we went back out on the terrace, I suggested we sit at an empty table where a row of imitation ficus trees offered at least a degree of cover.

"If you're all set here," Dal said, when I was seated, "I'm gonna go check in with the boss."

"Go," I said, and settled back, sipping my martini and watching the lights of the city turn the river into an ever-changing Rorschach.

Partially mesmerized by the shimmering water, I nearly jumped into it when I felt a tap on my shoulder.

I whipped my head around to find Adoree standing beside my chair.

"Billy, I startled you," she said. "I am so sorry."

"Nothing to be sorry about," I said, getting to my feet awkwardly. "It's great to see you."

I leaned forward and kissed her cheek.

"Please sit," I said, pulling out a chair for her.

She didn't sit. "I believe you know these gentlemen," she said. Standing just behind her were Charlie Dann the Puff Potato Man and his brother-in-law, Jon Baker. Charlie was dressed casually in a camel hair sport coat, a pale blue shirt, and chocolate trousers. Jon was in another beautifully tailored dark suit, with a white shirt and red power tie.

"Hi, Billy," Jon said, offering his hand. "This beautiful lady insisted on coming over here, even though we were charming the heck out of her without your help."

I shook his hand and then Charlie Dann's.

"Please join me," I said.

The two men waited for Adoree to sit, but she remained standing. "I have to go meet with the television and news people now."

"Come back after," I said.

"Of course. Save a place for me for dinner, please."

"She's quite a gal," Charlie said, taking a seat as we watched her move across the terrace.

"Very savvy about the food business," Jon said. "Her sister's partnered in a restaurant in Marseilles. But I guess you knew that."

As a matter of fact I didn't know very much about Adoree at all. But I merely smiled.

"Is Jonny here tonight?" I asked.

"No. He, ah . . . He's got his TV shows at night. I was hoping Jonny's brother, Dickie, might join us, but he's out at the plant, checking on something or other. The kid's all business. I sure wasn't at his age."

I noticed Dal standing at the entrance to the terrace, surveying the buildings across the river. Trying to ignore the chill on the back of my neck, I asked, "What do you produce at the plant?"

"The one where Dickie is? Farm equipment. He's checking on overtime production."

"Jon manufactures all sorts of stuff," Charlie said. "Cellphones. Semiconductors. The Bakers Best line of cooking products, which you may have heard of. Exercise machines. All this in addition to construction and real estate. Hell, with all the building, he's changing the face of Chicago."

The phrase was far from original, but there was something. . . .

"My brother-in-law is better than the press agents I hire," Jon said, with a smile. "The one business I'm not in yet is the one responsible for our dinner tonight."

"This restaurant?" Charlie asked.

"No. I want a few branches of our host's money tree. Instapicks. Derek's a tougher businessman than

I am, but I'm persistent. I'll wear him down. What about you, Billy? You're not a guy who stands still. An entertainer with your own restaurant, frozen foods, books. That's nice, but wouldn't you like a stake in the new gold rush?"

That reminded me of the offer from Restaurants International that could be a game changer, financially speaking. "You offering me a piece of your action, Jon?"

His grin grew wider. "No, sir," he said. "The only people getting a piece of my action are my boys."

The conversation went on like that while the terrace became more and more crowded and noisy and the night sky darkened. Carrie and J.B. sat at a table not far from the entrance. Dal eventually joined us, along with two Chicago Cubs teammates and their wives who knew Charlie and were devotees of his establishment.

Dinner was just being served when Adoree returned. I'd reserved the chair on my left for her. I introduced her to the newcomers to the table and sat back and watched her as she easily became the center of attention, answering their questions with grace and charm.

Yes, she loved America. In fact, her grandfather had been an American, a World War Two GI who'd fallen in love with a Parisienne and decided to return to her after the war. Adoree was diplomatic enough not to mention why he'd chosen to remain an expatriate in Paris with his white wife.

Her father had been something of a rogue, a professional gambler, who, during her and her elder sister's youth, had settled for a moderate but more secure income by working for casinos in Paris and Monte Carlo. The family had been well off enough for her sister, Jeanne, to attend Ecole de Cordon Bleu and for Adoree to study at the Conservatoire Supérieur d'art Dramatique, where she had been one of only three young women of color.

The dinner was fine, I suppose. But in Adoree's company, the enjoyment of food took second place, even when the appetizer was crab bisque made with coconut milk and the main course was New York steak with béarnaise sauce.

"The food is delicious, no?" she asked.

My plate was almost clean. Hers looked as if she'd barely touched it. "You should try some," I said.

"But I've tried it all. It is very good."

"I guess it must be that *French Women Don't Get Fat* way of eating," I said.

"Oh, that book? No, no. My habit of eating is more flexible than that. I . . . have no appetite when I am without a lover."

I heard Dal make an odd choking sound, which confirmed my suspicion that he was bending an ear our way. Ignoring that, I said, "And when you have a lover?"

"I am ravenous. I am as hungry as a dog."

"A horse," I said, without thinking.

She frowned. " You think I resemble a horse?"

"No. Not at all. I . . . It's the idiom. 'Hungry as a horse.' Or maybe 'Hungry as a bear.' I've never heard 'Hungry as a dog.' But I guess it works."

She continued to frown.

The young woman who'd greeted us at the door approached our table. She told Adoree that Derek

was about to say a few words to the guests and
wanted the cast with him.

"Excuse me," Adoree said brusquely, adding,
when I pushed my chair back, "Please do not get up."

And she was gone.

Dal was shaking his head. "Speaking of horses,"
he said. "The ass of a horse, that would be you."

"Thanks for your support," I said.

"Lady's an actress," he said. "Anything other than
a compliment is an insult."

Had what I said been that terrible? Not even
the arrival of dessert—*mousse chocolat caramel*—
brought me out of my funk.

With Derek and the cast assembling and several
camera crews setting up their special lights, I pushed
back my chair and stood.

"Going to apologize?" Dal asked.

"I'm going to the men's room," I said. "If it's all
right with you."

"It's your bladder," he said.

Crossing the terrace, I saw Derek make some comment that seemed to amuse the actors around him.
Adoree was laughing.

Maybe I was overthinking the whole thing, mis-
reading her reaction. Even if she thought I was calling
her a horse, how bad was that? Horses were handsome animals, right? Hadn't some famous artist
called attention to Katharine Hepburn's equine pro-
file?

I was still focused on my little faux pas when I
emerged from the men's room stall and began wash-
ing my hands at the row of basins. It took me a moment to realize something was off in the room. I

raised my eyes from my wet but now immaculate hands and, in the mirror, saw two men standing a few feet behind me. Staring at me. My old kidnapping pals—Ace and C-man.

I turned to face them.

They'd dressed for the occasion. Ace had traded in his country-boy duds for cleaned and pressed khaki pants and a bright yellow T-shirt that read: "She's with Stupid." C-man's bombardier jacket had been replaced by a black-and-white checked sport coat. I'd thought that he looked familiar the last time we'd met. Seeing him in the sport coat brought that into focus.

"Why were you in the audience at the Gemma Bright show?" I asked him. "A fan of Gemma's? No, I bet you were a fan of Pat Patton's."

He stared at me.

His coat bulged a little over his heart. He removed the bulge and pointed it at me. "I think we'll just pick up where we left off," he said. "With you coming with us to our van."

I have to admit that even though he was aiming the gun at my chest, the Kevlar vest didn't make me feel any less frightened.

"That reminds me," he said. He took a step forward and smashed the gun against the side of my head.

So much for the value of the vest.

First came shock, followed by loss of equilibrium, followed by pain.

My knees gave. I tried to grab the washbasin, but it was too smooth, and I slid to the tile floor. Head spinning, eyes out of focus.

"Get up," he shouted. A silly request, since he'd made it a physical impossibility.

"Chri' Pete, why'd you hit him, C-man?" Ace said.

"Payback for the knock his pal gave me. I got a bump big as an egg." What seemed to me like two C-men leaned down and shouted, "Stand the fuck up!"

I tried, but my legs were rubber.

"Get him up, Ace."

"An' then what?"

"Then you carry him out."

"Me and what derrick?" Ace said.

"Okay, c'mon. You take one arm, I'll take the other."

They were bent over, trying to pick me up, when the bathroom door opened and Dal stepped in.

C-man dropped me and, as I fell back down, dragging Ace with me, swung his gun around to aim it at Dal.

My bodyguard was a little too fast for that. He grabbed C-man's wrist, bringing it up behind his back with an ugly cracking sound. The gun clattered against the tile as Dal swung the unfortunate C-man face-first into a porcelain basin.

Ace scurried out from under me in time to see his partner's damaged nose sending a spray of blood across the tiles where he'd fallen. He got one step toward the door when Dal grabbed him by the collar of his T-shirt and yanked him backward off his feet. He hit the tile with butt, back, and head, in that order.

Dal grabbed my arm and lifted me. "How you doing?" he asked.

"Better than them," I said.

"Can you walk?"

"Give me a minute."

"That's all we've got. Our host is about finished doing his thing out there, and this place is going to see a whole lot of traffic." While he talked, he searched the pockets of the unconscious men.

"Wallets. Car keys. No phones."

"Maybe in their van," I said.

"No time to check, even if we knew where they parked it. I'd really love to chat up one of these a-holes about their employer, but that's not gonna happen. At least not right now." He slipped the wallets into his coat pocket. "You ready?"

My head ached and I was still woozy. I took a tentative step, and my legs seemed to be working again. "Ready," I said.

Dal looked down at the sprawled, bleeding C-man and kicked him in the stomach, without much reaction. "Bastard's lucky he didn't do anything to make me mad," he said.

Our timing was right. Derek's after-dinner display had just ended, and people were moving quickly in the direction of the restrooms. I caught a glimpse of Adoree talking with an outwardly appeased Madeleine Parnelle.

"It seems rude to leave without saying goodbye," I said.

Dal made a horse-whicker noise and shook his head. He whispered, "Save the romance for later.

We—Make that *I*—don't want to be anywhere near here when the cops come."

I took one more look at Adoree and followed Dal out.

Chapter
THIRTY-SIX

It had been quite a day.

Between the interview with the naked housewives on *Wake Up* and the moment at ten-thirty p.m. when I settled back on the soft chair at my hotel with an ice pack, a couple of aspirin, and a glass of water, I'd been kidnapped and rescued, almost shot in a South Side bar, hit with a gun ("gun-whipped" was the term Dal used), and nearly kidnapped again.

And all I could think about was the dumb thing I'd said to Adoree.

Pressing the ice against my throbbing skull, I washed down the pills and was wondering if I should call her when Dal said, "Want to take a look at this stuff?"

He was sitting at a flyleaf table that he'd opened up to spread the contents of the two wallets he'd taken from the hard-luck kidnappers. There wasn't much. Several hundred dollars in cash. No credit cards. No photos. No receipts. The only personal items were the driver's licenses. According to one,

Ace was Ashton Paul Killinek, a twenty-seven-year-old, six-foot-two, 172-pound blond male with blue eyes who lived at an address Dal said was near O'Hare Airport.

C-man was Claus Dieter Heinz, a thirty-five-year-old, five-foot-nine, 159-pound male with brown hair and brown eyes who lived in Evanston.

Dal had found another card, which he tossed onto the table. It identified Heinz as a private investigator licensed by the state.

"Heinz is a private eye?"

Dal responded with a derisive snort. "Like that's a step up from kidnapper? It just means it should be easier to get our hands on him again."

"What else do we have?"

"That's it. I wonder how long before the cops release 'em."

"They may not even be arrested," I said. "They might seem more like victims, the condition they were in."

"That's why I left their guns. Since we have their wallets, I know they're not carrying FOID cards."

"FOID cards being . . . ?"

"Firearm Owner's ID cards," Dal said. "Very big in this state."

"I'm going to bed," I told him. "You should, too. I have to be at Millennium Park by five-thirty a.m."

"You're shitting me! Five-thirty?"

"I'll be up at four-thirty," I said. "Want me to wake you then? Or would you rather loll around until four-forty-five?"

Chapter
THIRTY-SEVEN

"I can't find my shoes," Dal said, at approximately five a.m., just after I'd shaken him partially awake.

He was lying on the couch that he'd converted into a bed, reaching over to pat the carpet nearby, searching.

"Open your eyes," I said. I was without mercy. My head was sore and, though the ice may have kept the swelling down, there was a lump where the pistol had connected that looked like a stunted devil horn.

"Okay," Dal said. "My eyes are open."

"Now look down the length of your body. See? You're wearing your shoes. And your pants and shirt. You must've slept in them last night."

"Right," he said, rolling over to go back to sleep.

I considered dousing him with water.

By five-twenty-five, he was upright and more or less dressed in fresh clothes. His hair, still wet, hung down on his face, giving him the look of a Viking who'd been caught in the rain. "It's still dark out," he complained.

"How late was it when you got to sleep last night?" I handed him a cup of freshly brewed black coffee.

"Very. Mantata was pissed because I woke him up, so he got back at me by talking for over an hour."

He took a gulp of the coffee, winced at its heat, and put the cup on a table.

"I told you it was too late to call him," I said.

"It's his standing order that we let him know about things like the bathroom incident in, to use his words, a timely manner. He said he was going to check with his source at the CPD to find out what happened to Killinek and Heinz. And by now he's probably got somebody running down the addresses on the licenses. Whatever else he is, the old bastard's efficient."

Dal stood. He stretched, cleared his throat, and said, "Okay, Billy, you got me up. You threw water on me and burned my mouth with hot coffee. What's next on your torture list: Making me watch your show?" Ouch.

It wasn't bad, as shows go.

The highlight for me was a segment of Karma's featuring an excellent local singer who was promoting an upcoming swing festival in the city. In spite of our charming entertainment reporter's obvious disregard for the style of music ("Isn't swing sort of old-fashioned?"), the singer managed to remain upbeat and cheery. She'd brought along a seasoned trio, and they performed two of my favorite songs, both by Billy Strayhorn, "Lush Life" and "Take the 'A' Train."

Afterward, I caught up with Karma just as she began ranting to Trina about not wanting "to be stuck with any more nostalgia shit. Let Lance do it. It's more his age bracket, anyway."

"Let me explain something," our producer replied. "Lance Tuttle is a respected television journalist who interviews politicians, major celebrities, and, yes, what you call nostalgia shit, if and when he wishes. You, on the other hand, are a twit with big boobs, good hair and teeth, who interviews whomever I decide."

"You"—Karma's face reddened as she tried to think of the ultimate squelch—"liberal," she said, with hauteur, and departed.

"Aw, snap!" Trina said, then turned to me. "What do you want, Billy?"

"To talk to the twit," I said, and ran after Karma.

"My hair isn't good," she said, when I caught up with her, "it's great. Everybody says so."

"And your boobs aren't just big," I said, "they are spectacular, to quote the immortal line from *Seinfeld*."

"What do you want, Billy? And what the heck happened to your head?"

"A spider bit me," I said. "How late did you stay at the party last night?"

"I was there past the bitter end, with Sandford and Austin," the *Thief* movie's leading man and director. She squinted her eyes. "A spider? I hate spiders."

"I heard there was some kind of ruckus just as the party was ending."

She gave me a blank look. Well, blanker than usual. "What do you mean?"

"I don't know. Maybe police showing up?"

"Not that I saw."

"No ambulance?" I asked, thinking of the condition of the two men.

"Ambulance? Police? For Christ's sake, Billy. If there'd been anything like that, I'd have got my cameraman all over it. I'm not an idiot."

I thanked her for her kindness and was walking away when she said, "Are you talking about the drunks?"

"Maybe," I said.

"Well, when Derek finished his pitch on behalf of the movie, two of the guests who'd had too much to drink got into a little fight in the men's loo. They had to be helped to their car."

"Who helped them?"

"Derek and a couple of the other guests."

"Tell me about the other guests."

"What's to tell? Two of them. Just guys. They weren't celebrities."

"What'd they look like?"

"Who knows?"

"What were they wearing?"

"Who cares? Like I said, they weren't celebrities."

"Give it a little thought. It's important."

"Fuck you. I'm busy."

I watched her go, although I'd rather have kicked her in the butt. And it was a nice butt. Went with the good teeth and big boobs.

Dal was sitting on a camp chair in our little makeshift office, phone to his ear. "Can you pause that?" I asked him.

He said something into the phone and lowered it, staring at me.

I relayed the information I'd extracted from

Karma. He frowned, lifted the phone to his ear, and said, "Call you later." To me, he said, "Did she say—"

He was interrupted by Kiki rushing in, cursing me for hiding from her, and announcing I had twenty seconds to my interview with Willard Mitry, the author of *Da Mare*.

"I'll be back in a few minutes," I told Dal, and departed for the set, quick-scanning the notes I'd made on the book.

Mitry, a burly guy in his fifties with a mainly gray buzz cut and a matching mustache-Vandyke beard combination, was sitting before a camera, rigid as a wooden plank. He relaxed only slightly when I sat down beside him, freshly miked.

"They couldn't find you," he said, when we'd shaken hands. "The guy in the Hawaiian shirt said they might have to cancel the interview."

"That's just his way of relaxing the guests," I said. "Everything's okay. All we have to do is . . ."

I heard Gin McCauley introducing us. The camera directly in front of us blinked red. And we went live.

Fourteen minutes later, the network was peddling a diabetes product and Willard Mitry was being relieved of his mike. "On the air you mentioned your new project is a history of Chicago's gangs," I said.

"Right. *Gangland, Illinois* is the tentative title."

"That seems to be a hot topic these days."

"What do you mean?" he asked.

"Derek Webber is hoping to launch a television series about the gangs."

"Oh, yeah." He was obviously relieved. "I thought

you were talking about another book. I'm aware of Webber's project. When he heard I was researching the book, he wanted me to meet with him. My agent said no."

"Even before he heard the offer?"

"Jeb, my agent, Jeb Matthias, is probably a little conservative, but he's not a big fan of Webber's."

"He have a specific problem?"

"He doesn't trust the guy."

"Is that because of the stuff Pat Patton said about Webber?"

"Not at all. Nobody with any intelligence paid attention to Patton's rants. But speaking of Patton, that's gonna be one hell of a story when they find out who killed him. I bet it's Mob-related. Even way back, when I was starting out at the *Trib,* there were rumors that Patton was in Joe Nagall's back pocket."

That name rang a not-too-distant bell. Mantata had mentioned that Louis Venici, the man who'd killed Paul Lamont, had worked for Nagall. I longed to ask Mitry about Paul's death, but I didn't want him to wonder about my interest. Instead, I asked how Patton managed to keep moving up in the CPD.

"Like I said, there were rumors, no proof. And he wasn't the only cop on the . . . I think your assistant is looking for you."

I turned to see Kiki charging toward us. "Damn it, Billy, don't make me keep chasing you. It's 'Goofy News' time."

That was one of my newer segments, prompted by a friend of our CEO who mentioned over dinner that the news was simply too dreary. To combat that, and just maybe to grab some of that successful *Daily*

Show vibe, I was now, in addition to my other duties, the "Goofy News" reporter, essentially a voice-over chore accompanying odd people, things, and events captured on film. Edward R. Murrow would be proud.

"Gotta go, Willard," I said, "but I'd like to continue our conversation. Any chance you might be free for lunch?"

"I'm on Gemma Bright's show at noon, but I'll be out around one."

"Great," I said. "I'll meet you at the studio."

Chapter
THIRTY-EIGHT

The news was not particularly goofy that morning. A dog and a duck did a dance. A Brunhilda-type opera singer fell into the orchestra pit in the middle of an aria. A robber making his getaway from a bank tripped on his shoestrings, fell, and knocked himself out. Though to some it may have been the apex of hilarity, it didn't do much to counteract the real news about another rise in unemployment, more discord in the Middle East, and more gridlock in Congress.

But, looking at the positive side, it completed my work for the day.

Kiki was alone in the mini-office. "It's a lovely morning, don't you think?" she asked.

"Bright and beautiful," I said, staring at her.

"Sorry if I seemed angry before."

"No problem," I said. "What's going on?"

"Going on? Oh, you mean your schedule tomorrow." She consulted a sheet of paper. "At six-fifteen, you're interviewing a sausage maker named Armand Hutner."

"I mean what's going on with you?"

"I don't know what you're talking about."

"It's the first time, to my knowledge, that you've ever apologized for anything. I'm guessing you've met someone new."

"No. Well, Richard did call and invite me to dinner tonight."

"Richard being the guy who picked you up at the hotel?"

"I wish you wouldn't put it that way. But yes. That Richard."

"Good. I'm happy for you. Did you say I'm working at six-fifteen tomorrow morning?"

"With a sausage maker."

"Then I'm not booked on *Hotline Tonight*?"

"The whole show is going to be about the floods in California," she said.

"Floods in California?"

"Don't take this as criticism, Billy, but you could pay a little more attention to the news."

"Lady, I'm the go-to guy for news. Of course it's 'Goofy News.' "

Ordinarily that would have prompted an eye roll. Instead, she smiled. The power of Richard.

"Where's Dal?" I asked.

She returned to her notes. "He had to go. Said he'll call you later."

"Didn't say where he was going?"

"Nope," she replied.

I settled onto the campaign chair and dialed Dal's number. He answered on the second ring.

"What's up?" I asked.

"I'm at the gallery," he said. "Somebody broke in during the night. Doesn't look like anything was taken. Mantata wants me to stick around here and help him go over the place. Make sure they didn't leave a little surprise."

"A bomb, you mean?"

"I was thinking a bug. A bomb? Jesus, you're morbid. You finished there?"

"Let me find out." I looked at Kiki. "Am I finished here?"

"Meeting at ten," she said. "Then free as a bird."

I passed that news on to Dal, telling him I'd call when the meeting wound down.

Since our ratings hadn't had the surge our visits to Chicago had experienced in palmier days, it was less a meeting than an ass chewing. It lasted until after eleven, at which time I phoned Dal.

"Hiho's gonna pick you up, Billy. He'll be on the corner of Michigan and Randolph in fifteen minutes."

I'd been looking for a big white Escalade. Hiho had to hit the horn of the sleek, maroon Nissan to get my attention.

"Zeke did a good job," I said, buckling up on the passenger seat.

"Always does," the diminutive Portuguese said.

He was dressed in tan. Tan suit, pointed tan suede shoes, tan-and-white checked shirt. And a chocolate velvet hat with a tan band. "See something funny?" he asked.

"No," I said, squelching a grin.

Neither of us said another word for the rest of the drive.

The door at the rear of the gallery was locked. "When I left, was a guy here changing the lock," Hiho said. "Guess we gotta go around to the front."

As we circled the building, he added, "Gallery closed for the day. Mantata sent everybody home, except me and Dal. And the less-than-worthless guard."

The front door was locked, too. A sign echoed Hiho's comment about the gallery being closed. The security guard Dal had called Oakley was sitting at his desk near the glass door, staring at his cellular phone.

Hiho knocked on the door.

Oakley looked up, scowling. He stayed seated.

"Lout bastard," Hiho shouted. "Get off yoah ass and open the fucking door."

Begrudgingly, Oakley rose and walked toward us as slowly as if he were doing a Willie Best imitation. He unlocked the door, and Hiho pushed through it, nearly knocking the guard over.

"Little punk ass," Oakley mumbled.

Hiho wheeled on him, a thin knife sliding from his

cuff into his right hand. "I should gut you like a perch," he said.

"Lose the blade, Hiho," Dal ordered. He was standing near the door to the gallery's display area.

Hiho hesitated briefly, then literally made the knife disappear up his sleeve. "Just wanted to show the clown who's boss," he said, strutting toward Dal.

"No way that little Karate Kid's my boss," Oakley mumbled.

If Hiho heard him, he didn't react.

Mantata was obviously upset by the break-in.

His white hair was mussed, his lime-colored suit was in disarray, and his mood was testy. "I don't like this," he said. "It shows a lack of respect."

"They came in the back door," Dal said.

He and Hiho were sitting on the couch. I was on a chair beside Mantata's desk.

"I didn't see any damage to the door," I said.

"There's the rub," Mantata said. "There was no sign of force, not even the scratch of a pick. The only conclusion is that somehow the intruders possessed a key."

"Hell, boss," Hiho said. "You never even gave *me* a key."

"There are very few keys extant, which may help in identifying the Judas."

"Oakley have a key?" Dal asked.

"He's the kind of fucker who'd do it, boss," Hiho chimed in.

Mantata raised one white eyebrow. "Do either of

you have any substantive reason to think Oakley might be our traitor?"

"He's got no class," Hiho said. He hopped from his chair. "Lemme go get the bastard. We'll sweat the truth out of him."

"Sit!" Mantata commanded. "If by some chance Oakley is the culprit, it would be foolish to let him know he is suspect."

"Friends close but enemies closer, huh?" Dal asked.

"Very good. Do you know the source of the quote?"

"Michael Corleone," Dal replied, with a smirk.

"Perhaps. I would have thought Sun Tzu or Machiavelli," Mantata said. "In any case, we shall keep an eye on Oakley."

"It's possible the intruder didn't need a key," I said. "There are lock guys who can open any door without leaving evidence."

"It's not just the lock. Only I know the code that turns off the alarm, but the violators knew enough about the system to disengage it by force. And they knew the locations of the security cameras. We have several views of the back of their heads, but not one identifying shot. However, the cameras do tell us that they entered at a little after three and left approximately forty-five minutes later."

"How many?"

"Two. One short, one tall."

"Could be the same two who killed Patton."

"And tried to kill Billy and Patton's assistant," Dal said.

"Well, whoever they were, it will be difficult for

them to return," Mantata said. "The locks have already been changed."

"There was no reason for them to be in any hurry, but they left after only forty-five minutes," I said. "That seems to suggest mission accomplished. Is there anything missing?"

"Nothing, as best I can tell. Dal and I have found no evidence of bugs. A professional will be here shortly, to make sure."

He stared at me. "Since the break-in has occurred during a period when my only . . . extraordinary activity is on your behalf, Billy, I am assuming that to be the reason. The one thing in the building that might add to their knowledge on that point was here in this office, apparently untouched."

"What is it?"

He plucked something from the coffee table he used for a desk, a small, thin clear plastic box containing a mini-disk. "This digital recording of a conversation I had with Mr. James C. Yountz."

"Pat Patton's lawyer," I said.

"I was curious about his client's claim re Mr. Webber's financing. Mr. Yountz assured me that it was not manufactured out of whole cloth. Mr. Patton told him he had proof that Onion City Entertainment was in part financed by Outfit money."

"What was the proof?"

"Mr. Patton was not generous enough to provide him with that information. He thought that whatever it was might be in a bin Mr. Patton rented at Secombe's Storage. The police were sifting through its contents, but, as Mr. Patton's executor, he—Mr.

Yountz—would get a look for himself when they were finished."

"By then the police will probably have found whatever it was," I said. "Unless someone removed it shortly after Patton's murder."

I told them about the red files that Nat Parkins and Larry Kelsto had removed from the storage bin.

"You're sure Mr. Parkins actually possesses the files?" Mantata asked. When I nodded, he said, "Well, I assume he is still in need of cash. He'll call you again. Unless he's dead, of course. In which case, all is lost."

I turned to Dal. "Anything new about the two guys you roughed up at Pastiche?"

"Trejean's running down their addresses," Dal said. "Heinz moved out of the one on his licenses four years ago. Killinek didn't strike me as a long-term occupant, either. But you never know."

"So your associate saw Derek Webber helping them to their car," Mantata said. "I assume, Billy, you will no longer feel compelled to defend the man."

"He's too young to be Gio Polvere."

Mantata's eyes flickered to a Post-it on the table, then returned to me. "That is only significant if one believes in fantasies."

I felt my face heating up. Maybe anger, maybe embarrassment.

"Can you think of any reason Derek Webber may want you dead?"

"No. There's no past history. I just met the man two days ago. And I like him."

The old man considered that and changed directions. "It's nearing lunchtime," he said, "and I'm feeling peckish."

I glanced at the Post-it. There was just one word written on it: "flour."

"I'm thinking a nice submarine sandwich," Mantata said.

"I have a lunch date in about forty-five minutes," I said.

"Not with Mr. Webber?"

"No. An ex–*Trib* reporter who's written a book called *Da Mare*. His name is—"

"I am familiar with Mr. Mitry," Mantata said.

Of course he was. Mitry had been a crime reporter, and he was currently writing a book on gangland Chicago.

"I am sure you will be the soul of discretion, should my name come up during your luncheon chat."

"Absolutely. Mainly, I'll be listening. Mitry says he knows a lot about Patton's CPD history. He said Patton was taking bribes from Joe Nagall. And, as you told me, Venici worked for him."

"Nagall," the old man said and nodded. "Joe Ferriola, a very violent fellow. Very feared and respected."

"Whoa. How did we get from Nagall to Ferriola?"

"The I-ties all used a variety of names. Joe Ferriola was Nagall's real name. He was the boss of the Cicero crew."

A variety of names.

Mantata was smiling, as if struck by a pleasant memory. "Joe was an enforcer for Momo."

Momo. Sam Giancana. Mantata's pal. The guy rumored to have won Chicago, and the election, for

John Kennedy. But that wasn't what was piquing my interest.

"Paul's body was found in Cicero," I said, "where Louis Venici worked for Ferriola. If these guys had several names . . . ?"

He averted his eyes. "The records have Polvere dying in 1987. Ferriola died two years later. The thing the two men definitely have in common is that they're both dead. As is everyone involved in Paul's death, apparently."

"Then why is somebody trying to kill me?"

Mantata shook his head. "I don't know."

Why did I think he was lying?

He turned to Hiho. "Pick up some sandwiches from Graziano's. Just for you, Dal, and myself. Billy's got a luncheon date."

Hiho frowned. "The parking on Randolph . . ."

"Dal will go with and run in for the food."

Dal replied with a you-really-want-me-to-be-your-lunch-boy? scowl of disappointment. But he obediently followed Hiho from the room.

As soon as they'd gone, Mantata said, "There's something I've discovered about your good friend Mr. Webber."

"I'd like to know more about Ferriola and the Cicero crew," I said.

"There are times when the past has to bow to the present," he said. "Did you know that Instapicks International is now located in Ireland?"

"I thought it was in Winnetka."

"That's where the work is done. But the company is registered in Dublin, where the tax rate is a mere twelve-point-five percent."

"I saw something about this kind of thing on *60 Minutes*. It's an exploitation of a tax loophole."

"Precisely. Business can be conducted here, but the money is overseas."

"It is legal, right?" I asked.

"Absolutely."

"I don't see what that has to do with anything."

Mantata got to his feet. He seemed suddenly very old. He began gathering the scattered papers on the coffee table. "I'd better clear space for lunch," he said.

"What exactly are you trying to tell me, Mantata?"

He paused and considered the question. "I can't speak for people like Mr. Capone or Mr. Giancana as to why they chose to go against society's grain. I did it because it seemed the only way to achieve anything in a country where all the doors were closed to me. I was smart enough to know that being smart wasn't enough. I needed the power to gain the kind of freedom that allowed me to use my intelligence. There were many things I did of which I am not proud, but I achieved my goal."

"You don't have to—"

"This is not a confession, Billy. It's an . . . admission. There was a time when a wave of my hand could get a candidate elected to mayor of this city. Now I'm a toothless old lion who can't even keep the jackals from his cave."

"It was just a break-in," I said.

"It would have been, if they had not had a key and if the gallery was owned by an ordinary business-man. My point of this private chat, Billy, is that we're dealing with people who are more powerful than I'd thought. In my arrogance, I assumed I could keep you safe. I no longer believe that. I suggest you employ a reliable security firm."

"Dal seems to be handling the job," I said.

He smiled. "We have arrived at a time in this country's history when the real-life Monopoly game is heading toward its conclusion. The small group of ultra-rich winners has amassed nearly all of the property and money on the board. They can buy or destroy whomever they choose. Supreme Court justices, FBI agents, politicians, cops. Even presidents. When the cost of a gallon of gasoline is five dollars, men like Dal or Hiho or Trejean, no matter how loyal, will always have their price."

"You think one of them is responsible for the break-in?"

"Someone I trusted was."

"Maybe it's your guard, Oakley," I said.

"Though the others are not aware of it, Oakley is my great-nephew. He's no work wizard, but he's kept his nose clean and, according to my grandniece, he even goes to church on Sundays. I don't see him selling me out, but, the times being what they are, all things are possible."

"Well, Dal's rescued me twice," I said. "I'd just as soon stick with him."

"It's your decision, Billy," he said. "But bear in mind: Dal, Trejean, Hiho, and I are all sociopaths."

Chapter
THIRTY-NINE

Gemma Bright's show had just ended when Hiho braked the Nissan Z near the entrance to WWBC. Leaving him to deal with the illegally parked car, I worked my way through the crowd of departing ladies. Each was lugging a copy of the massive *Da Mare*.

Willard Mitry was still onstage, getting de-miked. But it was another of the show's guests who caught my eye: Adoree, engaged in conversation with Gemma and a woman with too much makeup whom I didn't recognize.

Gemma, whose roving eyes covered more territory than radar, was the first to spot me. "Billy!" she exclaimed, waving me forward.

I suppose Mitry must have turned in my direction, but I wasn't staring at him. Adoree was regarding me without expression.

"Adoree, you *must* meet Billy Blessing," Gemma said.

"We've met," Adoree said.

"Lovely of you to drop *by*, Billy," Gemma said. "Oh, and this is Will—"

"Billy interviewed me this morning," Mitry said.

"If you'll excuse me, I have to run," Adoree said. Without waiting for a reply, she turned and began walking away, followed by the woman in excessive makeup.

"Give me a minute," I said to Mitry and Gemma, and ran after them, catching up as they entered the greenroom.

"Adoree . . . ," I began.

She turned. "I'm in something of a rush, Billy."

"I'm Candy Mott, with RDL Publicity, Chef Blessing," the woman with Adoree said, extending her hand. "We're handling prepub on the film."

"A pleasure," I said, shaking her hand. "Could you give us a minute, Ms. Mott?"

"Not more than that," she said, walking away. "We have a key luncheon."

Momentarily alone, Adoree said, "Well, Billy?"

"Evidently I did something to upset you last night," I said. "I wanted to apologize."

"Fine," she said. "Apology accepted."

She turned to go.

"Wait. Clearly I've offended you, and I—"

"You disappeared last night," she said. "I was disappointed when you did not return. But that was probably a good thing. I do not need to make any more mistakes with men of your type."

"I didn't return because . . ." I paused before I could get the lie out of my mouth. "Men of my type? What the heck are you talking about?"

"Of course you would deny it."

"Deny what?" I realized I was shouting.

"You are a *voleur*. A thief."

"I'm a chef. I feed people. I entertain people. I do not rob people."

"Ah. Now, perhaps, you are a chef. *Mais vous êtes dans les rues a faire ses combines.*"

"I don't know what that means."

"You were—how do you say?—a hustler on the streets."

"Who told you this?"

"No one told me. I . . . overheard a discussion."

"A discussion about me? At the dinner last night?"

"It does not matter when or where. Do you deny you were a *criminel*?"

I hesitated, then replied, "No. I won't deny it."

"*Soit!*"

"No. Not *soit*! It was more than twenty-five years ago. Adoree, it's very important I know who was talking about my past."

"Why, if they spoke the truth?"

"Because their knowledge of things I've done may mean they are criminals themselves."

She smiled. "Now you are making fun of me."

"I'm serious," I said. "Do they know you overheard them?"

"I . . . I don't believe so. They were helping one of the guests into a car in the garage. I was sitting in another car, awaiting . . . someone."

"Listen to me. You must not let them know you overheard them. It could be dangerous for you."

"You're frightening me with this silly game, Billy. *J'en ai assez!*"

"It's no game," I said. "For both our sakes, tell me who they are."

And Candy Mott picked that perfect moment to return. "Sorry, Adoree. We have to go."

"*Au revoir,* Billy," Adoree said.

"I'll call you," I said.

She merely shook her head from side to side.

And was gone.

Chapter
FORTY

Willard Mitry and I had lunch at Terzo Piano, the antiseptic white-and-gray, sunlight-freshened restaurant located in the Art Institute.

Thanks to his stockpile of intriguing anecdotes, a lamb burger grilled to perfection and stuffed with goat cheese, and a formidable pile of hand-cut french fries, I had almost recovered from Adoree's rejection. Not to mention her potentially perilous situation. Especially if Derek Webber was the guy who'd been talking about me.

Well, maybe I hadn't recovered.

"You okay, Billy?" Mitry asked.

"Fine. I was just . . . What was it you said about Patton's murder?"

"That it's not even mentioned in the paper anymore. Still, when they find the killer or killers, that's going to be one sweet story. But it probably won't be the *Trib* that breaks it. Hell, it'll probably be TMZ."

"In researching *Gangland, Illinois,* have you come across the name Giovanni Polvere?"

He thought for a few seconds, then withdrew a small reporter's notepad from his jacket pocket. He flipped through several pages filled with tiny crabbed handwriting and paused. "Yeah. He was the Outfit's unofficial CFO during the eighties, starting with the last half of 'Joey Doves' Aiuppa's stint as front boss and continuing through most of Joe Nagall's run."

"Know when he died?"

"Eighty-seven, according to my notes. Went up in a fire. Why?"

"Your research show any direct connection to Patton?"

"Not direct. But as I think I mentioned, the rumor was Patton and Nagall had something going and Polvere was working for Nagall. What's your angle?"

"Suppose Nagall wanted to invest a sizable amount of the Outfit's coin in some scheme or other," I said. "Would he have to involve Polvere?"

"Sizable amount? Probably." Mitry had his head cocked and was looking at me with a half-smile on his face. "What's the story, Billy?"

I was beginning to see what might have happened back then—Paul approaching Venici with one of his cons, then, sensing an even bigger fish, expanding the con and drawing Joseph "Joe Nagall" Ferriola into the net. Ferriola takes the project to Polvere, who's controlling the big funds. And then what? The fact that Paul was killed without the loot suggests that Polvere saw through the scam and ordered his death. Then why were Venici and his cousin killed?

Did the Outfit bump off its minions for stupidity?

Wouldn't that have depleted the ranks long before the government did?

I had the feeling I was just a few pieces shy of the jigsaw puzzle of Paul's murder.

"You're spooking me, Billy," Mitry said. "Usually the food here is pretty good."

"The food's great, Willard. I'm sorry. Just a little distracted."

"It's Polvere, right? Is there something I should know? For the book?"

"Nothing right now. If anything develops, I promise to clue you in."

"Good enough," he said. "Meanwhile, if you're looking for a dessert to talk about on your show, you want to try the gingerbread cake and maple-bourbon ice cream."

"Let's get a couple, and you can tell me why your agent doesn't trust Derek Webber."

The dessert was a dream.

Mitry's agent's report on Webber was, like everything Mantata had turned up, not terribly incriminating and only vaguely supported by fact.

"Jeb didn't say Webber was a crook. Just a shark. The reason he wanted to meet with me was probably to pick my brain. And even if he did make an offer to purchase the film and TV rights of the book, it wouldn't be my talent he'd be buying. It'd be insurance that a rival project wouldn't get launched."

"How wealthy is he?"

"I don't know, but he and his partner, Luchek, are up there with guys like Branson and Malone."

"If they have all this money, why are they going out of their way to court backers for their movie?"

"Because the first rule any of these moguls learn is: Never use your own money."

If Polvere obeyed that rule, that could be the reason he closed down Paul's scam. Or maybe he hadn't thought of the money as his own.

"Know anything about Luchek?" I asked.

"He's not as high-profile as Webber, but I gave them both a Google when they expressed interest in my book. Luchek's family has money. Not as much as he has now."

"What's his father do?"

"He doesn't. He's retired. He was in banking. Mother passed about ten years ago. Alan's got two sisters, both older. One's unmarried, maybe divorced, living in the family home in Winnetka. The other's married and on the East Coast. Philadelphia, maybe."

"You got all that from Google?"

"Google and the sweat of my brow," he said. "I'm . . . I was a reporter, Billy. Research is what we do."

Chapter
FORTY-ONE

Dal arrived at my hotel suite shortly before nine on Thursday night. Kiki, Hiho, and I had just polished off a room-service dinner of pan-fried trout (Kiki);

filet mignon burger, well done (Hiho); and T-bone, rare (me), and were having coffee.

Dal seemed a little jangled and distracted as he passed along Mantata's instructions to Hiho. "He wants you to go home, get a good night's sleep, and pick him up at his place at seven."

"Why so early?"

"Beats me. He commands, I obey."

Hiho had removed his hat and coat for dinner. He retrieved them from the couch and, almost daintily, put them back on. Standing in front of the room's only mirror, he adjusted his hat just so, shaping and smoothing the brim with his hand. "You and the boss worked late, huh?" he asked.

"We had pizza at Uno's, then I dropped him back at the gallery."

"He don't want me to drive him home?"

"Said he'd take a cab."

"A cab? That seem right to you?"

"What do you mean by 'right'?" Dal asked.

"You know. Funny? He didn't seem to be acting like himself."

"Maybe. He's pretty shook up about the break-in."

"That bastard Oakley," Hiho said. Finished with the hat, he turned to Kiki, bowed, and said, "A pleasure meeting you, *madame*."

Then it was my turn. "Thank you for dinner, Billy. I will see you tomorrow."

At the door, he turned to Dal. "Seven in the morning, huh? My eyes will be major puffy."

Kiki left shortly thereafter. "See you earlier than seven, boys," she said.

* * *

Dal and I stayed up long enough for him to tell me that Claus Dieter Heinz's private eye license was legitimate, but his address had changed at least three times since he'd been issued his driver's license, the most recent as yet undiscovered. There had been a one-room office for Heinz Security and Associates on the West Side for eight years, but that had closed over two years ago.

There was no record of a license for his associate Ashton Killinek. The address on his driver's license was no longer valid, though neighbors recalled Ashton and his wife, Anne. The couple's public displays of affection had been either "disgusting" and "lewd" or "really sweet," depending on the eye of the beholder.

Hospitals were being canvassed in hopes of discovering a doctor who'd set Heinz's arm and packed his nose, assuming the broken bones had been attended.

On that note, I headed off to bed.

I didn't hear Dal's phone chirp. What woke me was the sound of his voice, sharpened by tension, as he said, "He can't be! He said he was going home!"

I staggered from the bedroom into the lighted sitting room. Dal was on his feet, dressed only in his shorts, holding the phone, looking dazed. "Yeah," he told the caller. "I'm on my way."

He clicked off the phone and began searching for

his pants and shirt. "That was Trejean. The fucking gallery's on fire. He thinks Mantata's inside."

By the time we arrived, there was an unnatural glow in the nightscape and smoke in the air, and the CFD and the CPD had the street traffic blocked.

Dal found a parking space on the periphery of the activity, and we worked our way along the sidewalk through the acrid night air, past a scattering of gawkers, some of them in robes and pajamas, a paparazzo or two, camera crews on the dog watch from local channels, yawning uniform cops and a weary firefighter trying unsuccessfully to keep a hastily dressed man at arm's distance. The man was demanding to know the extent of the damage to his shop, which I gathered was next to the main fire.

A cop stopped us before we got too close to the gallery, but we were able to see its display window blow out, sending sharp glistening shards into the street over the fire engine and firefighters handling the hose.

I remembered seeing a building burn a couple of years ago, recalled how loud the noise was, not just the roar of the fire but the creaking and cracking of the structure as it gave in to the heat and flames. That fire was set to cover a murder and to get rid of evidence in a case that launched me as a reluctant amateur sleuth.

Suddenly, the flames grew brighter. The firefighters on the ladder started shouting at those on the ground. As the earthbound members of the crew rushed back and away, the roof of the building seemed to cave in on itself, sending up a spray of burning embers.

"What a fucking mess," Dal said.

"Mos'def." Trejean had moved behind us.

"You sure he was in there?" Dal asked.

Trejean nodded. His eyes were wet, maybe from the smoke. "He call me. Say to come and drive him home."

"How long did it take you to get here?"

"One half the hour." He scanned the area, regarding the police with some apprehension. "Too much law. No place to be. Mi step out, yah."

"Let's step out to my car," Dal said. "I need to get a fix on all this."

The once bright yellow gallery was now a scarred skeletal framework. The firemen gave up on it and concentrated on saving what they could of the neighboring buildings.

"Tell me exactly what Mantata said to you." Dal made it more of a command than a request. He and I were occupying the Z-car's front seats. The Jamaican was in the rear.

"De ole man say: 'No trust cabs. I need you heah, to delivah mi to ma home.'"

"How did he sound?"

"What you mean? He soun' lak Mantata."

"Was he happy? Was he sad? Angry? Nervous?"

"Not happy. Mebbe sad. Oh, yeah. He say: 'It time I be goin' home.'"

Dal and I exchanged glances.

"There are less painful ways to go home," I said.

Dal nodded. "What was going on when you got here, Trejean?"

"Street empty. I see fi-ah in the window. Smoke. I stop car, run to doe-ah. Key no work. I run to back doe-ah. Key no work theah."

"We'd changed the locks."

"I bang on doe-ah, shout for Mantata. Then I run back to car an' phone him. All the while, the fi-ah grow biggah. Flames cover the wall. Mantata voice ansah, but not him, a record. I stop that, dial nine-one-one and tell them about the fi-ah. Then I drive away and park. I call you. I don't know what else to do."

"You didn't tell 'em your name?"

"Hail, no! An' mi speaky-spokey, like an American. But de ole man . . ."

"Not much else you could've done," Dal said. "The poor bastard."

Trejean made the sign of the cross.

We sat in silence for a minute.

"You finish wit me, Dal?" Trejean was staring at a policeman walking past the car.

"Yeah."

"Than mi step out, yah." He waited until the cop was well past, then opened the door and exited, melting into the night.

"We should step out, too," Dal said, and started up the Z.

Driving away, he repeated, "The poor bastard. Sitting up there on the third floor with all that flammable crap beneath him."

"There must've been fire alarms in the gallery," I said.

"And a sprinkler system. But from what I could see, the sprinklers weren't operational."

"Meaning what?"

"Meaning I guess we know now why those guys broke in this morning."

Dal was understandably silent on the drive to the hotel. When we were in my suite, I asked, "Isn't there stuff you've got to do?"

"You mean like find another gig?" He was sitting on the bed made from the foldout couch, holding a water glass half filled with the Glenfiddich we'd picked up on the way.

"I mean about Mantata. Somebody will have to arrange for the funeral. There must be business things. . . ."

"He's got family for that. A sister, I think. And there's a lawyer. I was just one of his employees."

"I got the feeling you and he were pretty close."

"Close? All the guy did was rag on me and demand that I be at his beck and call and . . . Aw, hell. I loved the son of a bitch more than I did my old man. He believed in me more than my old man. Do me a favor, Billy, and leave me the fuck alone right now."

I went into the bedroom and shut the door. But I could still hear him weeping in the other room.

Chapter FORTY-TWO

"How much was Mantata paying you to watch my back?" I asked Dal during the short drive to Millennium Park the following morning. Neither of us had been able to shower away all of the smoke odor, and its lingering presence did nothing to lift the melancholy mood.

"Why?"

"Because I want you to keep doing it, and—"

"I'm paid up through the end of the month, Billy."

"I'd still like to—"

"I've been paid," he said, ending the discussion.

He stopped the car at the park's entrance on Randolph. "I'd rather not sit around for the next three hours while you do your thing," he said. "There's stuff I should take care of. If that's all right with you."

"Sure," I said.

"Don't do anything dumb, like wandering off from the park on your own."

"I'll be good."

I had one foot on the ground when he said, "Billy?"

I ducked down and looked at him.

"You think it'd be all right if I talked to his sister? I met her once, a while ago, but she may not even know who the hell I am."

"I think it'd be fine."

"I'd like to straighten her out on that crap that was in the paper."

The morning's *Chicago Trib* coverage of the fire had reported that "Its only victim is thought to be the gallery's owner, an octogenarian reminder of this city's wide-open and corrupt past. Born Byron Gaines on March 4, 1925, he became, at the age of twenty-three, one of the South Side's most powerful gangland figures, operating houses of prostitution, gambling dens, the sale of narcotics, and other forms of vice, virtually untouched by the forces of law and order. It was not until the mid-1960s that he officially assumed the single name Mantata, an African word meaning dangerous. He was that and then some. . . ."

"My guess is his sister won't be surprised by anything in the article," I said.

"I just want her to know the stuff that wasn't in the paper. He wasn't an angel, but he was a hell of a lot better than some of the people that fucking rag praises for their civic duty. A hell of a lot better than the bastards who roasted him alive."

"You know who set the fire?"

"What?" His face paled. "How could I? But I know somebody set it. According to the fucking paper, a fire lieutenant says it was arson." He scowled. "You're gonna be late. Call me when you need me."

*   *   *

Before the show began, I asked Kiki to keep track of any news releases about the fire and its victim. Then I marched onto the set for seven minutes of bright co-host repartee, before the show switched to D.C., where our evening news anchor, Jim McBride, had risen early to interview a congresswoman who'd just introduced a bill that she felt would cut a fair amount of the nation's budget by allowing indigents and the terminally ill to end their lives legally.

With tongue in cheek, Jim had suggested the possibility of saving even more money by selling their remains to pet food companies.

The congresswoman, who was quite beautiful, by the way, considered that and said, "Perhaps, if we can come up with a fatal drug that would not affect animals."

I was considering the intelligence level of the voters who'd put the lovely congresswoman in office when Kiki cheerily reminded me to get ready for my segment with the sausage king of the Midwest.

It was a stove-top interview with a guy as round as he was tall and who spoke with an accent thicker than Schwarzenegger's. Fourteen minutes later, weary from straining to understand what the guy was saying and feeling totally stuffed from scarfing down three or four very tasty sausages, the best of which was the one stuffed with Gouda cheese and apple, I left the set only to be approached by Trina.

"What do you know about rap?" she asked.

"What do you know about the Planet Zorg?" I replied.

"Well, fortunately, I'm not going to be interviewing a Zorgean by satellite in seven minutes."

"There's no rapper on my schedule."

"There is now. Li'l Beatcakes. He's got the number one record in the country, but our favorite entertainment hostess refuses to talk to him."

"Isn't that what she's paid to do?"

"She claims his name is demeaning to women."

"Beatcakes? What does it mean in rap lingo?"

"Fucking doggie-style," Trina said.

"Didn't I just see that on a greeting card?" I asked.

"You're doing the fucking interview," she said, and walked away. Arf! Arf!

Kiki had no new information on the fire, she informed me, when I returned to the office. But she did have notes on Li'l Beatcakes, who had only recently returned from a two-year prison stretch for carrying a concealed weapon. Among the other things that happened to him while in the slams, he had found God. Hence his new hit on Dig Out Records, "Pick the Redeemer over the Reamer."

It was not my finest interview. I'm never at my best talking to a TV screen. In this case, I was talking to a TV screen that was essentially nonverbal. Li'l Beatcakes didn't so much talk as make growling noises, especially when one referenced his time in the slams. No matter. The interview was really just a warm-up to get him to sing his song, which was, to my ear, growling noises punctuated by *uhn*s.

But what do I know?

Still nothing new on the fire and no definite identification of the victim. And the media's interest was waning.

Gus Genovisi, the fresh-vegetable king of Chicago, was a subject more to my liking than Li'l Beatcakes. Charismatic, knowledgeable, and helpful. Ditto Danny DeBek, the creator of *Plum Tukker,* a comic strip about the dating life that was a sort of mash-up of *Doonesbury* and *Cathy.* I was about as au courant on that as I was on rap, but DeBek was not only verbal, he was funny.

Kiki was waiting for me after that interview. She held up my phone.

"Some bloke just called. Said he'd call back. Sounded frantic."

"Good," I said. "Frantic is exactly what I need this morning." But the events of the night made me think the call might be important. I took the phone. Its log listed the caller as "Private Number."

I handed the instrument back to her. "If he calls again, try to work your magic and get a name and a not-so-private number."

When I wrapped my "people online" segment, she was waiting. "He called again. Hung up as soon as I told him you were busy."

"Okay." I took the phone and walked to the tent where coffee and fruit and pastries awaited. I had black coffee and a bear claw, and I didn't feel in the least guilty about ignoring the apples and bananas. Well, maybe a little. Halfway through the second bear claw.

The phone rang, but it was Cassandra calling from Manhattan.

She was angry and puzzled. Her fiancé's operatives had followed the rat and roach-releasing busboy to the offices of Restaurants International, the conglomerate that was trying to purchase stock in the Bistro.

"Fuck that smarmy Frenchman Charles Limon and his cologne!" she exclaimed. "But I don't get it. Why would they want to ruin a business they want to buy?"

"They don't want to ruin it," I said. "They just want to make it more difficult for me to keep it going without their 'help.' It's a combination of the old protection racket and the new business morality."

"So we report them to the police, right?"

"Wrong. Ask your fiancé, A.W., if we've got enough evidence to make a case against Restaurants International. If not, we'll just give 'em more rope until we do. Then we turn the whole thing over to Wally Wing and whichever firm of legal sharks he wants to bring in to bite them in their bankroll."

"Wow, Billy. Speaking of the new business morality . . ."

"It's the world we live in," I said.

Chapter FORTY-THREE

At a little after ten, just as I was getting ready to call Dal, Lily Conover arrived at our temporary HQ. My cable coproducer was dressed down in a little white frock, draped with a zebra-stripe-patterned cape.

She'd flown in from Manhattan to oversee the

taping early next week of two *Blessing's in the Kitchen* shows focusing on the varying styles of Chicago's famous pizza, from the original deep dish to the more recent stuffed version, including thin-crust and pan-cooked pies.

"I assume you've seen the ad in the *Tribune* featuring tonight's show?" she asked.

I admitted I hadn't.

"I don't understand you, Billy. Don't you care anymore?" she asked, digging out a section of the morning paper from her black bag.

"I've had a few other things on my mind."

It was a nice quarter-page ad featuring a still from the show in which I'm holding up one of Charlie Dann's popular Puff Potatoes. The caption read: "Tonight, *Blessing's in the Kitchen* salutes Chicago's own Charlie Dann. Seven p.m., Wine & Dine Network."

"You are going to be at the party tonight, right?"

"Sure. What party?"

She turned to face Kiki, who was staring into her laptop with a dreamy half-smile on her face. Lily frowned, then returned to me. "I thought I'd asked Kiki to tell you, but maybe I was mistaken. There's a party tonight at Charlie's restaurant. He's giving away a lot of the Billy Blessing crap—the chef jackets with your picture over the heart, the kitchen essentials, the seasoning bottles. He was hoping you'd be there."

"Okay. What time?"

"The show's on at seven. Charlie would probably want you there at six-thirty, maybe?"

"Doable," I said.

"Excellent. You can chat up the customers, watch the show with them, and maybe answer a couple questions after. Then Charlie's putting on a feed for a few of us in a private dining room. It'd really be a downer if you didn't—"

"I'll be there."

"Good," Lily said. "Very good." She headed for the exit. "On to pizza land. Ta, Kiki—"

"Huh? Oh, right. Ta," my surprisingly mellow assistant replied.

"Lily's a breath of fresh air, isn't she?" I asked her, when the fresh air had blown away.

"Definitely."

"You okay?"

"Of course," she said, trying to seem blasé. "Don't I look okay?"

"You look like somebody with Cupid's arrow stuck in her. . . ."

I stopped because my phone was vibrating again.

"Private Number."

"Blessing. Who's this?"

"Who do you think?" Nat Parkins replied.

"Where are you?"

"You got the five thou?"

"I can get it," I said. It was in the hotel safe.

"How long'll it take you?"

I had to call Dal, find out when he could come pick me up. "A couple of hours," I said.

"That the best you can do?"

"Afraid so."

"Okay, then. What time you got?"

I checked my watch. "About ten-forty-five."

"Exact time."

"Ten-forty-three."

"Okay, I'll meet you at Lincoln Park at one. On the dot."

"At the zoo?"

He was silent, then, "Naw. There's this place called Grandmother's Garden. Where Lincoln Park West meets Belden Avenue."

I snapped my fingers to get Kiki's attention, then pantomimed writing on a piece of paper. Ordinarily, she'd have handed the objects to me before I'd finished miming. That day, it took nearly a minute.

"There's a statue of Shakespeare—"

"Hold on." As I wrote, I repeated his instructions. "Grandmother's Garden. Lincoln Park West and Belden Avenue."

"Yeah. I'll be waiting at the Shakespeare statue."

"I want something more than my file, Nat," I said.

He hesitated. "What else?"

"The file belonging to the guy who killed Patton."

"What are you going to do with it?"

"Save both our lives, maybe."

"Deal. But this time you come alone. Leave your honky leg-breaker at home."

"That's not—"

"I see anybody with you, I bolt."

He didn't bother saying goodbye.

"What's that all about?" Kiki asked.

"Meeting somebody."

"You mentioned 'money' and 'the guy who killed Patton.' Tell me you're not mixed up in murder again, Billy."

"I'm not mixed up in murder again," I said.

"You're lying, aren't you?"

"Not exactly," I said. "The thing is—"

Thank God my phone began vibrating again. "Hold that thought," I said, getting out the phone. "Actually, don't hold it."

"Private Number."

This time it was Dal.

"You don't need me right away, do you?" he asked.

I told him that I didn't need him until around twelve-thirty.

"Okay. It's official. The burn victim was Mantata. DNA verified it. And there was a leg bone. When Mantata was a young man, one of Jackie 'the Lackey' Cerone's hard cases beat the crap out of him. Snapped his right leg in two places."

Until that moment I'd been holding out the hope that the old man had faked his death.

"I'm trying to contact all of the crew, including the old-timers," Dal continued. "The ones I've reached are taking it harder than I'd thought. Guess we criminals aren't so tough after all."

"What about his sister?"

"I called her. Did you know fucking Oakley was the old man's nephew?"

"He may have mentioned it."

"He answered the phone when I called. Still lives with his mother. Talk about arrested development. Anyway, I'm gonna drop by their place for a few minutes. And there's some other stuff I'd better take care of. No problemo making it by twelve-thirty. I can get there earlier if you want."

"Make it by noon and we can grab a quick lunch somewhere around here."

"You're on."

I expected Kiki to pick up precisely where we'd left off, but she surprised me. "Could I depart now, Billy?" she asked. "There are a few personal things I should do, and I've a . . . meeting at noon."

"Go," I said. "I wouldn't want to keep you from your . . . meeting. With Richard, I assume?"

She smiled. "We'll name our first boy Billy," she said.

Chapter
FORTY-FOUR

Dal arrived at a quarter to twelve, looking as if his visit to Mantata's sister, Olivia Hudson, had worn him down a little. On the walk to The Gage, a nearby gastropub, he said, "She's a tough old broad. Tougher than her kid and maybe even tougher than her brother. She's got it all under control. The church. The service. When I left, she was lining up a choir."

I selected a light lunch, a seared sea scallops salad, while Dal tore into a grilled rib-eye sandwich. We were out of the restaurant at twenty after twelve. By twelve-thirty, I was at my hotel, withdrawing the cash from the safe. Fifteen minutes later, we were in the maroon Z-car on our way to Lincoln Park.

"I don't like the idea of you spending any time hanging around that statue by yourself," Dal said.

"Nat will run if he sees you. Anyway, you're going to be close. And I have the famous air horn to strike fear in evil hearts."

It was nearing one p.m. when he brought the car to a stop beside a knee-high wall of piled stones on North Stockton Drive. Because we did not want to risk Nat seeing Dal or the familiar maroon Z-car, we had not taken Lincoln Park West, as Nat had suggested. That street offered an unobstructed view of the statue of Shakespeare. Instead we'd traveled north on Stockton, the parallel street that ran along the other side of the narrow Grandmother's Garden.

From where we were parked, foliage in the garden partially hid the car from the view of anyone near the statue, which was a good thing. But it also meant that Dal would not be able to observe all the activity at the meeting scene, which was not such a good thing.

"Is that him?" Dal asked.

Someone was sitting on a bench facing the statue.

I checked my watch. Two minutes to one. "I might as well find out."

I opened the door.

"Got your air horn?" Dal asked.

"Yep," I said, amused by how much faith he had in it.

As soon as I reached the sidewalk leading to the statue, I saw that the man seated on the bench was not Nat. He was a rotund white man in his middle to late years, dressed in black. Black suit, black shirt. Ditto socks and shoes. He had a cherubic face surrounded by white hair on top and a matching Monty Woolley under his nose. One of his hands rested on the bench; the other held a black walking stick.

A primly dressed young woman and ten children, a mixed bag of preschool-age boys and girls, entered the garden area from Lincoln Park West and gathered around the statue. Some began climbing on the bard of Avon. A tiny girl sat on his lap.

Nat was nowhere to be seen.

"A little late, Susanna," the man in black chided the woman. His voice was a rich, theatrical baritone.

"We stopped to watch a game of horseshoes," the woman replied. "And how are you today, Durwood? Enjoying the park, as always?"

He looked up at the overcast sky. " 'True is it that we have seen better days,' " he said.

"I know that one," the woman said, evidently pleased with herself. "The duke in *As You Like It*."

The kids were creating quite a ruckus. The woman—their teacher, I presumed—tried to quiet them down, without much success.

I wondered where the hell Nat was and if I was being stood up.

It was ten after one.

The man in black looked at me and, referring to the kids, said, "Full of sound and fury, eh?"

I managed to come up with a smile. Then I saw that his pale plump hand was resting on a spiral notebook I'd last seen on a table at Nero's Wonder Lounge.

Walking toward him, I said, "This may sound like a strange question. . . ."

"Say no more. The answer is yes, I am the thespian Durwood Candless."

"Of course," I said, as if I knew who Durwood Candless was. "I've enjoyed your performances."

"My Falstaff?"

Behind me, the young woman was threatening to remove the kids from the park if they didn't behave.

"I've yet to have that pleasure," I said to the actor. "I was wondering about your notebook."

"Oh!" He looked down at it as if he'd forgotten it was there beneath his hand. "This isn't mine. It belongs to a young man who comes here often. He seems as fond of this tribute to the Bard as I. I was talking to him just a few minutes ago. Did you know that this statue is the first in which the great man was properly attired for his time? The collar. The cape. The leggings tied with bows."

"It's one heck of a statue," I said. "The young man. Is his name Nat?"

"Yes. You know him?"

"I was supposed to meet him here."

"Well, as I said, we were sitting here talking when he stood suddenly and ran off, over there toward the conservatory."

"Just a few minutes ago, you say?"

"Yes."

I looked in the direction he was indicating with his cane. Minutes. One minute would have been too late.

"Any idea why he ran away?"

Durwood Candless's attention had drifted to something just to the right of my crotch. A little boy stood there, staring at me. "It is him," he said.

"Matthew," the teacher called, "the gentlemen are talking. Come here."

"But it's him!" Matthew said. "The black guy from the morning show. The one my dad calls a no-talent asshole."

"Matthew!" the teacher almost screeched, silencing the other kids. "Don't ever use language like that. You apologize immediately to the gentleman."

"Why? It was my dad who said it." The others were gawking at the kid now.

"If you don't apologize immediately, Matthew, I will put you in Ms. Ordway's group."

Matthew hesitated, his deceptively cherubic face registering alarm. Then he gave up. Sniffling and staring at my knees, he said, "I'm sorry my dad said you're an asshole."

"I'm sorry, too," I said.

"This is so embarrassing," the teacher said to me.

"Don't give it another thought," I told her. "It's just one of the joys of being in the public eye."

She gave me an awkward smile, then gathered the brood, including Matthew. "There will be consequences," she informed them. "We're heading back to school now. No more climbing on the statue today. No recitation from Mr. Candless. No visit to the playground. All thanks to Matthew's rudeness."

The kids looked bummed as they walked away.

Durwood Candless looked a little bummed, too, watching them go. "I'd planned Polonius's 'Neither a borrower nor a lender' speech," he said.

If that was a hint, I had neither the time nor the inclination to act on it. "Do you know why my friend Nat rushed away?" I asked.

"Uh," the actor said, refocusing. "Clearly he was seeking to avoid the fellow who chased after him."

I stared at him, wondering if he was amusing himself at my expense. "The fellow," I said, calm as the day. "Tell me about him."

"There were three of them, actually. They pulled up in their dark green chariot right over there." The cane was now pointing at a spot where the sidewalk met Lincoln Park West. "One of the males rushed after Nat. The other male and the lady stayed with the auto. I gathered by their proximity that they were a couple."

"Could you describe them?"

"Indeed so. The young woman was lovely enough to be the modern incarnation of the Bard's dark lady, and the two men, were they thespians, I would have cast as Rosencrantz and Guildenstern."

"By 'dark lady,' you mean she was black?"

He mock sighed and touched his heart. "More a sweet caramel."

"And the men?"

"Caucasian. The shorter one, who pursued Nat, was stocky, the taller had a lean and hungry look. But regardless, there was a sameness to them. Hair. Coloring. As I said, they fit the characters of Prince Hamlet's false friends from childhood."

"Did the stocky man catch up with Nat?"

"Not that I saw. They both disappeared from view behind the conservatory. Then the other two got into their auto and drove off, north toward Fullerton Parkway, where I suppose they turned right. Assuming they were following the others."

This was not good news, and I must have showed it.

"Cheer up, dear boy." He held up the notebook. "Your friend will be returning for this."

"Probably not today," I said. "But I can take it to him."

"Excellent," he said, handing it to me. "The night air and morning dew would treat it badly."

I thanked him, promised to catch his next performance as Falstaff, and retired to Dal and the car.

"That doesn't look like a red folder," he said.

Working in live TV trains you in stretching information or condensing it. I brought him up to date in only three sentences.

"You figure it's the same guys who shot up this car at Nero's?"

"The description fits them better than the private eyes. And I doubt either of *them* would be doing any running."

"So the killers picked up a girlfriend. Wonder what her story is."

I was wondering the same thing. I knew a beautiful woman the color of caramel, but I couldn't believe Adoree would be joyriding with the pair who'd killed and tortured two men. Then again, she'd heard about my criminal activity from someone she knew.

"So? What now, boss?"

"Either they've got him or he's escaped," I said. "But we might as well circle the park and see if by some stroke of luck the green car is still around."

Starting the car, Dal said, "Might be luckier for us if it isn't."

Chapter
FORTY-FIVE

No green car. No Nat. No nothing.

By two-thirty we had retreated to my hotel suite. The housekeeping staff had restored it to its pristine condition, and Dal quickly began deconstructing their work by converting the couch into a bed and kicking off his shoes. "Excuse me if I grab a snooze, Billy," he said. "It was a short night and a tough day."

The idea was catching.

I went into the bedroom, sat on the bed, and kicked off my shoes.

I spent a few minutes going through Nat's notebook. I guess I should have referred to it as a sketchbook. It was more than half filled with nicely rendered pencil drawings. Patton in repose, on the phone, at the computer. Larry Kelsto looking wistful, watching TV, appearing onstage. Portraits of people I didn't recognize. Our ancient waitress at Nero's.

Of Nat's many subjects, the one that inspired the most drawings was the Shakespeare statue. There were separate sketches of the tilted head, the back of the head, the right elbow resting on the arm of the chair, the left arm casually draped on the left leg, the chair itself. There were drawings of the legs, nicely capturing right knee, left knee, thighs, ankles.

I was tired and my eyes burned. I closed the sketchbook and got out my phone. While waiting for Cassandra to pick up, I slipped down in the bed and rested my head against the pillow.

"Billy? Is everything okay?" she asked.

The question momentarily threw me. Had something happened I didn't know about? "I'm fine. Why?"

"You called at a time when I wasn't busting my chops working or fast asleep."

"Touché. How's the biz?"

"Very good, actually. Busy for lunch, and we're solid for dinner. TG for the TGIF mentality."

"Anything new on the evil busboy?"

"Nope. The lovely little Phillipe is merely biding his time. I don't see how he could possibly know we're onto him, but maybe . . ."

"I don't think so," I said. "If he did, he wouldn't bother coming in. He's probably searching for a way to up the ante."

"We have him covered. In addition to the undercover agent keeping her eye on him, I've reserved table twenty-three, the two-top near the swinging door, for circulating agents from A.W.'s office. And before you go into your Scrooge McDuck imitation, we get their services for the price of a meal. Booze and gratuities not included."

"Okay, but tell the waiters to try to talk them out of steaks and lobster."

"I hope you're kidding," she said, and hung up.

My next call was to Kiki, to inquire about our final week's schedule. Only after I was switched to her voice mail did I remember that she'd gone to a "meeting."

Good for her, I thought, yawning.

I put the phone on the night table, turned out the light, and lay back on the bed. I thought I might just fall . . .

The voice calling my name did not belong to Gabrielle Union, who had been urging me to search a nearby cave with her and forget about Halle Berry and Tyra Banks, my other companions with whom I was sharing a secluded cove.

"This better be good," I said, forcing my eyes open.

"It's six o'clock, bud," Dal said. "Time to get ready for the scene at Dann's Sports Den."

I rolled over, away from him. "Wake me again when you're through with the shower."

"I'm through. I'm dressed. And there's a blonde in the other room says you've gotta get moving."

"She wearing an outfit that looks like a Lady Gaga reject?"

"It's got feathers on the shoulders."

I groaned. "Tell her I'll be ready forthwith."

"I'll paraphrase," he said.

"You holding up?"

"I'm okay. I compartmentalize."

Twenty minutes later, shaved, showered, smelling like the piney woods, and dressed to the nines, I walked in on Dal and Lily Conover, who were discussing the relative merits of wearing apparel made from hemp and seriously depleting my bottle of single-malt.

"Hope you don't mind," Dal said, reacting to my picking up the bottle.

"Looks like you left me a shot," I said, wondering if I really was starting to sound like Scrooge McDuck.

"Well, you'll have to drink that shot later," Lily said. "We haven't much time, and the traffic is going to be fierce."

There was quite a crowd lined up in front of Dann's Sports Den when we arrived. Dal, preferring not to rely on the valets, dropped us off and rolled on in search of a place to park.

As far as the public is concerned, there is a big difference in arriving in a limo and being dropped off from a Nissan, even a Nissan Z. Some people on line recognized me, but the others, let's call them "the unenlightened," began shouting curses at us for busting the line.

Jonny Baker was waiting just inside the door, his face lighting up when he saw us. Tonight he'd dressed more formally. He was wearing a black Windbreaker with a white Onion City logo. "Billy!" he called. "Uncle Charlie's been worried. Come on!"

The place was packed.

Jonny began opening a path for us, pushing people aside.

"Easy on the customers," I told him.

"Uncle Charlie wants you to be with him," Jonny said, continuing to cut a swath through the throng, oblivious to their loud and profane complaints.

The lounge area smelled of whiskey and beer and, substituting for the cigarette smoke of yore, fried potatoes. With just a hint of perspiration that would undoubtedly grow stronger as the night and the crowd progressed.

Charlie Dann was at the far end of the bar, not looking terribly worried. He was keeping about twenty people enthralled with a sports story that ended with ". . . and with all that damned hair oil on the ball, it slipped right out of my fingers."

His listeners rewarded him with the kind of guffaw-laugh usually reserved for Chris Rock or Louis C. K. He looked past them at our approach and opened his arms wide in welcome. He hugged Lily, trying not to disturb the feathers, then put his arm around my shoulders and introduced me to the crowd as "The Man."

I'd never been called The Man before, and I have to admit it felt good. Especially in a sports bar.

"Billy's going to be watching the show with us," he said, gesturing to the monitor behind the bar and to an even bigger thin-screen TV secured to the opposite wall, temporarily covering a large rectangular section of framed memorabilia. Both screens were presently occupied by a former homeless man named Philo Markus who'd become the host of the Wine & Dine Network's show *Bin Diver Dinner*.

I looked away before Philo began feasting on a burger that had evidently been a little too super-sized for a McDonald's customer. I saw that Dal had made it inside and was settling in at the bar, a few drinkers down.

"If you've got any questions about cooking or TV or the show you're going to see," I told the crowd, "I'm here to answer them."

"Is *American Idol* rigged?"

"What's Snooki really like?"

"How can I get on *Survivor*?"

"Who the fuck are you, man?"

It went on like that until the show began. The crowd calmed down, watched for about five minutes, then began ordering more drinks from the bar.

By the time the show ended, there was so much noise in the room that I doubted anyone could hear the speakers. Charlie shrugged, said, "Well, the customer's always right. Especially when there are so many of 'em. Why don't we leave them to their booze and go get some grub."

He led us to a considerably more private dining room that he called the Bears' Cave.

There were only about thirty place settings on five tables. At ours, Charlie was to my left, Lily to my right. Dal was at a nearby table with a group of Dann's select customers.

Jonny was at a third table. But even before I was able to peruse the menu, he was up and at my side, handing me a slip of paper. On it, written in the same block-letter printing that had been on that sheet found in the deserted red Range Rover, was the terse message: "Come with me or your girl dies."

Jonny was grinning at me with the sweet innocence of the mentally challenged.

Charlie and Lily were chatting about something. Across the room, Dal was staring at me with some curiosity.

"Come alone," Jonny said. A simple statement, not a demand.

He was still grinning.

He leaned forward and whispered, "My brother says for me to wait for the count of ten."

He backed away and walked out of the room.

My immediate thought was that he, or, more likely, his brother, had played it wrong. They'd skipped too many beats, evidently overestimating my mental agility as I had underestimated Jonny's. It took me a few moments to fully understand the situation. Then it struck me that the squat man Nat had seen leaving Pat Patton's the night of the murder had been Jonny in one of his Onion City Windbreakers. I supposed he'd also been the man the old actor had seen chasing Nat Parkins through Lincoln Park.

Which left me wondering about my "girl." The Shakespearean dark lady who'd been with him in the park? Adoree? But how . . . ?

To the count of ten.

I placed my napkin on the table, stood, and left the room. Dal watched me go. I nodded and tried to look as serious as a man heading for the gallows. I hoped he would follow.

Jonny was waiting just outside the door, a phone to his ear. "Billy's here," he said into it.

He closed the phone. "My brother says we've got fifty minutes. Better zoom-zoom, huh?"

He beelined to the restaurant's rear stairwell, heading down the steps two at a time, assuming I was keeping up. Which I was, sort of. Then we were out through the exit and down an alley to the street.

"I'm around the corner," he said.

* * *

We were in his dark green SUV, seat belts attached, heading north, when I asked, "Where are we going, Jonny?"

"To where it's really nice. Right on the lake. You can swim. Or go out in the boat. I can even shoot my gun in the water. There aren't many neighbors, and they're pretty far away. But my baby brother, Dickie, says I should use a suppressor when I shoot so they don't freak out. It's this thing fits on the barrel. It still makes noise, but not as much and it sounds different, like a crack, not a gunshot."

I chanced a quick glance in the rearview mirror. The car directly behind us could have been Dal's maroon Z-car. Or not.

"I have many guns," Jonny said. "I brought one of 'em."

He reached inside his jacket with his left hand, keeping his right on the wheel. The gun he withdrew looked big and ugly.

"No suppressor?" I asked.

"No. It makes the gun not shoot straight. So I don't use it when I'm working."

"You need the gun for your work?"

"Sometimes. Depends on the job."

"You working now?"

He smiled. "Kind of."

"Who's my girl, Jonny?"

"I don't understand," he said.

"That note you gave me said that if I didn't come with you, my girl would be killed."

"I remember the note. I don't understand why you don't know who your girl is."

"Maybe I have more than one girl," I said.

"Oh. We only have the one."

"What's her name?"

"I don't know if I should say. My brother, Dickie, told me exactly what to write. He didn't say anything about telling you her name."

His brother, *Dickie. Damn it.* I didn't need Jonny to tell me her name. It wasn't Adoree.

Chapter
FORTY-SIX

The sky continued to darken as we drove north along Lake Shore Drive, catching the tail end of the going-home traffic. "Why don't you put the gun away, Jonny?" I said.

"It's okay. I know how to use it."

"Why would you use it?"

"Dickie said you might try something."

"That'd be pretty silly of me," I said. "If I did, Dickie would harm my girl. You know I don't want that. It's why I'm here with you."

"Makes sense," he said, and put the gun back into what I assumed was a shoulder holster under his jacket.

"There's a faster way to get there," he said, "but this is the way I know best."

The lake was to our right. I caught glimpses of it through the trees and shrubbery, turning black as ink under the night sky. "I'm a little disappointed," I said. "I thought you and I were friends."

"Aren't we?"

"Friends don't threaten friends."

"That's not . . . Dickie explained how that works. It's not personal. It's what you have to do to make everything turn out okay."

"How will my driving with you make that happen?"

"I don't know. But it will."

Belmont Harbor was on our right, a giant wall of high-rises to our left. "Is it your house we're going to?"

He nodded, concentrating hard on the road.

"Your dad going to be there?"

"Maybe. In the big house. Not where Dickie and I live. He never goes there. Cecil and Camilla take care of us."

"Will Cecil and Camilla be there?"

He smiled. "Of course not. They go to their daughter's in Wilmette on weekends. Unless there's a party, which there isn't tonight."

"So it'll just be you, me, and Dickie?"

"And your girl," Jonny said. "I better not talk anymore. I have to pay attention to my driving."

I looked at the rearview mirror. Too many cars and too many headlights to see anything more than vague shapes.

Eventually, the four-lane drive curved left and was transformed into a two-lane street called Sherman Road. Low-rise buildings were mixed in with the high-rises. Though the traffic was gradually falling off, Jonny slowed the SUV. A twenty mph warning sign explained that.

At one point, not long after passing Loyola University, a roadside establishment called Leona's Pizza appeared on our right. "We missed dinner," I said.

"No talking now. We're coming to the tricky part where I used to get lost. I need to concentrate real hard."

He was leaning forward, scowling at the road.

I loosened my seat belt a few inches and casually turned my body, taking a long but careful look at the road behind us. There were only a few cars following us now. The night made it impossible to gauge their colors. The one nearest was an SUV. But behind that was a smaller, sleeker car riding close to the ground.

As it passed near a streetlamp, I saw that it was maroon-colored.

Feeling almost elated, I settled back on my seat and contemplated the road ahead as we drove through what appeared to be a residential area, its sidewalks illuminated by old-fashioned streetlamps.

Jonny turned left down one street, then right on another. He began to mumble, then wailed, as if in pain. He pulled over to the side of the road, stopped, and pounded on the steering wheel in obvious frustration. "Stupid-stupid-stupid," he said, turning the word into a mantra.

The maroon Nissan Z was caught in our head-lights as it passed us by and continued on down the street.

Jonny didn't seem to have recognized the Z. He had his phone out. He pressed a button and held it to his ear. "Me," he said. "No. He's with me. That part's okay, Dickie. I . . . got lost."

He was silent for a few beats, then said, "Evanston, I think . . . Okay. Don't hang up."

He switched the phone to his left hand. With his right, he pressed a button on the dash that turned on the vehicle's tracking system. Immediately, a colorful street grid filled the little monitor screen. "Okay, now what?" he asked.

Squinting, he reached forward and pressed a button. A series of numbers in yellow circles appeared along the bottom of the screen, along with a circle filled with what looked like the drawing of a Monopoly house. Jonny pressed that button.

A digitized voice, British or faux British, announced that he was to drive forward until the route instructions began. He obeyed, and the British voice issued its first command.

Breathing easier, Jonny said into the phone, "It's working. We'll be there soon. I'm sorry, Dickie. I'll do better."

I could hear the tone, if not the words, of Dickie's harsh response.

Jonny put the phone away. He was sniffling, teary-eyed. He did not notice the parked maroon Nissan when we passed it by.

Back on track, Jonny used the sleeve of his jacket

to wipe his nose and eyes and asked, "Is it hot in here?"

"Not for us only children," I said.

As the route took us around and past the seemingly never-ending Northwestern University campus, Jonny said, "That's where my brother, Dickie, went to school. Studied architecture building and planning, so he could work with our dad. He says he's lucky I didn't get much smarts because that left more for him."

"What a nice, brotherly thing to say."

"Oh, yeah. Dickie's the best."

Once we'd entered the village of Wilmette, Jonny was able to find his way without the help of the grating British voice but blamed me because neither of us could figure out how to silence it.

It was still "recalculating" when he took a left turn onto a lane that led in the direction of the lake. Several feet from the lane's end, the disembodied Limey voice announced we'd reached our destination.

That wasn't quite accurate. There was still another left turn and then a lengthy drive through a forest of trees, at the end of which was the lighted gate of a high stone fence. Off the road to our left was a small windowed structure constructed with the same kind of piled stones as the wall. It was dark.

"Usually there's a guy out here who takes care of the gate," Jonny said, as he reached across me to

open the glove compartment. "Dickie sent him away."
He found a little plastic device, which he clicked
twice.

The gate opened smoothly and silently. It remained open only long enough for us to enter the
compound, and as it swung shut, I heard an odd bris-
tling, pounding sound. With heart-stopping sudden-
ness, the vehicle was attacked by two snarling German
shepherd dogs, their faces inches from our windows,
their paws scraping the paint on the door panels.
They'd evidently been trained not to bark.

"Adolph and Eva," Jonny said.

"Cute names," I said.

Jonny reached into the right pocket of his jacket.
Then the left. Then he dug into the pockets of his
pants, growing more and more upset. "I know I
had . . . Ah, here it is."

He'd finally found the object he'd been seeking, a
metal whistle. He placed it in his mouth and blew
three times. The only sound I heard was his breath
going through the instrument. But as suddenly as the
dog attack had begun, it stopped. The two animals
trotted off across a lawn the size of a soccer field.
They glanced back at us occasionally, as if they
weren't quite convinced that they were doing the
right thing by ignoring us.

Jonny put the SUV in drive. As we crunched along
the gravel road, I got a good look at the compound by
moonlight. There were three buildings that I could
see. The biggest, surrounded by a lush garden, was a
white two-story colonial home that, by my rough
count, beat the house of the seven gables by one. With

the exception of a room in the upper-left corner of the building, it was in darkness.

Behind that was a chain-link-fenced tennis court and an almost Olympic-size swimming pool. The smallest building, barely a cottage, was near the pool. Totally dark.

To our left was a large three- or four-car garage with what looked like living quarters above it.

"Chauffeur lives up there?" I asked.

He laughed. "We don't have a chauffeur. That's where Cecil and Camilla stay. But they're not here now."

"Probably went to visit their daughter."

He frowned. "You know Ce—" Then he grinned. "Aw, I told you that."

Our final destination was on a grassy knoll overlooking the lake, a miniature, less-gabled version of the main house. Its ground floor was lit up, and I saw the outline of someone leaning against the jamb of the front door.

"Dickie's waiting for us," Jonny said. "I hope he's not too pissed at me for getting lost."

He drove the SUV to within a few feet of the coach house, parking it on the lawn.

The man standing in the doorway was of average height, pale, dark-haired, and clean-shaven. He was thin, with a runner's body. Denim pants. White dress shirt rolled to the elbows. He resembled his brother, but while Jonny's face was unlined and full, Dickie's had sharp edges, prominent cheekbones, and dark smudges under his eyes. He looked tired, arrogant, and, at the least, annoyed.

"Here we are, Dickie," Jonny said, as we got out of the SUV. "Just like you wanted."

Dickie showed no response except to turn on his heel and go inside the house, letting the screen door slam back in place.

"This isn't good," Jonny said. "Dickie's angry. And he can be, well, mean when he's angry."

Terrific.

Chapter
FORTY-SEVEN

The coach house the brothers inhabited was furnished in early American—lots of wood, some chairs with cane bottoms, knit throw rugs on plank floors, walls a creamy off-white decorated with paintings by artists of the Grandma Moses school (maybe Grandma herself), dark beam ceilings, gingham pillows on tufted sofas. Not exactly what I'd have thought appropriate or acceptable for the Baker boys. But the furnishings were probably a decorator's idea, just as the neat-as-a-pin, fresh-tulips-and-roses-in-vases atmosphere was the work of their caretakers, Cecil and Camilla.

I took another look at the grounds, saw the two dogs stretched out by the pool, facing my direction, and wondered if Dal would be able to handle them, assuming he could make it past the gate.

"This way, Billy," Jonny urged me on, gesturing with his handgun. Its reappearance at this point was not unexpected. All signs—including the fact that Dickie had dismissed the staff—indicated the sort of night I'd be having. It reminded me of the old Woody Allen line: "The lion shall lie down with the calf, but the calf isn't going to get much sleep."

The others were waiting for us in what appeared to be a den. Ordinarily, it would have been overwhelmed by the giant TV screen that covered a full wall. But the screen was dark, and the two bodies—one on the floor, the other on the sofa—demanded attention in a way TV never would.

Nat was slumped near a cold flagstone fireplace, his body too brutalized and twisted to still be supporting life. His bloody face had a spongy, raw look. One eye was open, but it wasn't seeing anything.

The other body was very much alive, thank God. A forehead cut near her hairline had leaked blood down the side of her face. But she seemed otherwise unharmed, sitting upright on a wicker couch, her wrists and ankles bound by blue duct tape. Another blue strip had been pasted over her mouth, but a trickle of blood from the head wound had loosened an edge. She struggled against the bindings, watching me. Her dark eyes were full of fury, but I was pretty sure that this time, I was not the object of Kiki's wrath.

"Your girl can be a real pain in the ass, Blessing," were Dickie Baker's first words to me. "She likes to make things difficult for herself."

"I'm glad she's not as difficult as Nat Parkins," I said.

Dickie glared at Jonny, whose eyes dropped to the floor. "That was a mistake my retard brother made," Dickie said.

"He looked like he could handle it, but he just sort of came apart, Dickie." Jonny looked stricken. He seemed to have forgotten the gun in his hand.

"There's the problem, Blessing. Parkins *came apart* before he could tell us where the red files were. We're kinda hoping he told you."

"That's it? You seduce, kidnap, and brutalize my assistant and get me here because you hope I might know something? And you think you're the *smarter* brother?"

His face darkened. He took a step toward me, drawing back his hand. And stopped. He stared past me, his anger replaced by surprise.

Jon Baker Senior, in white silk pajamas under a black silk robe, was standing in the doorway. He was not happy. "Why the devil isn't there a security guard at the gate?"

"I sent him away," Dickie said.

"You what?" Jon entered the room and blinked when he saw Nat's body. "For Christ's sake, Dickie, what the hell . . . *Blessing?*"

I shrugged.

"Everything's under control, Dad."

"This you call under control? Is that man dead?"

"I told Jonny—"

"Don't lay any of this cock-up on Jonny. You're supposed to be calling the shots." He saw Kiki trussed up on the couch. "Who's this woman?"

"She works for Blessing. I've been using her to

find out what he's been up to. Stupid bitch hadn't a clue what I was doing."

"What's she doing *here*? Why are any of these people here? This is where we live, for God's sake."

I'd backed up a few steps until I was standing beside Jonny. His soft face was twisted in anguish. He was totally caught up in the conflict between his father and his brother.

"I'm sorry I'm not a genius like you, Dad," Dickie said. "Why don't you tell me where else I should have taken—"

"This is full-out idiocy. A key rule of life: You never put yourself in an indefensible position."

"I didn't—"

"What would you call it, if you got caught with a corpse in your own home?" His eyes swept over me and Kiki. "Or in this case, *three* corpses."

"We'll get rid of them, Dad. There's no chance anybody would—"

Jonny's cry interrupted him.

The comment about my impending corpsehood had been all the encouragement I'd needed. Jonny had forgotten both me and his gun. I just reached out, grabbed it with both hands, and twisted up. Hence the squeal.

"You hurt me," Jonny said, glaring at me with indignation. He began licking his scraped finger to heal it, animal-style.

"Dumbhead!" Dickie yelled at him.

Their father didn't seem very intimidated by my weapon. "What now, Blessing?"

"Now we discover how indefensible your position

is." Keeping the gun pointed in their direction, I got out my phone.

From the corner of my eye, I saw motion at the door. Then Dal slipped into the room with a gun in his hand. "Good timing," I said. "How'd you get . . . ?"

I was going to ask how he got past the dogs, but he more or less answered that by pointing the gun at me.

"Let it fall, Billy," he said. "At this distance I can put a bullet right between your eyes before you even start thinking about pulling the trigger."

Chapter
FORTY-EIGHT

"Do you get it now, Dickie?" his father asked, as Jonny reclaimed his weapon from the rug where I'd dropped it. "Do you see why Dal was worth every penny I paid him?"

"Okay," Dickie said, begrudgingly. "You were right, Dad. You're always right. Now can we get back to the business of cleaning up the mess *you* made?"

"Please do," Jon Baker said. "I'm anxious to see how you hope to accomplish that."

"Simple. We just let Jonny convince Blessing to give up the file."

Jonny was studying me like he'd been on a forced vegan diet and I was a three-inch porterhouse.

"Jonny seems up for it," his father said, "but it won't get us anywhere."

Dickie glared at him. "You're psychic now?"

"Dal, would you enlighten my impetuous son?"

"Like I told your dad this afternoon," Dal said, "Billy doesn't have the files. And he doesn't know where they are."

That wasn't quite true. I was pretty sure I knew their location. But this definitely was not the time to mention it.

"Why didn't you tell me what you were doing, Dickie?" Jon Baker said. "I could have saved you and your brother a lot of wasted effort. Now we have to dispose of three bodies. For no goddamn reason except your impetuosity."

Kiki managed to moan past the duct tape.

"So I'm clear on it, Dad, I have your permission to kill 'em here?" Dickie asked, not without sarcasm.

"Actually, no. We'll let Dal handle things now. He's the pro. You're not even an amateur."

Jon Baker started to leave.

"It's fingerprints, right?" I asked him.

He turned and raised an eyebrow. "You know what's in my red file?"

"You don't?" I asked.

"Actually, no. Patton was as cagey as he was crooked," Baker said. "He came here to see me last Saturday, said he had evidence linking me to . . . my past. He wouldn't be more specific. I said that if he had anything worth a hundred grand—that was his price—I didn't understand why he'd waited so long to collect. He told me he hadn't known what he had until you brought it to his attention earlier that morning."

Pat Patton, nature's nobleman, always happy to throw anybody under the bus.

"Is that what's in the red file, Billy? My finger-prints?"

Improv time. "The fingerprints of Giovanni Pol-vere," I said.

He nodded.

"Patton was no dummy," I continued. "And you were too cute with your new name." I might have been improvising, but there was some logic in it. "Lots of sons of Italy who are born Giovanni change that to John in this country. Just look at New York Mob boss Johnny Gambino. And 'polvere' is Italian for flour. John Flour. Jon Baker. Not a dead giveaway but much too close for a wise old bird like Patton not to see the connection."

"It's difficult to give up the past completely," Jon Baker said. "You want to keep something of what you were. I chose to do it with my name. I know you can understand that, Billy B."

So Patton had told him I was Billy Blanchard and, probably, how he and I were linked by Paul Lamont's death. The old bastard hadn't just thrown me under the bus, he'd given the driver a reason to want me dead.

"How much did you and Mantata find out about Gio Polvere?" Baker asked.

Did Dal tense up? I hoped he did.

"We pieced together most of the story," I said.

"Let's hear what you think you know."

"Dad, like you said, we should get moving."

"Shut up, Dickie. Billy's about to tell us how smart he is."

He gestured that I should begin.

"Gio Polvere. A bright young guy who convinced mobster Joe Nagall of his financial prowess and wound up the chief financial officer of Windy City Industrials, the Chicago Outfit's business umbrella."

"A guy that bright may even have suggested the creation of WCI," Baker said.

Hubris. Don't you love it?

"Not only that," I said, "he was shrewd enough to do his thing in the background, becoming a major player in the Outfit without posing for the cameras. The others enjoyed power and publicity and living the fast life. Gio was happy just watching the money pile up and waiting for the chance to grab as much of it as he could."

"Gio was a little more subtle than that," Baker said. "And it wasn't just about grabbing the money. It was taking what he felt he was owed to make up for the crap he'd had to endure from his loud, obnoxious, disgusting associates."

"Thanks for the clarification," I said. "In any case, in 1987, an Outfit lowlife named Louis Venici came to Gio and told him about a real moneymaker that some fool had dropped in his lap. Gio looked into it and realized that Venici was the fool and was about to be picked clean by a very smart con man named Paul Lamont."

"What's this crap all about, Dad?" Dickie asked.

"Shut up and learn something," his father said. "Excuse the interruption, Billy. Please continue."

"I was just going to point out how really clever

Gio was. He could have exposed Lamont. But where was the profit in that? Instead—and I'm guessing here—he went to the con man and suggested a partnership."

"He suggested more than that," Baker said. "Lamont thought big but not quite big enough."

The room was very quiet. Dickie was staring at his father with an expression of awe. This was all new to him. Dal seemed to be amused by his employer's openness. I hoped he understood what that candor meant to *his* life expectancy.

"So," I continued, "Gio—you—got Paul to add a few zeros to his scam, which you, as CFO, approved, and together you hit the Outfit's cash box pretty hard. As soon as the money exchanged hands, you had Paul killed, took the loot, set fire to your house, and caught the next flight out."

"It wasn't quite that easy," Baker said. "First I had to convince Venici that Lamont had played him. Then, when he and his cousin took care of Lamont and brought the cash back to me, I had to kill them. Not a walk in the park for a guy who'd never held a gun before in his life. I doctored their drinks first. Waited until they were unconscious, and used Venici's own weapon. But first I wrapped towels around their heads to minimize the mess."

"Jesus, that's cold," Dickie said.

"Cold? I'll tell you what's cold. Winding up on the bad side of a hard-core son of a bitch like Joe Nagall."

"How did he find out you had the money?" I asked.

"He didn't. Not for sure. I wasted fifty grand hiding it in Venici's closet, where I knew they'd find it. But there was just too much cash still missing. And Nagall never quite believed his old pal Venici would have gone against the Outfit."

"So you burned down your house."

"It seemed like the thing to do," he said. "I found a homeless guy about my size on Damen Avenue, fed him some cheap booze, and put him in my bed. Wasted a few more bills. Then woosh."

"Next stop, Southern California," I said. "That Hindu heaven on earth, where people go to exchange old lives for new. Exit Gio Polvere, mobster on the run, enter Jon Baker, wealthy young man of leisure."

I heard a whimpering sound to my left and saw Jonny was crying. "You're not our real dad?"

"Sure I am, son. I met your mom in California. We got married, and soon you boys completed the family. She wanted to come back here to live, and so did I."

"But not immediately," I said. "You had to wait until most of your old pals, like Nagall, were dead or in prison, and those still at large were too busy trying to deal with the burgeoning black gangs and the Russian Mafia to start wondering where a newcomer could have amassed all the ready cash needed to start building a little empire."

"I don't understand what you and Billy are talking about, Daddy," Jonny said.

"That's okay," Baker said. "It was a long time ago, son," he said. "Things were different."

"Right. Now you kill a better class of people," I said. "With your children as your accomplices."

"Eat or get eaten," he said. "It's the new American business motto."

"Only in your part of the zoo," I said.

"Enough!" He turned to Dal. "Take care of this."

I hoped I still had one card left to play.

"Did it feel like old times, Baker, seeing those flames again, feeling the warmth of the fire, getting that whiff of smoke and burning flesh?"

"What are you talking about?"

"The fire you set at Ubora Gallery. The one that killed the man who was helping me. Mantata." I forced myself not to look at Dal.

"I didn't—"

"No. I guess maybe you let the boys do it."

"Not me," Jonny said. "I don't like fire. I only watched while Dickie—"

"Shut up!" his brother shouted.

He barely got the words out before Dal shot him in the head.

Chapter FORTY-NINE

Baker watched, stunned, as his younger son crumpled to the floor. Then he wheeled on Dal in full fury.

"*Why?*" he cried.

Dal didn't answer. He stood rigid. Eyes glassy.

I remembered what Mantata and Trejean and even Dal had said about the way anger transformed him.

Baker clawed at something in his robe pocket.

I turned and ran past Jonny, who was raising his weapon. I grabbed Kiki and pulled her to the floor, covering her body with mine as the gunfire began.

It was over almost immediately.

Still, I stayed in place, Kiki wiggling under me. At first I was afraid that I had been shot and would feel the pain at any second. Then I was worried that someone was standing near us, waiting for me to move before firing.

"Billy . . ."

It was Dal.

I rolled away from Kiki and stood.

I was, literally, the last man standing.

Jonny was on his back about two yards away, hand still clutching his gun, open dead eyes staring at the ceiling. His father lay on his side, blood seeping through his silk robe. Dal was braced against the wall near the door. Still breathing, but not easily. Staring at me.

I pulled Kiki to her feet and deposited her back on the couch before going to Dal.

As I approached, he coughed blood. He'd been shot twice that I could see, a probably fatal chest wound and a gash along his right cheek. "Just . . . wanted . . . to find out . . . who . . ."

"I got that."

"They . . . all dead?"

I nodded.

"Get . . . outta here."

I took out my phone and dialed 911.

"No," he said. "Go . . . I'm . . . dead."

And he was.

* * *

The Winnetka Police Department has a chief, a deputy chief, and an administration staff of two commanders, four sergeants, and eighteen officers, nearly all of whom visited the Baker compound within the next twelve hours. Along with investigators from the North Regional Major Crimes Task Force (NORTAF), a forensics team, paramedics for Kiki, and Detectives Hank Bollinger and Ike Ruello, whom I'd notified.

The Winnetka officers were not overjoyed by the presence of the Chicago team, but my feeling was that since they were investigating the murders of Patton and Larry Kelsto, they deserved to be on the scene. And I wanted to be on their good side, in case I needed them later.

Kiki and I told the same story many times that night and on into Saturday morning. At Baker's request, his sons had murdered Patton and Kelsto, who'd been attempting to blackmail him with the knowledge that, under his birth name, Giovanni Polvere, he'd been a member of the Chicago Outfit in the late eighties. They'd burned down Mantata's gallery and killed him because they'd mistakenly thought he'd been in on the blackmail scheme. That's also why they kidnapped and killed Nat Parkins. As for Kiki, they decided to use her to lure me to their party to find out what I knew about their father's history. Which was nothing.

What made them think you did, Mr. Blessing?

From what Baker said, Patton told them I was involved. I have no idea why. I met him only last Friday on *Midday with Gemma*. We met once or twice after that and didn't exactly hit it off. But I can think of no reason why he'd want to get me in trouble with killers like these. Maybe he was just a man who liked to cause people trouble.

The investigators from the CPD, the WPD, and NORTAF seemed to accept that vague speculation. I guess Patton's reputation succeeded him.

Bollinger and Ruello drove us back to the hotel.

Kiki was uncharacteristically silent through most of the trip. But just before we arrived, she said to me, "There are two things we have to straighten out if I am going to continue working with you."

I saw the detectives suddenly snap to attention.

"Okayyy," I said, warily.

"You have to believe I didn't know—"

"Of course I do."

She kissed my cheek. Then she said, "And the next time we're in a greenroom and I tell you I'm getting bad vibes and you should pass on the show, you bloody well pass on the show."

I smiled at her. "Done," I said.

Chapter
FIFTY

The aftermath of what some press wag labeled the Winnetka Wipeout was bigger and more intense than either of my previous brushes with homicide had been. Both Kiki's life and mine were changed, if not forever, at least for the immediate future. Everyone wanted to use us for fun and/or profit. That included the police; district attorneys; my agent, Wally Wing, who seemed to think he was now representing Kiki, too; the network, who insisted I become a semipermanent part of *Hotline Tonight* while signing Kiki to a new contract that would kick in as soon as the show returned to New York.

During our final week in Chicago, we both needed security guards to get us through the media throngs at the hotel, our temporary site in Millennium Park, police headquarters, and—long story short—any place we tried to show our faces in the city. This made it difficult for me to run a couple of crucial errands. Difficult but not impossible.

On the last Tuesday, just after noon, the first time since the Winnetka Wipeout when I'd had more than a moment to myself, I donned a Cubbies cap, a chambray work shirt, rumpled khaki pants, and, the perfect touch, a battered backpack, and made an incognito escape from my hotel room, down the elevator, to a basic gray two-door Ford Fiesta in the hotel's subbasement.

From there I had no problem driving to North Sedgwick Street in Old Town, parking only a few feet away from the alley leading to the house that had been shared by the late Larry Kelsto and Nat Parkins. I entered the yard through the rear fence gate.

The house was still wrapped in yellow CPD tape. That was fine with me. What I wanted wasn't in the house.

I approached the chrome naked man and chair. As I'd realized, the man was seated in pretty much the same position as the Shakespeare park statue that Nat had sketched in such detail.

When I'd first seen the chrome man, I'd been a bit distracted by its protruding penis. Now I ignored that in favor of the gap in the chrome where Nat had been planning on placing the missing right leg. It was an ostrich egg–shaped cavity, approximately seven inches across. Its edges should have been jagged, but they weren't. I hoped they'd been purposely smoothed by one of the tools Nat had been in too much of a hurry to put away.

Gingerly, I poked my hand into the gap. Nothing. I moved it higher. I was into the sculpture up to my shoulder when my fingers touched something that felt like a rolled magazine. Eager now, I pushed one more inch of my shoulder into the gap, got the edge of the object between fingers and thumb, and yanked.

It was the first red file, folded in two. Three others, dislodged, came tumbling after.

Like a miser—hell, like Scrooge McDuck finding a pot of leprechaun gold—I carried my treasure back to the car. There I immediately examined my find. The folders' tags carried three-digit numbers, their significance lost on me. Two-eighty-four contained a DVD disk and Xeroxed pictures of a naked Carrie Sands. In some, she energetically worked the pole in a strip club. Others were considerably less wholesome.

File 137 featured pages from an accountant's ledger and copies of two sets of matching fingerprints. Damned if my guess at Baker's hadn't been on the money. One set was marked "Polvere—back cover financial records, Windy City Industrials, September 3, 1987." The other: "Baker—pencil from office, construction site North Franklin and West Monroe, May 4, 2011."

So he had tied Baker to Polvere over a year ago. Why did he wait to confront him? Had it been something I said, as he told Baker? I doubted I'd ever know. Not that it mattered anymore.

My file was numbered 112. Its contents were the original pages and the Xeroxed copies that Patton had shown me that morning at the hotel.

The final red file, 283, was devoted to Derek Webber. There was another Xerox, this one of a check made out to Onion City for one hundred fifty thousand dollars and no cents. It was signed by Jonathan Baker. A notation on the page said that it was for two points in the feature film *The Thief Who Stole Trump Tower*. "Onion City's connection to Outfit," Patton had written. This was something Webber should see, I thought. Considering the number of people in the city who did business with Baker, Patton's smoking gun wasn't even a cap pistol.

But then I noticed another of Patton's notes in the folder. There was a paper-clip indentation at the top. My guess was that at one time, it had been attached to the film script Nat shoved under my door.

Chapter
FIFTY-ONE

"Yo, Billy," Derek Webber called out. "You're looking pretty good for a survivor of the Winnetka Wipeout." Walking to meet me, he gestured toward the briefcase in my hand. "Homework?"

"You could call it that."

We were on Navy Pier. During its normal hours of operation it served as a "family-friendly" collection of restaurants, a children's museum, an IMAX theater, and, near where we were standing, a giant Ferris wheel. The wheel, like the pier, had closed for the night a while ago but was quite active all the same, with the movie crew getting it ready for a golden time, all-night shoot.

I'd called Derek around noon, asking if we could get together. He'd suggested ten that night, but I'd had a *Hotline* spot at ten-forty-five, so we'd settled on eleven-thirty.

"It looks pretty busy around here," I said. "I hope I'm not keeping you from anything important."

"Me? There's nothing for me to do here. I'm just one of the guys who own the studio. But I love watching them make movies. Austin—you've met our director, Austin Deware, of course you have—he's filming a key sequence where our beautiful thief meets our beautiful but sinister villainess on the wheel. Austin says it's his homage to Carol Reed's scene in *The Third Man,* where Orson Welles and Joseph Cotten have a chat on the Great Wheel in Vienna."

"Is there someplace we can talk?"

"What about on the wheel? It's just sitting there. Lars is playing with his crane. The sound guy's not ready. Let's take a ride."

"I'd rather not. There's something I want to show you."

"Okay." Webber seemed surprised but agreeable. "There's a Winnebago we're using for an office."

We walked to where several motor homes were parked near the pier entrance. The one we entered was occupied by Derek's partner, Alan, and Madeleine Parnelle. They were sitting before a computer monitor, going through a file with lots of numbers.

"B-B-Billy," Alan said. "B-b-been reading about you. Glad to see you in one . . . piece."

Madeleine merely granted me a quick artificial smile.

"C'mon in the back, Billy," Derek suggested.

"Actually, as long as Alan and Madeleine are here, this is something they should know about."

Alan cocked his head and looked bemused. Madeleine seemed annoyed but attentive.

I opened the briefcase and withdrew the number 283 red file.

"Seen this before, Derek?" I asked.

The puzzled look on his face told me that he hadn't. Alan, on the other hand, was frowning. I began to wonder if I'd missed a beat somewhere.

"This belonged to the late Pat Patton," I said to Derek. "Here's an item you and Alan should find interesting."

I presented him with the Xerox of Jon Baker's check with Patton's comments. He gave it more than a glance and handed it to his partner.

He watched as Alan read it carefully, passing it to Madeleine. "This is bullshit," Derek said. "Nearly everybody in Chicago has done business with Baker."

"That's B-B-Billy's point," Alan said. "Right?"

"Right," I agreed. "This should clear up any doubt anyone may have about your company due to Patton's claim."

"Patton," Derek said, as if the word left a bitter taste in his mouth. "What a son of a bitch."

"But he did have that gift some cops and reporters seem to be born with," I said. "He could look at a bunch of seemingly unrelated things and find a pattern. It's how he found out about Baker's past."

I removed the other page of the old detective's notes from the folder. "And this is something else he was working on when he was killed."

I handed it to Derek.

He read through Patton's neat penmanship and looked up at me. "Does this mean what I think it does?" he asked.

"You tell me," I said.

"This is nuts." He turned to Madeleine. "How tall is Gerard?" he asked.

"How tall? I'm not sure, exactly. Taller than I, I am confident."

"Take a guess," Derek said.

Madeleine and Alan exchanged glances.

"W-W-What's this all about? Let's see that p-p-paper."

"I'd say a little under six feet, right?" Derek said, keeping the paper. "How about moles? Did he have a little one just under his right nipple?"

" Madeleine said.

k Carrie, she'll agree?"

est-ce que tu fais?" Madeleine said. She lushed, splotches of red on her cheeks.

hen exactly did your husband fly home to ' I asked.

e blinked her eyes. "I am not sure of the exact . But it was several weeks ago. I can look it up."

"I remember exactly," Derek said. "He was sup-sed to have flown out on a Wednesday, four weeks go tomorrow."

"I am sure you are right," she said. "So?"

"Stop b-b-beating around the b-b-bush, Rek. What's this all about?"

Derek looked at me.

I said, "The day Patton, Carrie, and I were on the talk show, the main topic of conversation was the truncated body that washed up on Oak Street Beach. That's why Patton was booked on the show. He claimed to have some secret knowledge about the corpse's identity that he wasn't quite ready to share. I think that was a bluff. But by the end of the show, he did have the glimmer of an idea worth pursuing. That's because Carrie surprised our hostess with the news that Gerard Parnelle had flown back to Paris several weeks before."

"I repeat, 'So?'" Madeleine said.

"Your husband's success made him a celebrity," I said. "And the fact that Gemma Bright didn't know he'd flown home struck Patton as significant. It meant he'd done it under the media radar. No shaky TMZ shots at the airport. No comings and goings in show-biz journals. No photos in the tabloids.

"And there was the timing. One of the things Patton did know about the dead man was the approximate time he was dumped in the lake. It's all in his notes."

Derek handed her the page. I watched her eyes jump jerkily from sentence to sentence. Alan moved closer to her to read over her shoulder. I wondered if Derek was sharing my thought, that they looked like a couple. In this case, brought together by desperation rather than love or sex.

They were looking at the plans Patton had for an investigation he'd been unable to pursue. He had found a *Chicago Tribune* photo of Parnelle on the movie set earlier in the month. He'd written: "Get NV"—possibly a CPD friend, I thought—"to check airline passenger lists for a three-week period following date of photograph. Have MC make soft inquiry into the whereabouts of Parnelle in Paris. Check with doctor."

He'd included notations, apparently from the postmortem examination of the truncated corpse. The approximate height was sixty-eight to seventy-one inches. Weight, 165 to 174 lbs. Age, thirty-seven to forty-five. Hair, brown. The "mole under right nipple" was noted. As for the occurrence of death, an approximate date was noted. There was not even the speculation of a time of death.

Patton had underlined the cause, "AMI, acute myocardial infarction," and followed that with: "Check w. P's medical record, heart?, hypertension?, enlarged?, asthma?, etc."

Madeleine Parnelle suddenly crumpled the paper in her hand, squeezing it into a ball. "This means nothing."

"True," I agreed. "But you and I know Patton's hunch would have paid off. Your husband died of a heart attack at an inopportune time. There were the movie and future movies, television series, book contracts to fulfill. The temptation to keep everything moving forward must have been overwhelming."

"Jesus Christ!" Derek exclaimed. "You cut him up? Your husband? The guy you lived with for five years?"

The red spots had left her cheeks, leaving her face pallid, appropriate for the coldness in her voice as she turned to Alan. *"Trop sentimental."*

He didn't seem that pleased to be on her team. He took a step away. Looking at Derek, he said, "It's not like you think. She . . . we d-d-didn't d-d-do that to him. The whole thing was B-B-Baker's idea. His . . . kid did the c-c-cutting."

"You owe Derek no apology," she said.

"The hell he doesn't. You both do."

Alan sighed and started to say something, but Madeleine interrupted him. She apparently was in no mood to hear him struggle through an explanation. "It was the night you attended the filming at Soldier Field," she said to Derek. "Jon invited us for dinner on his yacht. Alan, Gerard, and myself. Jon and his son, the handsome one, not the *parfait imbécile*. We were in the midst of dining, and it happened like that." She snapped her fingers. "Gerard stopped eating. He complained of pain in his chest. And he fell forward. *Mort.*"

"We were shocked. B-B-But Jon was incredibly c-c . . . cool."

"He arose, approached Gerard, touched him here"—she pointed to a spot on her throat—"and shook his head."

"I g-g-got out my phone to c-c-call nine-one-one. . . ."

"But Jon stopped him, suggested that we consider the—how do you?—the implication of Gerard's death."

"We all had a g-g-great deal riding on Gerard."

"What are you talking about?" Derek asked. "You two maybe, but Jon only had two points in the movie. That was chump change to him."

Alan looked even more uncomfortable. "I g-g-guess it's g-g-gonna . . . come out now, anyway. He was t-t-taking over the . . . company. With my help."

"Christ, Alan," Derek said. "You know what Onion City means to me."

His partner couldn't look him in the eye.

"It wasn't just Onion City," he said. "I agreed to sell him my shares in Instap-p-picks."

Derek looked as if a magic finger had poked a hole in him, allowing all the air to escape. He backed to a chair and sat down. "We grew up together," he said, in a whisper.

"So much money," Alan said. "For you, t-t-too."

This was all interesting, in a big-business soap-opera way. But we'd wandered afield from the reason I was there. I was about to attempt to get back on track when Madeleine, brutally pragmatic Madeleine, did it for me.

"In any case, Derek, Gerard's death would have ruined everything."

"Just out of curiosity," I said, "what was the ultimate plan? You couldn't keep the man's death a secret forever."

"Not forever," she said. "There would be a prolonged illness, during which Gerard would undergo treatment in seclusion. I would assist him on his writing for perhaps two years. At which time he would, alas, succumb, leaving behind several completed works and many others in various stages that I, being his collaborator, would complete."

"The three of you concocted this plan with your husband lying facedown in his dinner?" I asked.

"That's a crude way to put it," she said. "But yes. Jon's mind is, was, very agile."

"Of course," I said. "The agile mind of a sociopath. What about Gerard's romance with Carrie?"

"How heartbroken would she have been to have her lover die so suddenly?" Madeleine asked.

"It could even have affected her performance in the movie," I said.

"Exactly," Madeleine said, my sarcasm evidently lost in translation. "So I have already been working on that. Gerard's emails to her have been growing less and less romantic. By the time filming ends, he will have withdrawn completely, telling her, in no uncertain terms, to move on with her life."

"Let's c-c-cut to the . . . chase. What do you want, B-B-Billy?"

"What have you got?"

It was a definite eye-opener. Alan looked like I'd tapped him with a cattle prod.

"Just a joke," I said. "Ever since I heard Brando ask that question in a movie, I've been waiting for an opportunity to use it. What made you think I want money?"

"You and P-P-Patton were working t-t-together."

"How'd you come up with that factoid? Jon Baker?"

"N-N-No. A couple of weeks ago, P-P-Patton offered to recant his b-b-blog about us. For a . . . price. I decided to . . . play his game instead. I hired . . . detectives to follow him, see if we c-c-could get something on *him*. One of them was at that . . . t-talk show. He saw you and him . . . getting all . . . c-confidential after the show went off the air. The next day, P-P-Patton went . . . to your hotel."

"Your guys Heinz and Killinek saw all that, but they didn't see Baker's sons go into Patton's house to kill him?"

"They figured he was in for the . . . night, so they went home."

"Some sleuths. Why'd you sic 'em on me?"

"The . . . morning after P-P-Patton's . . . murder, some . . . g-guy called, offering to sell me something P-P-Patton had that would . . . c-clear our . . . c-company's reputation. I thought it was you."

"They tried to kidnap me. Twice."

"I'm sorry about that," Alan said. "But I assumed you were a b-b-blackmailer and maybe even the guy who'd t-t-tortured and killed . . . Patton."

"What about that crazy who attacked me and Carrie?"

"He was only . . . supposed to scare you, f-fire over your head. It's why Heinz . . . dropped him off. He was worried a d-d-drive-by might be too risky, hitting a . . . pothole or something."

"The paper said the guy was a hired killer," I said.

Alan shrugged. "Heinz . . . p-picked him. Anyway, how do we m-m-make all of this go away? What do you want?"

"Transparency."

It was the code word Bollinger and I had picked.

The door to the Winnebago opened, and he and Ruello sauntered in, followed by several uniformed officers.

Not much later, as we watched the blue-and-whites take Alan and Madeleine away, and the police techs had removed the wireless transmitter I'd been wearing, Bollinger said, "Not homicide but a clean bust for all that. Guess we owe you a couple, Blessing."

"Always glad to help."

He offered his hand. I shook it, and he strolled off.

"I'm an even bigger fan now, Chef Blessing," Ruello said. He lowered his voice. "Frank's birthday's coming up. I think I'll get him one of your cookbooks. Maybe the barbecue?"

"Good choice," I said.

And Ruello hugged me. The first time I'd been

hugged by a cop and, considering the NYPD, probably the last.

Before leaving, I turned to look back at the Ferris wheel. It was aglow with light. The camera, high on its crane, was aimed at the two actresses sharing a seat. Carrie and Adoree. Glamorous. Poised. Playing their roles in a make-believe world that was about to collide with the real one.

I was partially responsible for that collision. But at least I'd eased Carrie's burden a little by turning her and my red files to ashes and letting the Windy City have its way with them.

I was sorry my promising beginning with Adoree had gone so haywire. Had I behaved like an idiot? Or was she just too French, and an actress to boot?

I sighed, realizing that my chauvinistic, not to mention jingoistic, second question had provided an answer to the first.

Chapter
FIFTY-TWO

Shortly before I departed Chicago, J. B. Kazynski called, ostensibly to wish me an uneventful trip back to the first city. But after the pleasantries, and a brief update on her cousin (he and his wife were now happy as clams with their Instapicks money), she began to question me about my network, Worldwide

Broadcasting Company. It seemed her landlord's niece had suffered a diabetic seizure while watching *Who's Your Daddy?*, the new hit comedy set at a Hollywood school for celebrity offspring. What she specifically wanted to know was if WBC used subliminal messages to sell high-fructose kids' breakfast cereals. I told her that my understanding was that the network held the line at product placement. At least for now.

Kiki and the rest of the *Wake Up, America!* team returned to New York on Friday, after our last show. I stayed for another day, to attend Mantata's funeral service at the Greater Salem Baptist Church on the South Side, the house of worship where Mahalia Jackson began her professional singing career. When she died, fifty thousand mourners passed her coffin at the church. The number of Mantata's mourners was closer to fifty, but his sister, Olivia Hudson, had arranged for the kind of elegant send-off, complete with a gospel choir, that the old boy would have appreciated.

After the ceremony there was a reception at Olivia's home, where tea and coffee and cake were served and people spoke in hushed tones. Trejean, Hiho, and I ducked out of that quickly and held our own celebration with beer and deep-dish pizza at a nearby joint. I enjoyed listening to their stories about Mantata, real or legendary, and stayed with them until their arguments and laughter grew so raucous we were asked to leave.

My flight to New York was scheduled for ten that night. I was at O'Hare early, nursing a soda in the frequent-flyer lounge, when Cassandra called from the Bistro.

"When do you arrive?" she asked.

I looked at my watch. "My flight leaves in forty minutes. You'll have to do the math. I'm too tired."

"We had an excellent night. Full up, both sittings. It's been like that ever since your participation in the Winnetka Wipeout went viral."

"I can't believe that name stuck. Winnetka Wipeout," I said. "It sounds like a headline for a paper-towel ad."

"I'm thinking Charmin," she said.

"That, too."

"Phillipe made another move tonight," she said.

"Roaches, rats. What was it this time, locusts?"

"He tried to put something in the soup du jour."

"What was it?"

"A very nice lobster bisque," she said.

"Not the soup. What did he try to put in it?"

"We won't know until next week. It has to be analyzed. He says it's just Epsom salts. He wasn't trying to kill anybody. Just give 'em the runs."

"Who stopped him? The security guy?"

"She's a security woman," Cassandra said. "But it was Maurice who stopped him."

"Oh?" Maurice Terrebone, my hot-tempered kitchen supervisor. "How'd that work out?"

"Billy, he tried to chop the boy's right hand off."

"He was probably just throwing a scare into the kid."

"No. The security woman almost had to use her Taser to get him to drop the cleaver. But he definitely did scare the kid. Scared him straight. Phillipe wrote out a very readable detailed confession that rests on your desk, signed and notarized."

"Where is Phillipe now?"

"In a hotel room with one of A.W.'s male agents. They'll be serving papers on his employers tomorrow, at which time he can go wherever he wants."

"How much is this costing me?" I asked.

"Well, Unca' Scrooge, a lot less than if he'd put the laxative in the soup."

She continued rattling on about the efficiency with which A.W. had taken care of the problem. But I was barely listening. Unless I was imagining it, a lady seated at the bar with her back to me was Adoree.

I stood and clicked off the phone while Cassandra was still talking. I walked across the room until I was beside the woman and tapped her on the shoulder.

She turned. Definitely not Adoree. But nearly as beautiful. I was about to apologize, using the old "I thought you were someone I knew" line. But I didn't have to. She smiled and said, "My goodness. Aren't you the television chef, the one who helped solve the murders?"

"That would be me," I said, taking the seat beside her. "You aren't flying to New York, by any chance?"

"Yes, I am. And I want to hear all about the Winnetka Wipeout."

Funny how much better that name was beginning to sound.